LEFT COAST LEFT

LEFT COAST LEFT

A Brandon McStocker Novel

TERRY STAFFORD

The characters and events in Left Coast Left are fictitious. Any similarity to real persons, living or dead, is coincidental and not intended by the author.

Copyright © 2020 by Terry Stafford

All rights reserved
Printed in the United States of America

The scanning, uploading, and distribution of this book without permission is a theft of the author's intellectual property. No part of this publication may be reproduced, stored in a retrieval system, or transmitted in any form or by any means—for example, electronic, photocopy, recording—without the prior written permission of the publisher. The only exception is brief quotations in printed reviews. Thank you for your support of the author's rights.

Published by Tipperary South
4216 S. Mooney Blvd., Suite #317
Visalia, CA 93277-9143

ISBN: 978-0-9859655-6-3 (trade paperback)
ISBN: 978-0-9859655-5-6 (trade hardcover)
ISBN: 978-0-9859655-7-0 (eBook)

Library of Congress Control Number: 2020932939

Cover Design by JD&J Book Cover Design, LLC
Interior Design by JetLaunch, Inc.
Editing by Harshman Services

May the elected servant leaders of these
United States of America
always do what is right for the people.

This book was released during the COVID-19
Global pandemic of 2020. While it was tempting to
change the storyline to incorporate the events that
occurred during this time, I elected to remain clear
and let the truth of the matter reveal itself.

TABLE OF CONTENTS

Chapter 1 1
Chapter 2 15
Chapter 3 30
Chapter 4 46
Chapter 5 60
Chapter 6 75
Chapter 7 89
Chapter 8 102
Chapter 9 117
Chapter 10 132
Chapter 11 146
Chapter 12 159
Chapter 13 172
Chapter 14 185
Chapter 15 199
Chapter 16 213
Chapter 17 228
Chapter 18 242
Chapter 19 257
Chapter 20 271

CHAPTER 1

Lucinda opened the heavy steel door and walked out onto the expanse of the rooftop, heavy equipment and solar panels scattered everywhere. She continued walking and let the door slam behind her. After the long trek to the edge, she stopped and looked out over the new city.

"Lucy!"

She turned to see who was shouting at her. Her long dark hair whipped around in the stiff wind so common in that part of the country.

"Lucy, what are you doing up here?"

"Mena, please. I just want to be alone. You shouldn't have followed me."

"Maybe. But you left the meeting so abruptly. I was worried about you." Mena, McClellan and McStocker's executive secretary, arrived at Lucy's side near the edge of the four-story office building. "Are you okay?"

"Your boss makes me crazy."

"Brandon? Why?"

"Does he really believe Civil War II is imminent?"

"Apparently so. Are you going out to California with him?"

"I don't know. I'm starting to believe I should go back to D.C. Maybe I can find a project to work on back there."

"But there's nothing left back there. There *is* no D.C."

Lucinda Reagan, a middle-aged senior manager at McLellan and McStocker, continued her scan of the city through her dancing hair, thinking back over all the challenges they went through to move the federal government from Washington, D.C. to this new city that grew from the cornfields of North Central Kansas. Lebanon, Kéntro District, or K.D. as it had come to be known.

"I could try private industry."

Mena turned and put her hand on Lucinda's arm. "You love him, don't you?"

Lucinda paused, then smiled as tears filled her eyes. "Oh, jeez. Yes. What's not to love. Look at this." She threw her arms up, looking back over the city. "I can't believe he built this. All of this."

Brandon McStocker, the president and only remaining partner of McClellan and McStocker Engineering Services, was still down in the executive conference room presiding over his weekly staff meeting.

"It *is* pretty amazing when you think about it," Mena said.

"Come on. I mean, who does that? Who builds an entirely new city to relocate the federal government? Who builds another man's dream?"

"Let's go back down to the conference room. It's freezing up here."

"I'll be down soon," Lucinda said.

"How did you even find this place? I've never been up here before."

Lucinda smiled. "He brought me up here once to show me the view."

"Wow. Who knew!"

"I told him he needs to build a little patio up here as an escape. But now, we aren't even going to be here."

"Is that what's bothering you?"

"Maybe. I've really fallen in love with this place—the people, the relaxed attitudes. It's different."

"That, it is," Mena said.

"I can't tell what my future looks like . . . you know . . . with Brandon."

"Seriously? You have become his world, pretty girl." Mena lifted the cell phone she was holding and read the text message.

Where are you?

"Sorry, it's Liv." Mena smiled at Lucinda and pecked at the face of her phone.

I'm on the roof with Lucy.
I'll be right there.

"I guess she's coming up here."

"The more, the merrier," Lucinda chuckled.

After a few minutes, the steel door from the vestibule flew open, and the wind launched Olivia onto the roof. Olivia McStocker, an attractive, smartly dressed executive, was Brandon's oldest daughter and the firm's deputy project manager. Her long strawberry blonde hair immediately started pitching in the wind. "What are you guys doing up here? Dang, it's cold!"

"You left, too?" Mena asked.

"We took a break. Daddy told everyone to take fifteen minutes. You okay, Luce?"

"I'm fine. All that talk about Civil War II kind of freaked me out."

"Yeah. Tell me about it." Olivia walked up close to Lucinda and held her arm. "Are you and Daddy all right?"

"I think so."

"Don't give up on him, okay?"

"I just keep thinking about . . ." Lucinda turned her head and fell silent.

"Keep thinking about what?"

"Oh, nothing, Liv. Never mind."

"He loves you, ya know," Olivia said.

"I know. Are you okay with all this? You and Susan, I mean?" Susan was Brandon's other daughter.

"Truth be told, we love you too. You've been the best thing to happen to Daddy since . . . well, since Mom died."

"But he hasn't . . ."

"Hasn't what?"

"Come on, let's get back inside. This is nuts," Lucinda said.

The three of them crossed their arms together, tucked into the wind, and walked back across the roof and through the door into the dimly lit stairwell leading down to the fourth floor.

"Thank you, everyone, for getting back in here promptly," Brandon said. "Given the circumstances . . ."

The conference room was full, with occupied chairs lining the side and back walls. The conference table was surrounded by the company department directors from finance, legal, engineering, human resources, operations, and many others, along with city officials from nearby Manhattan. Near the front of the table sat the Governor of Kansas. Lucinda and Olivia quietly made their way to the front of the table while Mena returned to her place at the back of the room where she took notes of the proceedings.

"Wait! What circumstances?" Governor Redman interrupted. "You keep talking like the whole damn country is going to hell in a handbasket. I thought moving the entire seat of government from D.C. out here was supposed to fix everything. The president sold us all on that premise."

"Yes, Governor. That's true," Brandon said. "And it has gone a long way toward that. As you are well aware, the upheaval at the California border caused by pulling the roadblocks from the Mexican border back to the state line has caused its own set of problems."

"What has that got to do with Kansas?"

"Governor, this issue has everything to do with Kansas," Senator Beecher chimed in. It has everything to do with everybody. Please, Governor; allow Mr. McStocker the chance to get to his point." Senator Beecher was assigned by the Central House, what used to be known as the White House, to lead the committee overseeing Brandon and his company's relocation of the U.S. Government facilities.

Brandon stood and began to pace back and forth in front of the displays on the wall of the high-tech conference room. "Senator, has the president ruled that the Kéntro Project is complete?"

"Pretty much," Beecher said. "OMB signed off on it last week. No open contract issues. We know you're still working off punch lists."

"A ton," Brandon smiled. "Thank you, Senator. So, again, under the present circumstances, I've invited some folks to this meeting that you haven't seen in a while. Don, will you come up and join me, please?"

A gentleman in the back of the room stood tall and straight as he walked to the front and stood next to Brandon.

"For those of you who don't know, this is Don Greene. Before the president waived several regulations, taking control of the company to expedite the oversight of Project Kéntro, Don was the chairman of our board of directors. We have gone a long time without the board's leadership, but things are about to change, and I've asked President Richland's blessing to re-form the board and get Mac & Mac back in compliance with FTC regulations.

"I'm not sure how to make it official," Brandon continued. "So, the rest of the previous board members are free to come up and sit in these seats along the wall to take over these proceedings."

"Wait. What's changing?"

"Stew, give it a rest," Senator Beecham told the governor as the others in the room chuckled.

Brandon smiled and looked at the governor. "Sir, we're getting to that." Then he took his seat, and Don Greene ceremoniously moved to where Brandon had been standing.

"Ladies and gentlemen, I call this meeting of the McClellan and McStocker Engineering Services board of directors to order. Our first order of business is to reseat the board of directors and reaffirm the membership into their previously held positions with all of the associated duties. All in favor."

"Aye." Those sitting along the front wall responded.

"All opposed." Everyone looked around the room and smiled. "Hearing none, I declare this board reseated and back in session. Does anyone have a gavel in their pocket?" A chuckle rose from everyone in the room.

Don sat in the chair at the head of the table, rolled it forward, and opened his notebook. "For the next order of business, I have a guest waiting in the print room next door that will be quite a surprise to everyone, I would imagine. Mena, would you invite our guest in, please?"

Mena looked puzzled as she stood and walked to the door at the side of the room. She turned and looked at Brandon with a questioning eye. He shrugged his shoulders, also confused. She opened the door and saw who was sitting at the work desk. Mena covered her mouth, and tears welled up in her eyes. Again, turning to look at Brandon, she shook her head. Mena motioned for the guest to come in.

"Ladies and gentlemen," Don said. "I would like you to join me in welcoming Anne McClellan, wife of the late Bob McClellan."

A gasp went up, followed by an explosive cheer as everyone stood and applauded Anne's entrance. She smiled with the grace of a dignitary and walked slowly to join Don in front. As she walked by Brandon, she began to cry and wrapped her arms around him. The applause got louder, and another cheer erupted. Mena, Olivia, and Lucy were all standing with their hands covering their mouths, tears running down their faces.

When Anne saw Olivia, she walked to the other side of the table to hug her.

"Olivia, my dear, you are the most beautiful sight I've seen in a long time. You are certainly your mother's daughter."

"Oh my God, Miss Anne. What a wonderful surprise!"

The room slowly quieted as the attendees returned to their seats. Senator Beecher pulled a chair out for Anne between him and Brandon. "Mrs. McClellan, it is truly an honor to have you join us," he said.

"Indeed, it is," Governor Redman echoed.

When Brandon finally sat down, Anne took his hand and held it tightly as the chairman continued. "Thank you, everyone. Please, let's continue."

"Yes. Thank you," Anne said. "I'm in shock. I'm sure Bob is laughing at me right now."

The room erupted into laughter.

"It's good to have you here, Anne," Don said. "So, let's get back down to business. Mrs. McClellan is here for a very specific reason."

Anne squeezed Brandon's hand tighter, and he reached across to take her hand with both of his.

"As you all know, Bob McClellan started this company when he was in Huntsville, Alabama. He wanted to be part of the space program. Not long after, he partnered with his favorite engineer, Brandon McStocker." He gestured toward Brandon as the others nodded and smiled. "Bob had such respect for Brandon that he put his name on the front of the building when they moved to Fairfax, Virginia. The rest, as they say, is history.

"We all know—especially those of us who have been watching from the sidelines all these years—we know the value that Brandon has brought to this company, and indeed to this country, since Bob's unfortunate passing." Anne lowered her head, and Brandon put an arm around her. She looked up at him and smiled, nodding her head.

"Then, when Brandon brought his daughter, Olivia, onboard, new lights began to come on around here."

The room began to chant, "Liv. Liv. Liv. Liv."

Olivia grinned and covered her eyes. Then she smiled across the table at the man she'd been dating, Tim O'Neil, an aide to the governor.

Don called the room back to order. "To honor that partnership and to recognize the unprecedented leadership they have both provided, Anne has asked the board to consider renaming and rebranding McClellan and McStocker. The new company will be called McStocker and McStocker Enterprises, Incorporated."

Brandon and Olivia looked at each other with gaping mouths.

"The board has consulted with counsel and have agreed to move forward with the change effective immediately. All legal documentation and FTC-required notifications are in work as we speak." A buzz came over the room.

Brandon leaned in, speaking quietly into Anne's ear. "Are you sure about this?"

"Son, I've never been surer about anything in my life. This is your company. I could see it even before Bob left us. It's only right, and he would agree. Brandon, he would be so proud of what you've done here. I know Kéntro was his dream and his vision, but you made it happen."

"But Anne. You know what's going on next, right?"

"Of course. Don told me all about it—which makes it all the timelier. This needs to happen, son."

"Brandon. Olivia. Congratulations on your new company," Don said. Everyone in the room stood and applauded the change. Anne leaned into Brandon's side and put her arm around his waist as they rose. Olivia walked around the end of the table, tears streaming down her face, and joined her father and Anne in a long hug.

"I know you two have traveled a long, hard road," Senator Beecher said. "This is well-deserved. Congratulations."

"Thank you, Senator," Brandon said, looking over the heads of the two ladies.

A chant began to grow in the room. "Speech. Speech. Speech. Speech."

Olivia looked up blushing. "Daddy?"

Brandon turned and looked at Don, who was motioning for him to come back to the head of the table.

"Okay. Okay. Fine," Brandon shouted as he made his way to the front. "Please. Sit."

Everyone applauded again and took their seats. Olivia took Brandon's seat and held Anne's hand.

"Thank you, everyone," Brandon said. "I really don't know what to say. I did not see this coming. I think Liv and I will have to sneak away and gather our thoughts on this. But, one thing is certain. I can't tell you how proud I am of my little girl, all grown up and living her dream—working with her slug of an old man."

Everyone chuckled and began applauding again. "Liv. Liv. Liv. Liv."

"Shut up," Olivia laughed while wiping the tears from her face.

"But really," Brandon continued. "You all know as well as I do what an amazing partner Liv has become. There is no way I could come close to running this company without her. I just overheard Anne telling her that she is her mother's daughter. There's no doubt about it."

Olivia smiled and blew a kiss to her father as the room applauded her once again. He motioned for her to stand to receive her honor. Her face blushed red, and she stood, pointing at him. The room finally quieted, and Olivia sat back down.

Brandon continued. "Thank you all. Anne, thank you for this honor. You know I had the utmost respect for Bob, and we will not take this lightly. I'm so proud of the entire team here at Mac and Mac. Bob would be proud as well."

He paused for several seconds, changing the mood of the room. "But now we have more work to do. I have to leave here shortly to meet with the president. As hard as this move of the federal government has been, we may be embarking on something even bigger."

Everyone looked at each other and whispered, shaking their heads.

"I know. I know. What could be bigger than that? I'm not at liberty to go into details yet, but I hope, after this meeting with the president, I'll be able to share more with you. I just don't want you to be concerned about not having work to do now that we're closing out the Lebanon, K.D. project.

"Before we break for the day, I have one more thing I need to do. But before I do that, I want to invite one more guest into the room. Mena, will you ask our other guest in, please?"

Mena smiled and walked to the back of the room and opened the door. Olivia and Anne looked at each other and shrugged their shoulders. The room erupted into laughter and applause when Susan, Brandon's younger daughter, entered the room. They all knew Susan and watched her grow up. She was always the fun-loving kid getting into mischief around the office. She had grown into a beautiful young woman and everyone loved her.

"Hey, everybody!" She smiled and walked quickly and confidently to the front of the room to hug her father. "Hey, Daddy."

"Liv, will you come up and join us, please?" Brandon asked.

Olivia squeezed Anne's hand, shrugged her shoulders again, then stood and walked up to join her sister and father.

"Thanks, girls. As you all know, these two are my pride and joy. Before my wife, Cassandra, left this world, these two kept her going during my many absences. And since Cassandra's passing, they have kept me in line. It is with their blessing that I am going to do something that has never been done in the history of Mac and Mac. Lucy, will you come up and join us, please?"

Olivia and Susan stepped to the side, and Lucinda stood by Brandon with a perplexed look on her face. She glanced at Olivia with squinted eyes. Olivia shrugged and whispered something to Susan.

"I think most of you know Lucinda Reagan. She has been working with us for quite a while now, coordinating the final move of the federal offices into their new homes here in K.D. What you probably don't know is how rocky things were when we first met."

Lucinda lowered her head and giggled, then looked over at Olivia, who was also giggling.

"Trust me, everyone. You don't want to know," Olivia said.

All the attendees in the room laughed as Brandon continued. "That being said, I want to do something to make this partnership a little more permanent."

At that moment, Olivia and Susan realized what was about to happen. They both covered their mouths, and tears welled in their eyes. Brandon pulled a small box from his coat pocket and lowered himself to one knee. Lucinda's jaw dropped, and she too, covered her mouth. Gasps filled the room.

"Lucy. I think I've loved you from the minute I saw you. I'm pretty sure Liv knew it before I did."

Lucinda glanced over at Olivia to see her nodding through her tears.

"And as you know, what's just as important is the fact that these girls of mine love you too. You have become their friend and confidant. So, we're all in this together."

Lucinda began to nod her head and bob up and down at her knees, crying even harder.

"Lucy . . . will you marry me? Will you become a permanent part of our family?"

She couldn't get the words out quickly enough. "Yes! Of course, I'll marry you!" She held out her hand so Brandon could put on the ring. He stood, and Lucinda threw her arms around his neck.

Everyone in the conference room jumped to their feet and applauded with loud cheers. Olivia and Susan walked over to join in the embrace. Anne pulled a handkerchief from her purse to wipe her eyes. Olivia turned and motioned for her to join them.

Brandon saw Anne walking toward them and moved from his embrace to greet her. She reached up to hug him.

"Oh, Brandon. I am so happy for you. I couldn't be prouder if you were my own son." Then she turned to Lucinda. "You've got quite a catch here, young lady." She turned to hug her.

"Oh, I know, Miss Anne. I'll take good care of him. I promise."

"I know you will, Sweetheart. I know you will."

"I'm not sure about the whole *Mom* thing," Susan said as she laughed and wrapped her arms around Lucinda.

"Don't even think about it, Kiddo," Lucinda chuckled.

CHAPTER 2

Later that day, Brandon arrived at the Central House, the new facility in the heart of Lebanon, K.D., where President Richland worked and lived.

"I have a meeting with the president," Brandon told the gate guard.

"Of course, sir." He waved Brandon through to the front entrance where Senator Beecher, who had arrived ahead of them, was waiting. Sonny Langston, Brandon's bodyguard, driver, and friend got out of the car and walked around to open Brandon's door, but Brandon was already halfway out when he arrived.

"I told you, man. I can do this."

Sonny looked at Senator Beecher and shook his head. Beecher laughed and greeted Brandon.

"You ready for this?"

"Well, I'm not completely sure what to be ready for, but I suppose."

"That was quite a show you put on this morning," the senator said with a chuckle and patted Brandon on the back.

"Well, I strive to keep the troops entertained, you know."

"So, you're going to be a married man."

"So, it would seem."

They both laughed as the attendants held the front doors open for them to enter into the lobby.

"Good morning, Kathryn," Senator Beecher said to the receptionist. "I believe the president is expecting us."

"Yes, sir. Please have a seat." She picked up her phone. "Mr. President, Senator Beecher and Mr. McStocker are here to see you, sir."

She returned the phone to its cradle. "It'll be just a few minutes."

The senator nodded and smiled, then opened his briefcase. He removed a phone from his coat pocket, turned it off, and threw it in the briefcase, then pulled several file folders out and closed it.

Brandon smiled. "So, you know what this is about?"

"Pretty much. Don't you?"

"I have a hunch."

"That's the impression I got when you mentioned it in the meeting this morning."

"Well, I guess I know the topic. Just not sure of the direction of the topic."

The huge door to the new Oval Office swung open, and President Richland walked out with a smile and loud voice. "Good afternoon, gentlemen. Come on in."

Brandon and Senator Beecher stood, smiled, and nodded at Kathryn as they walked past her and the president into his office. He followed them in and closed the door.

"Help yourself to something to drink over there if you like."

"No, thank you, Mr. President. I'm fine." Brandon said, walking toward the couch.

The senator shook his head and followed Brandon. They sat across the large coffee table from the president's wing-back chair.

"Thanks for coming to see me, gentlemen. Brandon, everyone is thoroughly pleased with their new offices. You and your team did an excellent job here."

"Thank you, sir. I'll pass along your kind words."

"Is it safe to assume that you know why I asked you to come over here?"

Brandon and the senator turned to each other and smiled.

"I thought so. Yes. It's California. We've got to do something out there."

"Sir, I know you mentioned it a few months back, but I'm just not sure what I can do out there."

"I'm not sure yet either, Brandon. Governor Truly has a hell of a mess on his hands. San Francisco is about to boil over."

"Moving the border checkpoints up to the state line seems to have slowed illegal entries," Senator Beecher said. "But the protests around L.A. and the Bay Area are getting worse," Senator Beecher said. "While Truly's predecessor really screwed things up with his self-righteous antics, we think Truly may actually want our help."

For several years, a move had been afoot to remove California from the United States. Many progressive residents wanted to see it on the ballots. Mexican Drug cartels were taking advantage of the unrest by increasing their insurgencies into the state. Protests against the federal government were increasing in number and intensity around the major coastal cities of Los Angeles and San Francisco.

"What kind of help does he want?" Brandon asked.

"That's what we need you to find out," the president said. "I want to send an envoy out there, and I want you to head it up. You'll be able to see the big picture without a preconceived political agenda. Take a few people with you."

"How long do you think we'll be out there, sir?"

"As long as it takes. Do you have any major irons in the fire?"

"We have taken on several development projects, but nothing Liv can't handle. I'll take Lucy with me."

"Good. How is Miss Reagan doing?"

President Richland was the one who assigned Lucinda the task of leading the actual move of each of the government offices to K.D. He sent her from Washington, D.C. without warning Brandon.

Senator Beecher glanced at Brandon and smiled. "Mr. President, Brandon proposed to her this morning right there in the conference room in front of God and everybody."

Brandon blushed and laughed while the senator slapped him on the back.

"Is that right? Well, congratulations, Brandon. That's excellent. But did she say yes?"

Brandon laughed. "Yes, sir. She said yes."

"That's good. That's good. You two will be a force to be reckoned with."

"Thank you, Mr. President."

Brandon had become a friend and trusted "non-political" advisor to the president through the years of challenges and near tragic events during the Kéntro project. Brandon was instrumental in helping him navigate through a host of sticky wickets.

"When's the big day?"

"Well, sir. We haven't really had time to talk about it yet."

"Not to be a pushy influence or anything, but you might want to do it sooner than later."

"Sir?"

"You need to get to California fairly soon, before Truly loses complete control. We need to get a handle on it, and soon."

"Of course, sir. I'll have a talk with Lucy as soon as possible."

"Take her out to a nice dinner at Barney's Diner on me. I know that's your favorite meeting place."

"True, but it's not exactly five-star cuisine," Senator Beecher said.

Brandon chuckled. "She's not hard to please. She actually loves the food there. We'll do it in a day or two."

"Good. I'll have Kathryn give Susan a call to arrange payment."

"That really isn't necessary, Mr. President."

"Think nothing of it. It's my pleasure. You two have a lot on your plate to talk about."

"Thank you, sir."

Sonny drove the black limo into the parking lot of Barney's Diner just as the sun was setting over the plains of North Central Kansas. He parked the limo and jumped out with a smile on his face and a skip in his step. He ran around the back of the car to open the door for Brandon and Lucinda. Brandon got out first, wearing his usual dark gray suit and tie, then turned to help Lucinda, adorned in a tight-fitting short black dress.

"Thank you, Sonny," Lucinda said.

"Of course, ma'am."

She smiled and poked her finger into Sonny's chest. As they walked toward the front door of the diner, Sonny closed the car door and walked over to take his usual position, leaning on the front fender. He began his scanning of the parking lot.

"Hey, guys!" Susan shouted from behind the counter as the couple walked through the door, the bell ringing over their heads. "Your table is all clear back there. Nobody around it." The other customers turned their heads, wondering what she was talking about.

Susan bought the diner that she had fallen in love with from Barney after her failed attempt to be a recording artist in Nashville. She decided she didn't like her producer or the politics involved in the industry. Barney agreed to stay on as her cook while bringing her up to speed.

Brandon and Lucinda hung their coats and walked to the back corner of the dining room, where Brandon always sat, usually conducting business of some sort. He often joked that it was from there that he managed the Kéntro Project. They sat as Susan came up behind them with glasses of water.

"Dang, Luce. You look hot tonight!"

"Well, thanks. I'm told the president is buying, so I assumed it was a special night. I thought you would be off by now."

"Hey. The president's buying." They laughed, and Brandon shook his head, lowering his gaze behind a menu. "Why are you even looking at that, Daddy? You know what you're going to order. And trust me, you're overdressed for it."

"Overdressed? How can you be overdressed at Barney's?" he asked.

Lucinda choked on her water and laughed. "Seriously?"

"What are you going to have, Luce?" Susan asked.

"I'll just have one of Barney's salmon salads."

"Tea?"

"No. It's too late for tea. Just water is fine."

"You got it." Susan started to walk away.

"Hey, wait," Brandon said. "You didn't ask *me*."

She turned and smiled at Lucinda, then glared at Brandon, pointing her finger at him. "It doesn't take a genius to know you want a BLT and onion rings."

"You didn't ask me what I want to drink."

"You want sweet tea."

He paused and smiled. "Okay. I want sweet tea."

"And it's going to keep you up all night," Susan said.

"Maybe."

"And you're going to be in here for breakfast in the morning bitching about it."

The three laughed as Susan turned to continue her walk back to the kitchen.

"That girl of yours is such a hoot," Lucinda chuckled.

"She has her moments."

"So, what's the big deal? What prompted Richland to buy our dinner?"

"Oh, Senator Beecher told him about the marriage proposal the other day, and he just wanted to do something nice."

"And?"

"And what?"

"And what else? I've been around here long enough to know when you go see the president, something is about to hit the fan."

"Seriously? Can't we just enjoy a quiet dinner?" He smiled.

"Yeah, right," Lucinda chuckled.

After several minutes, Susan brought their food to the table while grinning at Lucinda. "So, what do you have planned for the big wedding day?"

"You know what? I don't even know. Something simple, I suppose."

"Have you set a date?"

"Girl! This is the first time we've even had a minute to talk since your daddy proposed."

"I can pull up a chair and help you plan it all out," Susan said.

"Go away," Brandon laughed.

She smiled and walked away. "You're no fun."

Lucinda shook her head and smiled. "I guess we do need to figure out what we're going to do."

Brandon stared at his food and became sullen. "Yeah, we do."

"You okay? Brandon, honey, we don't have to do this now if your heart is still with Cassandra. I'll understand."

"Oh, no. No." He reached across the table and took her hands in his. "That's not it at all. I love you, Lucy, and there's nothing I want more than to spend the rest of my life with you."

She smiled. "What then?"

"Well . . ."

"Well? Well, what? Brandon, what is it?"

"Well . . . we may have to do it sooner than you want."

"What do you mean? Like, how much sooner?"

"Like . . . now."

"Now?"

He nodded.

"California?"

He nodded again. "I'm so sorry. I know you wanted time to plan this out, and . . ."

"Stop." Lucinda smiled. "Now works for me."

"What?"

"Honey, I knew something like this would happen sooner or later. It just happens to be sooner than later. I know what I'm signing up for here. So, what's happening?"

"The president wants me to go to Sacramento and meet with Governor Truly—find out what he's dealing with. I'd like you to come with me. I actually think the president expects it."

"You think they're going to secede, don't you?"

"It might be time."

"Of course, I'll go with you. When do we leave?"

"Next week?"

"Are you serious?"

"He wanted to give us time for the wedding." They both laughed.

"Well, of course," Lucinda said.

"You kids doing okay over here?" Susan asked as she approached the table with a pitcher of water in one hand and a pitcher of iced tea in the other. She noticed that neither one of them had started eating. "Whoa. Must be some serious chatter happening over here. Sorry to interrupt."

"No, Sweetie. It's fine," Brandon said.

"I think it's time for you to sit," Lucinda chuckled.

"I was just kidding. Really."

"Please." Lucinda stared up at Susan with begging eyes.

"Damn." Susan turned and placed the pitchers on the next table over and pulled a chair out to sit down with them. "What in the world is going on?"

"Lucy has a problem," Brandon said.

Susan reached across the table and held Lucinda's hand. "Oh, no. You poor thing. What is it?"

Lucinda laughed at Susan's concern and shook her head. "No. No, honey. It's nothing that traumatic."

"Oh, thank God."

Brandon shook his head and took a bite of his sandwich.

"We need to get married . . . now."

"Now? Lucy, what do you mean, now?"

"Like, within the week, now."

Susan looked at Brandon. "Now?"

He nodded and continued chewing and staring at his onion rings.

"SSShoot! Can I call Liv?" Susan asked. "I have to call Liv!"

"I think you probably should," Lucinda said. "Any idea where we might be able to have a quick ceremony?"

Susan thought for a few seconds, her eyes shifting back and forth in her head. Then she looked around the dining room.

"What?" Lucinda wondered what she was looking for.

"Here! Get married here!"

"Really? Can we do that?"

"I own the place. Of course we can do that. I'm sure Pastor Emmet will do the official stuff."

"Official stuff?" Lucinda smiled.

"Hey. We can do it Friday night during the bluegrass jam."

Brandon choked and put his napkin over his mouth. He could barely get his words out. "You're nuts, Kiddo."

"What do you think, Luce?" Susan's face lit up.

Lucinda looked at Brandon with her head slanted like a curious puppy. "Could be fun."

Brandon pitched an onion ring into his mouth, smiled, and shrugged his shoulders. Then he nodded in agreement.

"Yay!" Susan shouted. "It's a plan. I need to call Liv and let her know. I'm going to go out and tell Sonny. Do you know if he's eaten anything?"

"No idea," Lucinda said.

"I'll be right back." She picked up the pitchers and walked behind the counter and into the kitchen.

"Hey, Barn. Can you throw a burger and some fries in a box for Sonny?"

"On it!"

Susan grabbed a Styrofoam cup and filled it with ice and a soft drink. When the food was ready, she scooped up the box and the drink and rushed out, pushing the front door open with her backside and a swift kick behind her, then went into the parking lot.

"Hey, you!" she shouted.

Sonny looked up from the paper he was reading and threw it through the open car window into the front seat. "Hey, pretty girl. What are you doing out here?"

"Brought you some supper."

"How did you know I was hungry?"

"You're always hungry."

He laughed and took the box and cup from her, placing it on the hood of the car. The burger filled his face within seconds.

"Got news."

"Yeah?" he said through his chewing.

"Yeah. Daddy and Lucy are getting married."

"Not news."

"Friday."

Sonny started choking and reached for his drink. He took a long sip and swallowed the food. "Girl, what are you talking about? This Friday?"

"Yep."

"How can that be?"

"Apparently, they have to do it fast because they have to leave town."

"Really?"

"Yes, sir. Crap. I need to call Liv." She pulled the cell phone from her pocket and punched in the numbers. "Hey, Sis. You busy?"

"Not too. What's up?"

"Where are you?"

"Just left the office a little bit ago. Headed toward town. Why?"

"You need to stop by the diner."

"I do?"

"You do."

"I could eat."

"Not for that. Well, you can eat, but we've got to talk. Daddy and Luce are getting married."

"Duh. Not news, Kiddo."

"Friday."

"SSShoot! What? What are you talking about?"

"They have to do it quickly because of something Daddy has to do."

"California."

"Apparently so. I suggested they just do it here at the diner Friday night with Pastor Emmet during the jam."

"And Lucy bought into that?"

"I think she actually liked the idea."

"Huh. Who knew?"

"Right? Anyway, stop when you get here, and we'll work out some details. I sure hope Emmet is available."

"Not to worry, Sis. It'll be fine. I'm almost there. Throw a salad together for me?"

"Sure. See you in a bit." Susan pressed the end button and slid the phone back into her pocket.

Sonny swallowed the last handful of French fries and wiped his fingers.

"Dang, dude. You *were* hungry."

"Maybe a little. So, you two got this wedding thing figured out?"

"She's almost here. We'll do something. They'll love it."

"No doubt in my mind, sweet girl. No doubt in my mind."

They chatted for several minutes before Olivia pulled into the parking lot. She saw Susan waving and parked next to the limousine. "Hey there, Sis," she said, getting out of the car. "Hey, Sonny."

"Hey, Liv. Working late, I see."

"Yeah. Trevor and I were going over some of the work he's doing with the Genius Pods. It would seem that Daddy has already put a bug in his ear about California. Maybe something there with technology. I don't know."

"Boring," Susan said as she grabbed the empty box and cup from the hood of the car. "I'll take this, sir."

"Well, thank you."

Susan smiled and poked Sonny in the chest with her finger. "We're going in now. Don't shoot anybody."

They all laughed, and Olivia looped an arm around Susan's as they walked toward the front door.

"I take it you haven't been back in to make a salad for me?"

"Oh, crap. Sorry, Sis. It'll just take me a minute."

"No problem. So, they're back at *the* table, I presume?"

"Of course."

"Should I join them back there?"

"Tell you what. I'll take a break so you and I can go back to the kitchen to eat."

They walked into the diner, and Olivia removed her coat. She walked halfway across the dining room and waved. "Hey, Daddy. Hey, Luce. You guys enjoy your supper. We're going to grab a bite back in the kitchen. We'll let you know what we come up with." She smiled and followed Susan behind the counter, where they disappeared behind the large metal swinging door.

"Uh, oh. What have you done?" Brandon chuckled.

"They're *your* daughters. You don't trust them to cook up something?"

"Oh, they'll cook up something, all right."

CHAPTER 3

Sonny drove into the parking lot of the new headquarters building in Lebanon, K.D., where the company had resided for less than a year. From the back seat, Brandon looked up at the large sign over the main entrance into the lobby—*McClellan and McStocker Engineering Services.*

"It's going to be strange seeing that sign come down," Brandon said.

"It hasn't even been up there that long," Sonny chuckled.

"No, it hasn't; not here, anyway."

"When does the new one go up?"

"I'm told they'll be here this afternoon," Brandon said. "You gonna be in your office later this morning?"

"Yes, sir. I don't have anything going on."

Sonny stopped at the front door of the building and jumped out of the driver's seat to open Brandon's door.

"Thanks, Sonny. I'll see you in a bit." Brandon grinned when he saw Sonny shaking his head, obviously wondering what Brandon wanted to talk to him about.

When Brandon entered the lobby, he looked to the right and noticed that there were already visitors waiting to get into the museum and gift shop. It was called *Cassandra's Garden*, named after his late wife. The museum primarily consisted of American Indian relics that had been excavated from the site that the new building sat on. Olivia had done some timely negotiations with the local tribes to pull off an unprecedented agreement for the construction.

He turned and walked past the cafeteria toward the elevator. *Cass's Place* adorned the sign over the door—again, named for his late wife by the people who run the kitchen. He smiled as he walked onto the elevator and pressed the button for the fourth floor. He wondered what Cassandra would think of Lucinda and the whole wedding thing. *I think she would approve*, he thought.

Even after all that had happened over the previous several years, Brandon was still amazed that he ended up running the company. He thought back to when he sat in the conference room at the old headquarters building in Fairfax, Virginia when he first learned that his friend, Bob McClellan had been murdered.

He leaned against the side of the elevator and rubbed his eyes. Such a great leader was taken away from us way too soon, he thought. And for what? Some stupid attempt at political control. It was an inside job by an employee he trusted.

He thought he would never recover when Cassandra met the same fate—murdered by the very agent that was supposed to have been protecting her. The reach of the corrupt power brokers in D.C. had to be stopped and President Richland did everything he could to rid the country of the scourge. He went as far as befriending Bob McClellan and contracted him to design and build an entire new city in the middle of nowhere to relocate the entire federal government. They worked together to make it happen through the unprecedented 28th Amendment to Constitution. What an achievement. How sad that Bob never got to see his dream project through to completion, Brandon thought, tears welling in his eyes.

It was after Bob was murdered that the president asked Brandon to take over the company and assigned a Secret Service detail to his family. It was then that they met Sonny Langston, the agent in charge of the detail and assigned as Brandon's personal bodyguard. Sonny was a tall, confident black man, and a highly trained Navy SEAL. His huge stature overwhelmed Brandon's two daughters, who were just little girls at the time. But they adored him almost immediately and the feeling was mutual, especially with Susan.

But would it be appropriate for me to ask him to be my best man? Brandon thought. What will everyone think? He's supposed to be my protector, my driver, not my friend. Is this too much?

The opening doors jarred him from his trance. Brandon walked off of the elevator and down the long empty hallway, his footsteps clicking on the highly polished terrazzo floors echoing as he approached the executive offices. He looked into Olivia's office as he walked by.

"Mornin', Liv."

"Mornin', Daddy . . . I mean, Brandon."

He smiled and continued walking past his executive secretary's desk.

"Mornin', Mena."

Good morning," she said, laughing. "That poor girl's never going to get it. You know that, right?"

"I know, but it's fun to watch her keep trying."

Mena shook her head. "Oh, the challenges of your daddy being the boss."

"I suppose. Any messages?"

"Nope. Nothing."

Brandon walked into his office and threw his briefcase and jacket on the small conference table that sat near the floor-to-ceiling window overlooking the city to the north. Then he turned and walked out again, past Mena and into Olivia's office, closing the door behind him.

"Uh . . . good morning . . . again," she said.

He sat at one of the chairs directly in front of her desk.

"Daddy? What's up? You look . . . well . . . serious?"

"Do you think it would be appropriate for me to ask Sonny to be my best man?"

She laughed. "You must be stressing over it."

"Maybe."

"Too much, I think."

"Probably."

"Why is it such a hard decision? I think it's a great idea. Yes, he's your security guy and your driver, but he's also your friend. Probably the closest one you've got. Don't be silly."

"Do you think your mom would be okay with Lucy?"

"Are you kidding me right now? Mom would want you to be happy. Susan and I adore her. Don't think for a second that this wedding shouldn't happen. And yes, I think Mom would like Lucy . . . a lot."

"I suppose."

"You crack me up," Olivia said.

"What?"

"All the crap we've been through over the last several years, and this is what makes you nervous?"

"Hey, Liv?" A voice came over the intercom.

"Yeah, Mena."

"Your dad . . . I mean, Brandon needs to take a call in his office."

"Oh, shut up. He heard you."

Brandon laughed, clapping his hands as he stood. "I love it!"

"Get out of my office!" Olivia said, blushing.

He opened the door and walked into the hall, where Mena was laughing.

"You'll get yours, Mena!" Olivia shouted through the door.

Mena shook her head. "It's Senator Beecher's office on one."

"Got it." Brandon continued to smile and shake his head as he walked back into his office, closing the door behind him. He sat at his desk, pressed the flashing button on his phone and put the call on the speaker, then swiveled his chair to stare out of the window at the city. "This is Brandon."

"Mr. McStocker, please hold for Senator Beecher."

Within a few seconds, the senator was on the phone.

"Brandon. Good. I'm glad I caught you in your office. Got a few minutes?"

"Of course, Senator. What's up?"

"When are you going to Sacramento?"

"Soon, but I don't know exactly. Why?"

"I need to get you connected with one of the senators out there. Somebody on our side."

"Does such a person even exist out there?" Brandon asked. And why am I still getting calls from you? No offense, but the Kéntro Project is over."

"None taken. I was just buttoning things up with the president, and he asked me to get you in contact with friendly forces out there. I have a couple of ideas I'm following up on. Things are going nuts in San Francisco right now. Have you seen it?"

Brandon reached for the TV remote at the edge of his desk. "No, I haven't."

"It's a powder keg. No doubt about it. If the president federalizes the National Guard to send in, it's going to flash."

"I'm watching it now."

An explosion had obviously just occurred as Brandon watched black smoke towering over a city block as hordes of people ran past the camera operator screaming and covering their noses and mouths. He turned up the volume.

"The source of the explosion is unknown at this time," the reporter said. "But we will stay on location until we find out more from the authorities." Brandon could hear sirens wailing in the background. Then he saw what was presumably a young mother pulling her two children along behind her, all three crying with black soot covering their faces.

"Oh, God," Brandon said.

The reporter continued, "This is the third explosion in this part of the city in as many days. The mayor doesn't seem to be able to get this under control."

Brandon turned the volume back down. "I don't suppose the president has heard from Governor Truly?"

"He didn't say, but I don't think so," Senator Beecher said.

"What are they protesting anyway?"

"The checkpoints at the state line? Secession? Civil rights? Hell, I don't know. You name it. When is your wedding, by the way?"

"Well, Senator, do you like bluegrass music?"

"Huh?"

"What are you doing Friday night?"

"You're kidding, right?"

"Not in the least. Frankly, it has become quite the inconvenience, considering everything that's going on—for Lucy and me both."

"Yeah, I get it. That's gotta be rough."

"You're telling me. Sid, you can make it, right?"

"I'll be there. I need to run, but I'll get back to you with a contact for California."

"Thanks, Senator."

Brandon hung up the phone, stood, and walked to the window. He scanned the horizon, thinking about what might be ahead during his trip to the West Coast. After several minutes, he smiled, turned, and left his office walking faster than normal.

"I'm going downstairs, Mena. I'll be back shortly."

"Okay, Boss. Is there a fire?"

"Not yet."

Olivia, hearing the fast footsteps, walked out of her office to see what was going on. "Where's he off to in such a hurry?"

"Didn't say."

"Maybe he's going down to see Sonny."

"Why is that?"

Olivia shrugged her shoulders and smiled, then turned and walked back into her office.

Brandon walked across the lobby on the first floor and into the museum, where he had given Sonny a small office. He tapped on the open door and walked in.

Sonny looked up from his desk. "Hey, Boss. What's up?"

"Sorry to interrupt. Got a sec?"

"Sure. Have a seat."

"Nah. I'll make it short."

"Uh . . . okay."

"I wanted to mention this earlier, but it just didn't feel like the right time. But things are happening fast."

"Brandon?"

"Sorry. I know it's going to be a really small deal and all, but would you consider being the best man at my wedding?"

Sonny leaned back in his chair, mouth gaping open. Then he smiled and stood.

"Are you kidding me? Brother, I would be honored." He walked from behind the desk, grabbed Brandon's hand, then hugged him. "What do you mean it's going to be a small deal? Man, that's huge! So, Suze tells me it's Friday at Barney's?"

"Yep."

"Dang. This is so cool. Lucy does know what went down at Barney's a few years ago, right?"

"Yes, she knows. I think enough time has passed. What about you? You okay with it? I don't see you going inside much."

"Oh yeah. I'm fine. I just like to hang back and keep an eye on things outside, you know?"

"I suppose. Thanks. I appreciate it."

"Man, it's an honor. I'm blown away that you would ask me."

"Dude, you've been the one constant friend in my life. From the moment Cassandra referred to you as family, and you almost cried, I knew you weren't going anywhere. You even stuck around after shooting that lunatic, Jimmy, in the diner."

"Well, you know I had to do that. I hate it, but I had to."

"I know you did, man. Susan wouldn't be here with us if you hadn't."

Brandon's phone vibrated in his pocket. He took it out and looked at the text.

"Crap."

"What is it?" Sonny asked.

"It's Senator Beecher again. I guess San Francisco is blowing up."

I know ur getting married Friday, Beecher texted. *Any chance of you two being on a plane to Sacto Saturday?*

He texted back. *ur kidding, right?*

not even a little. The prez is freaking and Truly needs help.

great. will talk to Lucy.

plz do. Keep in touch. This thing is moving fast.
ok

"Well. Looks like I won't be around to celebrate much. He wants us in California Saturday."

"What the heck!"

"I know. Luce is not going to be happy. I'll go up to three and talk to her. She's been helping Trevor with the Genius Pods, and I know he called a meeting with some of the guys up there. I don't suppose you'd want to tell her for me."

Sonny chuckled. "Not a chance. Grab me after while if you want to do lunch."

"Sounds good. Maybe I can get Lucy to join us if she's still talking to me by then."

"I got your back."

"Right."

Brandon left Sonny's office and noticed some flowers on display at the checkout counter in the gift shop. "Can you put one of these on my account?" he asked the cashier.

"Of course, sir."

He took the tiny vase with a single pink rose and walked through the lobby back to the elevator. When the door opened, Olivia walked out and saw the flower.

"Uh oh. Are you in trouble?"

"Maybe." He entered and pressed the button for the third floor then turned and looked at her as he straightened his coat.

She smiled as the door closed between them.

When Brandon arrived on the third floor, Lucinda saw him coming through the glass in the enclosed conference room. She rolled her eyes and looked at Trevor, sitting at the head of the table. Trevor caught her stare and turned to see Brandon coming.

"What did he do?"

"I don't know, but I think I'm about to find out."

Brandon stuck his head in the door. "Hey, Trev. Can I steal Lucy from you for a minute?"

"Am I going to get her back?"

Brandon and Lucy chuckled. "I think so," Brandon said.

"What are you doing?" Lucinda asked as she walked into the hallway to join Brandon.

"Let's go in the break room," he said. "I need to tell you something."

"Great. You've changed your mind."

Lucinda had been hurt badly several years earlier when she lived and worked in Washington, D.C. Her love for Brandon ran deep, but she had a hard time shaking the fear that she was in for another painful let down.

"No. I haven't changed my mind."

They sat at a small table in the empty break room, and Brandon slowly slid the small vase across the table toward Lucinda. She smiled and pulled it to her. "That's very nice. So, tell it. What have you done?"

"Oh, ye of little faith."

"Hey, I may be the newbie around here, but I'm not an idiot."

They laughed, and Brandon started telling her about what was going on in San Francisco and his text message from Senator Beecher.

"Wait. Is that all? You got nervous enough to bribe me with a flower just because we have to leave Saturday?"

"Well . . . yes."

"Unbelievable."

"What?"

"I told you, Brandon. I know what I'm signing up for here. I learned to expect the unexpected from you a long time ago. Give me some credit. I love you. I'm all in."

"I'm sorry. It's just that Cassandra always—"

"Stop!"

Brandon opened his eyes wide and fell silent.

"I'm not Cassandra. I know you loved her and probably always will. But just because she had issues with all of your weird priorities doesn't mean I do. Don't you think your girls have warned me about all this? Why do you think I love those two so much? They trust me, Honey. Why can't you?"

She was intense, but he could tell she wasn't really angry. They sat in silence for a long few seconds waiting for the air to calm.

"My girls talk to you about me like that?"

"Yes. Frankly, I think they were afraid you were going to mess this up if they didn't help things along. I'm not so sure their thinking was that far off."

He chuckled and stared at her across the table. "You amaze me; you know that? Hell, all three of you amaze me."

"Well, from all I've been told, those girls had a pretty incredible mom."

"Yeah. They did."

"You still want to go through with this?" she asked.

"I do."

"So, bluegrass and balloons it is, then."

"Yep. I guess it is. I'll get Mena on the travel arrangements to California."

"Sounds good. Now, I need to get back to work."

"What are you guys working on, anyway?"

"Oh, Trevor had called a few members of the Technology team in from out of town to brainstorm ways that Tech might be able to help at the state line."

"All right. I'll let you get back to it. I'll be up in my office."

They stood, and Lucinda gave Brandon a quick kiss as they went in opposite directions out of the break room.

Brandon arrived back on the fourth floor. "Hey, Mena. You need to get Lucy and me out to Sacramento this Saturday. It'll be one-way."

"Really?"

"Yep. And get a place for us to stay with long-term options."

"Will do. Liv taking over in your absence?"

"Good point. Yes. Hey, Liv!" he shouted.

"Yes!" Olivia shouted back as she appeared from her office door.

"Can you come to my office, Sweetie? We need to talk about something."

"Are you allowed to call me that here?"

Mena shook her head, snickering as she turned back around to face her computer monitor.

"Oh, hush. Go get your notebook and come on in," Brandon said.

After a few minutes, Olivia arrived in Brandon's office and closed the door behind her. She joined him at the small round conference table near the window, dropping her notebook loudly before she sat. "This view never gets old."

Brandon opened his notebook and smiled at her. "I hope not. You're in for the long haul."

"What are you talking about?"

"What's up with you and Tim?"

"What?"

"Is it serious?"

"Daddy! Really?"

Brandon dropped his head, shaking it and smiling. "Never mind. You know Luce and I are going to California, right?"

"Right. I knew that."

"We're going Saturday."

"What!"

"San Francisco is blowing up, and the Central House wants us out there now."

"Well, that, I know. Trevor and I have been keeping tabs on it to report to the guys in the Genius Pod. But, Daddy—so soon after your wedding? Lucy must be freaking out."

"Actually, she isn't . . . at all. Apparently, you girls prepared her well for such things. She's good with it. Mena is making the arrangements now."

"How long?"

"I have no idea. We're getting one-way tickets and open-ended lodging."

"I suppose it could be a honeymoon of sorts."

"Of sorts. Yes."

"So, where does that leave this brand new McStocker and McStocker?"

"Well, since Mr. McStocker isn't going to be here, Miss McStocker is going to have to take over."

"Really? Is it going to be that long? Daddy, are you sure I'm ready for that? You've got this place running like a well-oiled machine."

"Everybody here respects you, Honey. You'll do great. The firm will continue to get government engineering design and construction contracts just like we always have. If anything unusual comes up, pick up the phone like you always do. I'll just be a little further away. Maybe you should start grooming Trevor to pick up more of your load as you pick up mine."

"That's probably not a bad idea. Our portfolio isn't all that big right now."

"No, but it's growing. The phones in Contracting are ringing off the hook now that people are learning Kéntro has been closed out. But you and Trev can handle that growth. If you need HR to start hiring, we've got plenty of room in this building to expand. Hell, the second floor is still practically empty."

"I know. I don't even like going down there; it's so depressing."

"Brandon. Sorry to interrupt," Mena said on the intercom. "Sonny is on the line."

"Put him through." Brandon stood and walked to his desk to turn on the speaker.

"Hey, Boss. Sorry to bug you, but I think it's important."

"No problem. You're on the speaker. I'm here with Olivia."

"Oh. Hey, Liv."

"Mornin', Sonny."

"You guys, I just got a call from our buddy, Clyde Baldwin, over at the Secret Service. He said he got word that the FBI intercepted and took down a hit attempt on Governor Truly."

"Damn! Are you kidding me? Drug cartel?"

"He's pretty sure."

"I assume the president already knows?"

"I would think so, Boss. Now that I'm no longer in the Service, I'm not all that privy to what's going on minute-by-minute. Clyde just let me know about it because he tries to keep up with us."

"I understand. So, everyone is okay out in Sacramento?"

"Yes, sir. As far as I know."

"I'll tell you what, Sonny; see if you can get in touch with Truly's security people and get a SITREP. Then let them know we'll be out there Saturday."

"Will do. You're taking the jet?"

"No, I think we need to keep it low key. Not that anyone out there would give a rip about some random project manager showing up in California. But who knows who's watching. I've probably gotten way more attention with Kéntro than I need or want."

"Yes, sir. I'll let you know what I find out."

"Thanks, Sonny."

"Talk later, sir. See ya, Liv."

"Bye, Sonny."

Brandon pressed the speaker button to hang up the phone and sat on the edge of his desk. "This is getting nuts."

"Who's this Baldwin guy, again?"

"Lieutenant Commander Clyde Baldwin. Retired Navy. He was on the SEAL Team with Sonny back in the day. He's the Secret Service Director now, since the FBI took down Bill Cortez."

"Oh, I remember that name now that you mention Cortez. That was really scary when we learned the cartels got to a couple of people in the Secret Service. I don't even know how that's possible."

"It was a shock to everyone, Kiddo. But I'm sure that won't happen again."

"What about California?"

"Lord, I don't even know where all that's headed."

CHAPTER 4

Sonny drove the limousine into the parking lot at Barney's Diner. The lot was full, so he drove to the front door and got out to open the car door. Brandon emerged from the back seat dressed in a tuxedo. Olivia and Susan had already escorted Lucinda into the diner several minutes earlier.

"You ready for this, Boss?"

"I don't know that I've ever been more ready for anything, my friend." Brandon turned and stared into the sky, then closed his eyes for several seconds before he was pulled away from his memory of Cassandra by Susan crashing out of the front door.

"Hey, you guys. It's about time." She hugged Brandon. "You look great, Daddy."

"Thanks, Sweetie. Let's get this show on the road."

The three of them walked into the diner, where many of the tables had been moved against the walls to clear a path from one end of the dining room to the other. The place was packed with people standing around and cheering for them. Brandon waved at Pastor Emmet Cleveland standing at the other end of the small diner, where an arch of flowers had been erected.

Susan walked across the room. The crowd parted so she could get through, revealing Olivia standing with Lucinda, conservatively clad in an antique cream-colored dress. He gasped. His eyes filled with tears at the sight of her beauty. She smiled and pointed to the other end of the room, behind where he was standing.

Brandon looked at Emmet, motioning for them to come and stand next to him. Brandon and Sonny made their way through the crowd. Sonny nervously looked around the room and then looked at Susan. She whispered to Olivia and quickly walked down the makeshift aisle to Sonny's side. Everyone watched her, apparently wondering what was going on.

She grabbed Sonny's arm. "Are you going to be okay?"

He nodded.

"Are you sure? We shouldn't have forced you to come in here."

"I'm fine, really. Let's just get it done."

Susan brushed his coat and patted his chest, trying to calm her dearest friend. Sonny had always been her hero—her guardian. As a seasoned Secret Service agent at the time, Sonny shouldn't have been affected by the shooting like he was. But Jimmy, a good guy turned bad, and an employee at McClellan and McStocker, had been holding a gun to Susan's head. Sonny had no choice but to unleash a nine-millimeter round straight into Jimmy's forehead, mere inches from Susan. Sonny had avoided going into the diner since that day, opting instead to guard the parking lot whenever Brandon visited there, which was often.

But this day was different. It was a day of joy and happiness. He squeezed Susan's hand and smiled. "I'm fine."

"Well, alrighty, then. Let's do this." Susan turned and walked back across the room to rejoin Olivia and Lucinda.

Sonny, Brandon, and Emmett stood staring at Lucinda with Olivia and Susan standing on each side of her in deep burgundy dresses, all three each holding a bouquet.

Emmet whispered in Brandon's ear. "Ready?"

"Let's do it."

Emmet nodded toward Trevor, a senior manager at the firm who had moved there from Kentucky several years earlier. He was standing in the corner with his guitar. He began to strum as his wife, and Mena's cousin, Darcy, began to play an old waltz on her fiddle. The room fell silent except for the music. Brandon's three girls strolled across the makeshift chapel. Everyone in the dining room was mesmerized by the stunning trio. They stopped in front of the three men.

"Who gives this woman to be married to this man?"

"I do."

Everyone looked toward the door to see who the booming voice was coming from.

"Oh, my God! Dad?" Lucinda shouted.

Brandon and Lucinda both thought Olivia and Susan were going to say, "We do," in unison. At least, that was the plan. But the sisters had plotted to find Lucinda's parents to sneak them into the ceremony instead. Only her father was able to attend.

Lucinda covered her mouth, and tears flowed down her cheeks. Olivia and Susan left her side and took their places next to Emmet as Mr. Reagan walked slowly through the crowd to join his daughter, peering at Brandon the whole way. They hugged, Lucinda cried, and the crowd sighed. They eventually regained her composure.

"I give my daughter to this man," Kevin Reagan said as he reached out to shake Brandon's hand. "Good to meet you, son."

"You as well, sir. Can I assume I have your blessing?"

Mr. Reagan looked at his daughter, and she smiled at him. "Of course. My little girl is happy now." He reached down and kissed Lucinda on the cheek and walked back into the crowd. Brandon took his place at her side as she handed her flowers to Olivia.

Emmet proceeded with the ceremony, finally ending with the pronouncement to the crowd; "May I present to you Brandon and Lucinda McStocker."

The crowd erupted in applause and shouting. Together, Lucinda, Olivia, and Susan all threw their bouquets across the room. Then, at the top of her lungs, Susan shouted, "Let's pick!"

The wedding party quickly moved to the restrooms to change clothes. The rest of the attendees were asked to dress for the jam, not for the wedding. Trevor and Darcy had already made their way back to the circle of chairs set up in the far corner of the dining room. Trevor took his banjo from its case and began picking an old-time tune. Darcy joined in on her fiddle. Others started taking their instruments out of the cases they had previously lined up on the floor along the wall.

The roar of bluegrass and old-time music was soon filling the room.

When Susan came out of the restroom, she got the guitar that she always kept in the kitchen and joined in the circle, sitting next to Darcy. Lucinda joined a few minutes later with her mandolin. Brandon stood back and watched.

"You aren't playing, Daddy?" Olivia leaned into him as they stood against the wall near the front door.

Brandon put his arm around her. "No, Sweetie. I just want to listen for now."

"It's pretty amazing, you know."

"That it is. I love it when this kind of fun breaks out."

"I mean you and Lucy being married," she giggled.

"Oh, that. Yeah. I suppose it is. It wasn't long ago when I would never have seen this coming."

"Oh, I know. Suze and I discussed it often."

"I bet you did."

Sonny walked up and shook Brandon's hand. "Hey, Boss. I'm headed outside. I'll be around the limo. You know . . . keeping an eye on the parking lot."

"Got it. Thanks so much, Sonny. You're the best."

"It was my honor."

"Did you get something to eat, Sonny?" Olivia asked.

"Nah. I'm not really hungry."

"Well, I'm sure Susan will bring you something eventually."

"I'm sure." Sonny opened the door and disappeared into the parking lot.

"Hey, Brandon," Mena said. "That was a pretty neat little ceremony. Simple but beautiful."

"Yeah. That was on these girls."

"Well, you did a wonderful job, Liv."

"Thanks, Mena."

"Hey, Boss. All the travel has been taken care of for tomorrow. I texted you the tickets and itinerary."

"Thanks."

"Congratulations. Have fun tonight."

"Thanks, Mena," he said as she stepped away into the crowd.

"So, aren't you going to pick at all?" Olivia asked.

"I don't know. Maybe later."

"I take it your mind is on California."

"I suppose you could say that. I guess I better go speak to Mr. Reagan."

"Yeah. You better do that. I never thought we would find him without Lucy knowing."

"You took a bit of a risk there, you know," Brandon said.

"I know. But when we spoke to him on the phone, I didn't sense any bad mojo."

"Wish me luck."

"I'll be there if fists start flying." She laughed and disappeared into the crowd.

Brandon made his way across the diner to where Lucinda's father was sitting. "Mr. Reagan, mind if I join you?"

"Not at all, son. Sit. And it's Kevin."

"Got it. Kevin, it is." Brandon pulled out a chair and sat across the table from him.

"So, Lucy tells me you two are headed out tomorrow. Big plans?"

"Well, it's kind of a working vacation to California."

"It's crazy what's going on out there," Kevin said.

"That, it is."

"Does that have anything to do with your trip?"

"Hey, Dad," Lucinda interrupted. She leaned over and kissed Brandon on the forehead. "What are you boys up to?"

"Just shootin' the breeze," Kevin said. "Care to join?"

"Sure!" She pulled out a chair and sat next to Brandon.

"You tired of pickin' already?" Brandon asked.

"Well, you weren't there, so I lost interest."

"I'll go over there shortly."

"So, Dad, did you tell Brandon what you do for a living?"

"Oh, he's not interested in what an old coot like me does."

"Well, now I *have* to know," Brandon chuckled.

"Go on, Pop. Tell him."

"Okay. Fine. I run a drone business."

"A drone business," Brandon repeated.

"Yes. A drone business."

"You mean like, taking-pictures-of-real-estate drone business?"

"Among other things. But yes."

"Sounds like fun. How many drones do you have?" Brandon asked.

"Fun. Right."

"He has tons of them back in Virginia," Lucinda said. "He has so many he has a warehouse to keep them in."

"Dang. So, you're serious about it, then."

"Serious. Yes."

"He does work for the government on occasion."

"Nice. Has the move by the feds messed up your business any?"

"It has complicated matters. Yes. I'm thinking about moving the operation out here to be closer to the action."

"Might not be a bad idea," Brandon said.

"But if you and Lucy are moving to California, I don't know if I'd want to be here, not knowing anyone."

Brandon looked at Lucinda, then back at Kevin. "We aren't actually *moving* to California. It's just a temporary job. But I can introduce you to some of the movers and shakers around here if you like. The new GSA offices aren't far from ours if it's government contracts you're looking for."

Kevin looked at Lucinda for an uncomfortably long few seconds. She smiled and looked over at Brandon.

"What?"

"Oh, nothing," Kevin said. "I have some friends at the CIA that can probably help me out if I need it."

Brandon's smile dissolved, and he tilted his head in curiosity. "Oh. I understand."

"Son, I don't think you do, but we'll just leave it at that. Lucy here shouldn't have said anything about my hobby."

"So, I take it we're bumping up against top secret SCI here," Brandon said.

"Again, we'll just leave it at that."

"Sorry, Pop. I just wanted Brandon to know a little bit about what you do. We've never really talked about you, ya know. I didn't exactly leave D.C. under the best of circumstances."

"Hell, you left and didn't look back. Your mother has been crazy worried, and you barely talk to her.

You *could* call her, at least when she knows what planet she's on."

"I know, and I'm sorry. Things here just got spun up way faster than I expected. How is she?"

"About the same. More bad days than good. She hardly knows anyone anymore."

Lucinda looked at Brandon and put her hand on his arm. "Mom has advanced Alzheimer's."

"I'm really sorry to hear that," Brandon said. "It must be hard."

"Hard. Right."

Brandon shook his head. "Sir, have I offended you in some way?"

"Brandon," Lucinda said, squeezing his arm.

"Sir, if I've offended you, I'm really sorry. It was never my intention. I thought you were okay with us getting married . . . not that it would have mattered. But we would prefer to have your blessing."

Kevin stared at Brandon. "You know what. I came out here to stop this."

"Then why did you say it was okay earlier?"

"Because I didn't want to embarrass my daughter in front of her friends."

"Dad? What are you talking about?"

"Honey, I'm sorry. I just thought you would be coming home. I hoped that Brandon was trouble and that you would come to your senses." He looked at Brandon and continued. "I had some people look into your background after your daughters contacted me. I couldn't believe what I was hearing, and I got scared."

"Dad! What the hell?" Lucinda shouted, getting the attention of a few people sitting around them.

"Hang on. Hang on," Brandon said to her, then looked back at Kevin. "And what did this little investigation of yours turn up?"

Kevin looked down at the table and fell silent.

"Dad?"

"Nothing. Well, a little drinking problem a while back. But other than that, squeaky clean."

"So, you were disappointed then. You were looking for a reason to turn Luce against me?"

"You could say that."

"I don't believe this! This is low even for you, Dad." Lucinda jumped to her feet, almost knocking over her chair.

"Wait. Wait. Wait. Sit down. Please," Kevin pleaded.

Brandon looked up at her and nodded. "It's okay, Lucy."

She sat down, glaring at her father.

"Look. So, I didn't find anything, and I'm sorry. I was a jerk, okay?" He looked at Brandon. "I know Lucinda is a grown woman, but I set out to get her away from you. But when I read about the things you've done, I was impressed. I knew I had lost her. And now that I've met you face-to-face, I see what kind of man you are, and . . . I still didn't want to believe it. I see how much she loves you, and I know I have to let go." Kevin's eyes turned red and watery.

"So, you've got some serious ties in the CIA, then?" Brandon smiled. Lucinda chuckled at him, masterfully changing the subject. Her tension disappeared.

"And you've got some serious ties at the Central House," Kevin said.

"You might say that."

"If the president ever needs a drone, you think you could put in a good word?"

They all laughed as Susan walked up with a tray full of champagne.

"Load up, y'all. We're about to have a toast."

Brandon looked at her and then looked around the room. "What are you talking about?"

Susan placed two fingers from her free hand in her mouth and let out a blood-curdling whistle that was probably heard all the way out to the street. The room fell silent. "Hey, everyone," she shouted. "We're going to have a toast!"

The room erupted in shouts and cheers. Those who were sitting at the tables stood. Susan pointed across the room toward Olivia. She began to speak.

"I want to thank you all for coming to help us celebrate the marriage of our dad to this wonderful woman, Lucy," Olivia said. She was interrupted by another round of cheers.

"This was a long time coming. And to see my daddy so hap—" Olivia choked, and tears filled her eyes. The room fell pin-drop-quiet, and several seconds passed while she regained her composure.

"I'm sorry. To see my daddy happy again has just brought so much joy to Susan and me. Lucy has been such a blessing to our family, and I know Mom is looking down with a smile, too."

Lucinda wiped her eyes and blew a kiss to Olivia and then wrapped her arm around Brandon's.

"We all agreed that the title of mom would not enter into this deal," Susan shouted. The room exploded into laughter, and Lucinda reached over and kissed Susan on the cheek.

"So, let's raise a glass to Brandon and Lucy!" Olivia shouted.

"To Brandon and Lucy!" Susan repeated.

Then everyone in the room shouted, "To Brandon and Lucy!" All of the champagne glasses were raised, and everyone took a sip. When everyone returned to their conversations, Kevin, Brandon, and Lucinda sat back down at their table, and Susan went back into the crowd.

"That was great," Kevin said. You two are clearly loved. Congratulations." The three of them raised their glasses for another private toast.

"Thanks, Pop. That means a lot to me."

"So, is that what I call you, then?" Brandon asked. "Pop?"

"Uh . . . no," Kevin smiled. "Kevin will do just fine. Perhaps Mr. Reagan on occasion."

They laughed as Brandon and Kevin shook hands.

"So, you guys are headed out tomorrow, then?"

"Yes, Dad. We're leaving pretty early."

"Where do you fly out of?"

"Topeka," Brandon said.

"You need a ride to the airport?"

"No, thanks. My guy, Sonny, is taking us."

"You have a guy?"

"It's his driver and friend, Dad. You saw him briefly standing up with Brandon during the ceremony."

"Oh. The big black guy. He looked kinda nervous when I came in."

"He has his reasons. But I trust him with my life. He's been a friend of the family for many years."

"It's always good to have that kind of friend," Kevin said.

"Time to pick?" Lucinda asked.

"I believe it is," Brandon said.

"You guys go ahead. I'll be over shortly."

Brandon and Lucinda stood and made their way through the crowd to the other side of the dining room, where everyone in the jam circle was playing music and singing. Susan had sat back down with Trevor and Darcy and was playing her guitar. Eight or ten other musicians were sitting around the circle.

"Come on in here, Daddy. Your guitar is there against the wall. Lucy, I hid your mandolin here behind me."

They walked through the circle, and Brandon opened his case to get his guitar. Trevor began playing a roll on his banjo, and Lucinda picked up on it with her mandolin. Then Darcy started playing Grigsby's Hornpipe. Brandon sat next to Lucinda and began strumming his guitar. After several minutes of playing, Lucinda elbowed Brandon and motioned with her chin for him to look at the back of the room. Her dad was leaning against the wall and tapping his foot to the music.

When the music stopped, someone from the crowd shouted, "Angel Band!" Susan looked over at Darcy, then in the other direction toward Lucinda and Brandon.

"Let's do it," Brandon said and started strumming a slow waltz on his guitar while Darcy played a beautiful intro to the song on her fiddle. Susan joined in, singing the first verse.

"My latest sun is sinking fast. My race is nearly run. My strongest trials now are past. My triumph has begun."

Brandon, Lucinda, Darcy, and Trevor all joined in singing with Susan on the chorus.

"Oh, come, angel band. Come and around me stand. Oh, bear me away on your snow-white wings to my immortal home. Oh, bear me away on your snow-white wings to my immortal home."

Other than the music, there wasn't a sound in the room. Some people quietly moved their lips, singing along, while others listened and smiled. The Friday night bluegrass jam went on late into the night, most people forgetting that a wedding had taken place that day.

CHAPTER 5

"If you guys need me to ship anything out to you, let me know," Sonny said as he drove the limo east on I-70 toward Topeka.

"I think we've got most of what we need—at least to start," Brandon said. He smiled at Lucinda. "She has those two monster suitcases back there. I think she'll be fine."

"Shut up," Lucinda chuckled.

Brandon's phone vibrated in his coat pocket. It was a text message from Senator Beecher.

Great time last night. Congrats. Sorry I had to leave early.

Brandon turned the phone for Lucinda to see. Then he tapped out his response.

Glad you made it.
You guys on your way to arpt?
Yes. Almost there.
Prez wants you to let him know the second you make contact with Truly.
Will do.
Safe travels.

Brandon slid the phone back into his inside coat pocket. "I wonder what he's nervous about now." His phone vibrated again. "What the heck! Oh, it's Liv."

He pressed the speaker button. "Yeah, Sweetie. What's up?"

"Sorry to bug you, Daddy. If I asked, I forgot what you said. Where are you guys flying into out there?"

"Straight into Sacramento. Why?"

"It looks like the protesters are about to close San Francisco down, and I was worried about you two."

"Jeez. That sucks. I suppose the feds are headed over there too?"

"I would assume so, but I haven't heard for sure yet."

"Okay. We're almost at the airport. Text or call if you hear anything. Of course, we'll be incommunicado while we're airborne."

"Yeah. It sucks not using your own plane, eh?"

"Oh, I don't mind the inconvenience on occasion."

"Yeah, right."

Lucinda giggled. "He isn't too spoiled, is he, Liv?"

"Oh. Hey, Luce. I'm surprised he isn't giving Sonny fits, kicking and screaming all the way out there."

"He's all right, Liv," Sonny shouted from the front seat. "We got him calmed down."

"Hey, Sonny. Are you coming back here after you drop them off?"

"Yes, ma'am."

"Consider this limo yours, Honey," Brandon said.

"At your service, Mrs. McStocker," Sonny said with a swoon-inducing voice.

"Well, I hadn't thought about that, but that's cool. I'll take it."

"I'll see you in about an hour, Liv. We're pulling into the terminal now."

"Okay, Sonny. Come see me in my office when you get here, please."

"Will do."

"I'll text when we get to Sacramento, Sweetie. Hold the fort down."

"Will do, Daddy. Have fun, Lucy!"

"Bye-bye, Liv."

Sonny stopped at the departure terminal, jumped out of the driver's seat, and rushed to the back of the car. He had popped open the trunk lid. Brandon leaped out of the back seat and ran around behind Sonny to get to Lucinda's door. He patted Sonny on the back as he galloped past him. "Thanks, man. I appreciate this."

"My pleasure, Boss," Sonny said as he took the suitcases and Brandon's briefcase from the trunk and placed them on the sidewalk. "You guys have a good flight. As I said, let me know if you need anything out there. I can get a car for us out there if you want me to come and do the driver thing."

"I don't think that'll be necessary, but I'll let you know." Brandon slapped Sonny on the shoulder, then threw his briefcase on top of the suitcase and started toward the automatic doors to the terminal. Lucinda followed behind him, pulling her two large suitcases.

"Bye, Sonny. Thank you."

"Enjoy your flight, ma'am."

Sonny jumped into the car and drove off as Brandon and Lucinda disappeared into the terminal.

When the plane landed in Sacramento, Brandon turned on his phone and immediately received a text from Olivia.

Three more dead in San Francisco.

Not good, he replied. *We're taxiing in now. Any arrests or suspects?*

Not good at all. No arrests yet.

Guess that'll be the first order of business with Truly.

No doubt. Cartels suspected of instigating the whole thing.

Not surprising. Keep me posted.

K

"This is heating up faster than I thought it was going to," Brandon said to Lucinda. When the plane stopped rolling at the gate and the seatbelt sign was turned off, they stood to retrieve their carry-on bags from the overhead compartment—something they hadn't had to do in a long time.

"Is it San Francisco?" she asked.

"I'm afraid so. It isn't good, but at the moment, I'm just not sure what to do about it." Brandon put his briefcase down on the seat he had been sitting in while waiting for the flight attendant to open the door. He texted Mena.

Arrived safely. Contact info for Truly's office, please.

On it.

"This is just so weird," Lucinda said.

"What's that?"

"Why you? With everything that's going on, why is the president sending you to fix something so far outside of your field of expertise?"

"Don't think I didn't push that when I met with him," Brandon said. "Truthfully, I don't think he knows who to trust. Expertise or not, the president trusts me. I'm outside of the federal bubble. And I think that's all there is to it."

After several minutes, the contact information he requested arrived in Brandon's phone. He and Lucinda made their way through the terminal in Sacramento, picked up their luggage from the carousel, and exited to the ground transportation area. Their rental car was waiting.

"Don't you think it was pretty risky to come out here without having set an appointment with the governor first?" Lucinda asked.

"Probably. But the president seems to think he wants our help. So, we'll see."

They loaded everything into the small, unassuming rental car and left the airport. Brandon handed Lucinda his phone. "Give Mena a call, and ask her to set something up. I was going to do it myself, but she might have better luck just working with the governor's secretary."

"Good idea." Lucinda made the call, and Mena started working on the appointment. While they waited, Lucinda began tinkering with the Bluetooth functions in the car's stereo system. She was able to get Brandon's phone synced just in time for Mena's call to come in, startling them both.

"Crap!" Brandon said.

"Sorry about that," Lucinda chuckled as she turned the volume down. She pressed the green answer button.

"Mena?"

"Hey, Lucy. Yeah, it's me."

"Hey, Mena," Brandon said. "She was just figuring out the Bluetooth in here. You hearing us okay?"

"Just fine."

"Good. What have you got?" Brandon asked.

"Can you be there by three?"

"Today?"

"Yes."

"Dang! Uh . . . well, yeah. We're only about twenty minutes away from the State Capitol."

"Okay, then. His secretary said they'll be waiting for you, and the entry guards will be notified."

"Thanks, Mena. Is our girl pulling her hair out yet?"

"Not a chance. She's got this, Boss."

"I'm sure she does. We'll check in after the meeting, once we're at the hotel."

"Okay, Brandon. Bye now."

Brandon drove down Interstate 5 and exited near the State Capitol. When they arrived, they parked the car and walked to the front entrance and through the security checkpoint where they asked directions to the governor's office.

"Right this way, sir." The aide escorted them to the annex on the first floor where the governor was located. When they arrived at his office, the secretary stood to greet them.

"Mr. McStocker. Mrs. McStocker. Welcome. The governor is expecting you and asked that I show you in as soon as you arrive. Right this way."

Brandon and Lucinda followed behind her and through the doorway she opened for them.

"Mr. McStocker. It's a pleasure to meet you finally."

"You as well, Governor. This is my partner, Lucinda Rea . . . uh, McStocker."

"Ah. Another McStocker, eh? Interesting."

"Yes, sir."

"Can we get you two anything? Something to drink, perhaps?"

"No, thank you. I'm fine." They looked at Lucinda and she shook her head.

The governor's secretary walked out and closed the door.

"Please. You two have a seat here on the couch."

"Thank you, sir. To be frank with you, I wasn't quite sure how our visit would be received."

"I understand. A few weeks ago, things may have been different. But as it stands, I think we might be able to use all the help we can get, since the president is insisting." The governor sat in a chair on the opposite side of a long coffee table.

"Have you been keeping up with what's going on in the Bay Area?" the governor asked.

"Yes, sir. I'm sorry there were more lives lost."

"Me too. It has escalated far beyond what any one of us thought it would."

"Governor, do you have a plan to counter the cartel's threat?" Lucinda asked.

His brows pulled in as he tilted his head, "Cartel? What makes you think it's the cartels doing this?"

"I'm sorry, sir. We assumed you knew," Brandon said. "We've been tracking this for several years now. When we started building the Kéntro District, we worked to eliminate the corruption standing in our way. Some people went to prison, and some lost their lives. Each time we thought we were getting a handle on it, we learned the perpetrator was working for someone, even some of the highest offices in the country. It turned out, the only people with enough power to threaten the families of those charged with the security of the country had to be someone with a long reach and deep pockets."

"Drug cartels."

"Exactly. Sir, you didn't know about any of that?"

"Mr. McStocker—"

"Please. Call me, Brandon."

"Okay. Brandon, I don't pay much attention to what goes on outside of California. I just don't have the time nor the inclination. We've created our own infrastructure because the feds never gave a rip about what goes on out here. Whenever some stupid congressional mandate comes down, we create our own office to handle it. Over the years, we've learned that trying to work with a government all the way across the country was way too burdensome."

"Has the move further west helped matters any?" Brandon asked.

"Doesn't matter."

"Sir?"

"We've already got what we need to sustain ourselves. Hell, we grow most of the country's food supply here in the valley as it is. We've built our own infrastructure and have learned to live without federal handouts."

"How can you afford to keep doing that?" Lucinda asked.

"Missy, we have taxes for that—just like everybody else."

"With all due respect, Governor, you can call me Mrs. McStocker . . . just like everybody else."

He glared at her and then turned his attention back to Brandon. "Why are you here, exactly?"

"We've come as a kind of a nonpolitical envoy for the president, sir."

Governor Truly looked at Lucinda and back at Brandon. "What in the hell does that even mean? I'm told you're just a project manager for an engineering firm. What does that have to do with anything?"

"I like to think I've built an unusual amount of trust with the president over the years. We have access to an unprecedented network of experts around the country that the president would like to offer you."

"To what end?"

Lucinda shook her head. "Governor, he's offering his help to put a lid on this powder keg of a state you're running."

Brandon covered his grin as the governor jumped to his feet. "Watch it! You're about to wear out your welcome. I'd hate for that to happen so soon after you got here. Granted, San Francisco has turned into a bit of a ground zero for state politics right now. But California as a whole is doing just fine."

"Governor, the fact that your ballots keep showing up with proposals to split the state in two and all the chatter about leaving the Union kind of speaks for itself," Brandon said. "How is that doing just fine?"

"Most of the residents of this state are standing together and support what we're doing here at the Capitol."

"Are you kidding?" Brandon stood and walked closer to the governor. "If there's any unity in this state, it's with the east side of the state believing that the whole left coast is absolutely nuts!"

"Right along with the rest of the country," Lucinda said as she stood and walked around behind the couch, crossing her arms in front of her.

"Mrs. McStocker, have I done something to piss you off?"

"Governor, do you want our help or not?" she asked.

Brandon smiled. "Hang on. Hang on. Governor Truly, we really are here to help, not to attack your state. I'm sorry. It's just that the evolution here through the past several governors has left the more conservative constituents hanging out to dry. Most everyone in the Central Valley and all points east have been left with little or no representation in the state. You pride yourself in the state's agricultural achievements, yet your farmers are leaving the state in droves because you're taxing and legislating them out of business."

"I'd say the tree-huggers have you by the balls, Governor," Lucinda said.

"Look. That's enough. I'm not going to stand here in my own office and listen to this crap. I want you both gone. Now! Brandon, if I do decide to invite you back, and that's a big if, you come alone. Got it?" He glared at Lucinda.

"I understand, Governor. Please think it over. We have a lot of technology and other resources we can bring to bear to help control the borders and find the cartel that's causing this unrest. I'll leave my number with your secretary. We'll show ourselves out."

Brandon and Lucinda walked toward the door. Governor Truly walked around his desk and silently sat, lowering his head into his clenched fists.

They closed the heavy office door behind them and walked past the secretary's desk. "Here's my card for when the governor is ready to talk to me again."

She smiled. "Of course, sir."

The two walked out onto the front porch of the State Capitol. "What are you laughing about?" Lucinda asked.

He looked around and then down to his feet as they hopped down the steps. "What in the hell was that?" he asked with a chuckle.

"What?"

"That. That thing you did with the governor. You had it out for him the minute we walked into his office."

"Oh, jeez," Lucinda said. "I wanted to slap that smug look off of his face so badly I could taste it. What an arrogant ass."

"Go easy on him. He's got a lot on his plate."

"Maybe. Do you think he'll call you back?"

"I'm sure he will."

"Whoa! Has his arrogance rubbed off on you?"

"Look. He needs federal help here, and he knows it. But didn't you find it odd that he acted surprised to the hear a drug cartel is behind all this?"

"It didn't help matters. Talk about sticking your head in the sand."

"Something tells me he knows more than he's letting on." Brandon unlocked the doors, and they got into the car.

"Wait. Do you think he's hiding something?" Lucinda asked.

"He's the governor of California. Of course he's hiding something."

"But do you think maybe the cartel has gotten to him?"

"Wouldn't surprise me." Brandon's phone vibrated. "Here. See who this is," he said, handing it to Lucinda. He started the car and drove away.

"It's Beecher. Says the president wants to know if we've made contact."

"I guess just tell him, yes, but no progress. I wonder why the impatience. Hell, we just got here. Let's go get checked into the hotel and rest up a bit."

"Sounds good to me. I'm starving."

"Me too." Brandon turned onto the street toward their hotel. "Tree-huggers have you by the balls? Seriously?"

They started laughing so hard Brandon could barely keep the car in his lane.

When they arrived at the hotel, a bellhop took all of their luggage up to their room. They had already been automatically checked in. When they got into their room, Brandon tipped the bellhop and closed the door behind him. Lucinda fell backward onto the bed.

"I'm freakin' exhausted. Can we just order in?"

"Room service?" Brandon asked.

"Absolutely."

After they had eaten, Lucinda fell asleep on the bed, and Brandon dozed in the chair while watching the news on TV. He was in and out, but a live shot showing the chaos in San Francisco got his attention. He sat up straight and rubbed his face to wake up.

The reporter was interviewing people on the street near the riots that had broken out. "Sir, what can you tell us about what's going on here?"

"We want to live our own lives, but the government is out here getting in our business."

"How is that, sir?"

"They're the ones creating all of this. They're out here getting everyone stirred up. Their laws, their taxes, everything. We just want to be left alone. We should be able to marry who we want to marry, do what we want with our bodies, and smoke what we want to smoke."

The reporter smiled at the camera. "Back to you in the studio."

This can't be serious, Brandon thought.

It had gotten dark outside, and Lucinda was still sound asleep. Assuming that she was out for the night, Brandon pulled the covers over her and laid in the bed beside her. They both slept throughout the night in their clothes.

Brandon awoke to a knock on the door. He ignored it, thinking he must be dreaming.

"Brandon." Lucinda reached her hand across the bed, tapping on his stomach. "Brandon. What time is it?"

"I don't know, but the sun's up."

"What? You mean I slept all night?"

"Yes, you did." The knock on the door became louder and more intentional. "Who in the hell can that be at this hour?"

"What hour is it?" Lucinda asked again.

Brandon looked at his cell phone on the nightstand. "It's only seven." He sprang up from the bed and went to the door. He looked through the peephole. "I have no idea who this is." He attached the security chain and cracked the door open. "Can I help you?"

"Brandon McStocker?"

"Yes. Who's asking?"

"Mr. McStocker, I'm Bruce Talbot. I'm with the governor's office—with the CHP security detail actually. Governor Truly sent me. He didn't think it was safe to come himself."

"And why's that?"

"Sir, can I come in?" He pulled a badge from his inside coat pocket and showed it to Brandon.

Brandon turned and looked at Lucinda. She jumped up from the bed and straightened it, then nodded.

"I suppose." He unlatched the chain and opened the door.

Bruce walked in and raised a box he had been holding in his other hand. "I hope you don't mind. I took the liberty of bringing you some bagels and cream cheese. Coffee is on its way up. You like bagels, don't you?"

Lucinda opened the curtains and sat at the small round table in the corner of the room. "Sure. I'll have a bagel. Is this some kind of peace offering from the governor?"

"I suppose you could say that. He just wants to make sure you two are comfortable."

"So, he doesn't want us to get out of his state after all?" Brandon asked.

"No. In fact, he seemed a little worried that you might leave after yesterday's meeting."

Lucinda snickered as she reached into the box for breakfast. "So, he told you about that, eh?"

"He did. But I still think he's in denial."

Brandon and Lucinda looked at Bruce simultaneously, sensing a breach in his loyalty.

"What I mean is, I think some operatives are paying many of these protesters to come in from different parts of the country. All these people aren't from California. Mercenaries, if you will."

"Really," Brandon said. "You really believe that?"

"I do. We're looking into it."

"Do you think it might be a cartel?" Lucinda asked.

"What? You mean like a drug cartel . . . from Mexico?"

"That's exactly what I mean," she said.

"Why in the world would you think it's a cartel?"

"Well," Brandon said. "After the president closed off your state borders, it may have given the drug lords the motivation they needed for a full-scale move-in."

"You basically report to Senator Beecher, right?"

"Well, my board of directors does, I suppose—in a way. Why?"

"You might want him to get you in touch with one of the congressmen out here, so you have someone looking out for you."

Lucinda dabbed some cream cheese from her cheek and swallowed the bite of bagel in her mouth. "Is this the governor talking, or you?"

"It doesn't matter. Look, we do have people in this state who are supportive of President Richland's administration and his agenda. You just have to find them. They've been so badly beaten; they've given up on trying to share any kind of message out here."

"Yes. We have that in work," Brandon said. "Mr. Talbot, did the governor really send you, or did you come here on your own?"

"I'm sorry. I have to go. It was a pleasure meeting you both. Please; enjoy the bagels. Brandon, you need to call Senator Beecher." He rushed out of the room, closing the door behind him.

CHAPTER 6

Lucinda cut another bagel in half, spread cream cheese on it, and slid it to the other side of the table for Brandon. He sat down and, without looking up, sent a text.

Senator Beecher. Please call me when you can.

"Just put your phone down and eat."

"Fine, Lucy. I will. I just want to talk to the senator. So, what do you make of it?"

"I don't really know. That guy seemed awfully nervous."

Brandon's phone vibrated on the table. He turned it over. "Beecher." He read the text aloud. "Have you heard of Cártel del Mundo?" He looked at Lucinda. "I have not. Have you?"

She shook her head while chewing another bite of her bagel.

There was another knock at the door. Brandon continued to study the text he received from Senator Beecher and stood to see who it was. He looked through the peephole then opened the door. A server from the kitchen rolled a cart into the room with a silver carafe and two cups. "Your coffee, sir."

"Thanks. You can put it right over there next to the table."

"Yes, sir."

Brandon took the wallet from his pocket and started to take some cash out.

The server held up his hand and smiled. "Oh, no, that won't be necessary, sir. A gentleman who said he was with the governor's office has taken care of it."

"You sure?"

"Yes, sir. It's good." He nodded his head and left the room.

"Honey, look," Lucinda said.

"What?"

"Is that a receipt under the saucer, or is it a note?"

Brandon pulled the piece of paper from under the saucer and unfolded it. He read it aloud. "Cártel del Mundo."

"Are you serious?" Lucinda said.

Brandon picked up the room phone and called the front desk. "Hi. Can you put me in touch with the server who just brought coffee to this room?"

"Hold a moment, sir."

"Room Service."

"Hi. This is Brandon McStocker in room six eleven. Can you put me in touch with the server who just delivered coffee for two to this room?"

"I'm sorry, sir. We haven't delivered coffee to that room."

"There must be some mistake. Are you sure?"

"Absolutely sure, sir. I'm here alone this morning. Any such order would have had to come to me."

"Is there anyone else who could be delivering coffee? An outside service, perhaps."

"No, sir. That would be against company policy."

"Of course." Brandon looked at Lucinda, shaking his head. "Okay. Thank you." He hung up the phone. "Well, that's just weird."

"Could that Bruce guy have gotten it from somewhere else?" Lucinda asked.

"He said the hotel doesn't allow outside caterers."

The phone rang, and Brandon picked it up. "Yes?"

"Sir, you just called about the mysterious coffee service?"

"Yes."

"Well, I got curious after we hung up and did a quick inventory. Sir, I am missing a service cart and a silver carafe. I'm guessing a couple of cups and silverware are missing as well. Of course, I haven't actually inventoried that."

"Of course. Well, consider it all found. You have no idea how this might have happened?"

"No, sir. Not a clue. I'm really sorry."

Brandon's cell phone started vibrating on the table, and Lucinda looked over at it.

"Beecher," she said.

"Thanks for calling back up here," Brandon said to the attendant.

"You're welcome, sir. I'll let you know if I figure out anything else."

"Thank you." Brandon hung up the room phone as Lucinda tossed him his cell phone. He pressed the speaker button.

"Hey, Senator. Thanks for calling. I have you on the speaker. Lucy is here with me."

"You guys settling in okay?"

"Yes, sir."

"So, have you heard of that Cártel del Mundo?"

"Well, I hadn't, sir, until right after you texted me. Do you know a Bruce Talbot?"

"I've heard the name. Why?"

"He paid us a visit. Apparently, had some coffee smuggled up to us. Said he was with the governor's security detail. Then he told us we needed to call you about getting some local support out here."

"Oh, damn. You know what. Brandon, I need to get you in contact with a congresswoman by the name of Val Strickland. I have to wonder if he's her guy in the governor's office."

"A mole?"

"Something like that. I'll get back to you. Have you had any of that coffee?"

"No. Why?"

"I'd stay clear of it, just to be safe. Oh, and check with your guy, Sonny. He might have some insight into this Bruce Talbot."

"What? What are we dealing with here, Senator?"

"While you're at it. You might want him to join you out there. I'll get back to you." The call disconnected.

"How in the world would Sonny know anything about Bruce Talbot?" Lucinda asked.

"No idea, Luce. No idea." Brandon called Sonny.

"Hey, Boss. What's up?"

"You busy?"

"Let me see. You're there. I'm here. Nope. Not busy."

"Funny. I thought Liv might have you hopping."

"Ah. Yeah, I don't think she's found her groove yet. I'm a little surprised you called so soon, though."

"Yeah. Your name just came up, and I need to check on something."

"Okay. Shoot."

"Does the name Bruce Talbot ring a bell?"

"Wow. I haven't heard that name in a while. Yeah. We went through training in Glynco together. Last I heard he left the Service and was working out there in California. From what I heard, he was in pretty deep."

"What do you mean?"

"Well, like doing regular security work for key government officials while at the same time doing dark ops for someone else."

"Someone else? Like who?"

"Well, I have no idea who Bruce is actually working for, but the CIA often operates that way."

"You mean like a double agent?"

"Mm. I suppose it's something like that, but not really. Talbot's a good guy from everything I knew of him. The CIA, if that's who it is, wouldn't have taken him to do harm. How did you come across him, anyway?"

"He paid us a visit to rep the governor. Said he was head of his security detail."

"Yeah, I think the highway patrol has something to do with it out there. Strange. What makes you think he's gone deep?"

"Just a weird vibe we're getting. He smuggled some coffee for us from the kitchen and then left a note under one of the saucers."

"A note?"

"Yeah. It just said, 'Cártel del Mundo.' When we spoke to Senator Beecher, he said you would know about Talbot."

The line fell awkwardly silent for several seconds. "Sonny?"

"What else did the senator say?"

"Well, he did mention that you should probably join us out here."

"Exactly what I was thinking."

"Do you really think that's necessary?"

"I don't know, Boss. But if Talbot is a CIA plant in the governor's office, something is up."

"Sonny, do you have access to Talbot? Do you know how to get in touch with him?"

"No, but the Secret Service can probably find out. I'll pay Clyde a visit."

"Good. What do you know about Cártel del Mundo?"

"Not a lot. Only that they might be the biggest distributor of illegal drugs on the planet. Serious drug lords. Boss, do you know that encrypted server that Liv had set up a while back?"

"Sure. We've only used it once. Why?"

"We might want to wipe the dust off of it. I'll go upstairs and talk to Liv about it."

"Uh . . . Okay."

"Let's shut it down here. I'll meet you over there. Text her when you have it loaded up."

"Will do." Brandon disconnected the call and scrambled to get his computer out of the briefcase on the bed.

"Now what's going on?" Lucinda asked.

"Apparently, Sonny wants to start communicating on a secure network."

"Seriously? You guys have a secure network?"

"It's something Liv was messing with a few years ago. I guess she had her reasons."

"Brandon, are we safe here?"

"Frankly, at the moment, I don't really know." He placed the laptop on the table, sat down, and opened it. "C'mon. C'mon. C'mon." Once he finally got the secure application running, he saw the name *M&M2* blinking. He logged in to his M&M1 account and sent a chat message.

Liv?

Daddy. Yes. I'm in the car with Sonny, and we're headed to Secret Service Headquarters.

Does Clyde know you're coming?

Yes. Sonny said if Cártel del Mundo is operating in California, they're probably connected in Sacramento in some way.

Okay. Let me know what Clyde says about Talbot.

Will do. I also get the impression Sonny is planning to head your way soon.

Doesn't surprise me.

He's in that Sonny-mood.

Oh, crap.

Yeah.

Honey, I don't know what's going on, but be careful, and keep close tabs on your sister.

Of course, Daddy. We're pulling up to the gate at SS HQ. I'm shutting down.

Okay.

Brandon closed his laptop and spun his chair to stare out of the hotel room window.

"Brandon?"

"Sorry, Luce. I think there's a lot more going on here than just the president wanting me to help the governor. Way more than we signed up for."

"Do you think the president knows about all this?"

"Not a chance. He wouldn't have withheld it from me. Not something like this."

"Well, I do want some coffee. Just to be safe, I'll order another tray myself."

"Good idea." Brandon reached for another bagel from the box, sitting on the edge of the table. "Sure hope these aren't laced with anything."

"Oh crap!" Lucinda said. "I didn't think of that."

"I'm sure they're fine. We'd be dead by now."

After half an hour, the fresh tray arrived with coffee and cups. The server that Brandon had spoken to earlier that morning delivered it himself. Brandon's phone vibrated on the table. He looked down at it and spun it around. "Beecher."

Congresswoman Strickland wants to meet with you. Okay now?

Sure. We're here.

I'm giving her your cell number.

Okay.

Brandon sent the address of the hotel to Senator Beecher and threw his phone across the room onto the bed.

"What's wrong?" Lucinda asked.

"Beecher is sending a California congresswoman to us now."

"Now? Why?"

"Beats me."

"I'm getting in the shower."

"I'd join you," Brandon grinned, "but I don't know how soon we'll be getting a knock on the door."

She smiled and walked into the bathroom, carrying one of her suitcases. Brandon finished his bagel, brushed off his hands, and moved over to the bed. He sat leaning against the headboard, his legs spread straight out in front of him. He reached across the bed and picked up a newspaper that was brought in on the coffee cart. He unfolded the paper to a headline that stunned him.

San Francisco Ground Zero for Civil War II?
"What the hell!"

"Did you say something, Honey?" Lucinda shouted through the bathroom door. After a few seconds of silence, she opened the door and walked out wrapped in a towel. "Honey?"

He slowly looked up from the paper.

"My God, Brandon. What's wrong?"

"Luce, when I used the term Civil War II last week in the conference room, I was just halfway kidding."

"Right. I guess I got that."

He turned the paper around to show her the headline.

"What the . . . Honey, do you think it's a coincidence?"

"I hope so. I would never have planted that imagery in anyone's mind. This is awful. I assumed everyone in the room would have taken it the way I intended."

"Well, to be quite honest, it scared the crap out of me."

"Is that why you left the conference room?"

"Oh, you noticed that, eh? Yes, I had to take a break and went up to the roof for some fresh air."

"And Mena followed you."

"Yes. She came out after me. I think she thought I was going to jump."

They both laughed. There was a knock at the door. Brandon jumped to his feet. "I guess that's her."

"I'll finish up in here." Lucinda turned and walked back into the bathroom and closed the door.

Brandon looked through the peephole and opened the door. "Congresswoman Strickland?"

"Hi, Brandon, it is so nice to finally meet you. Please, call me Val. A lot fewer syllables." She chuckled. She was a young, attractive woman dressed in a business suit with a smile that lit up the room.

"Please, come in, Val."

"Thank you. I have to admit, I've been a fan of yours for a long time."

"A fan? I guess I didn't know I had any."

"Are you serious? Mr. McStocker, you're like a legend in government circles—at all levels."

"Don't tell him that. It'll go to his head," Lucinda laughed as she walked into the room.

"Hi!" Val said. You must be the famous Lucy Reagan."

"Famous?"

"The one that took him off the market."

They all smiled, and Brandon shook his head. "Val Strickland, yes, this is my wife, Lucinda Reagan . . . I mean, McStocker.

"Please, call me Val." She extended her hand.

"Hi, Val. Lucy is fine. It's good to meet you." They shook hands.

"You, as well. Can I get you some coffee or something? I can call down to room service to get more."

"No, thanks. I've had my fill."

Brandon rushed over to clear off the table where they had been eating breakfast. "Have a seat, Val. Sorry for the mess. We probably should have met downstairs somewhere."

"This is fine. When you meet in someone's hotel room, you have to assume it's going to look lived in. It's all good."

"So, how do you know Senator Beecher?" Brandon asked

The senator sat and pulled her chair in, placing her handbag on the table. "Oh, Sid and I go way back. I interned for him back in the day. He's the one who got me genuinely interested in politics."

"So, you've been at it a while?"

"Oh, yeah. We worked hard out here to help get President Richland elected. But in the end, I guess we weren't much help. It *is* California, after all."

"Right. But it was a noble effort."

"I suppose."

Brandon sat in the chair across from Val, and Lucinda sat on the edge of the bed, facing them, rubbing her hair with the towel she had wrapped around her head.

"Why did the senator send you to us, Val?" Lucinda asked. "It just all seems a bit out of the blue. Cloak and dagger stuff, you know?"

"Yeah. I get it. But it isn't quite that dramatic. Politics in California is a strange thing, especially when compared to the rest of the country. You can't just meet issues head-on. You have to look at things through the lens of Haight-Ashbury."

"Haight-Ashbury?" Brandon took a drink of his coffee.

"Well, we just call it that. The counterculture that sprang up around the Bay Area in the sixties. All those kids you saw on TV that everyone was afraid might be in office someday?"

"Right?"

"Well, they're in office. In a big way out here on the left coast. Anyway, Sid gave me a call and filled me in on what's going on. He thought you might need some insider help navigating all that."

"So, that counterculture. You seem way too young to be part of all that," Lucinda said.

"Oh, yeah. But my dad was square in the middle of it. You might say he was one of them, except that he saw early on where it was going to lead. He peeled off and became part of a counter-counterculture, trying to thwart the—she curled her fingers in air quotes—'do what feels good' insanity."

Brandon looked past Val and out of the window. "So, we have a whole generation of our youth having to decide whether or not to accept this crap."

"Basically. But the fact that Richland is even in office means there's hope for a better future for all of us."

"That's true, I guess. Look, I'm glad you're on the team and all, but what does Senator Beecher want you to do for us?"

"Well, watch the inside, I suppose. I'm sure questions will arise while you're here. Maybe I can help. Sacramento can be a tough place to navigate. Not many people trust the state government here, and for good reason. They've earned their reputation for making backroom, self-serving deals."

"Okay," Brandon said. "Let's start here. Do you know the name Bruce Talbot?"

Val's eyes widened, and her jaw dropped. "Wait. What? Did the governor give you Talbot?"

"I'm not sure if *given to me* would be accurate, but he showed up here this morning, first claiming to represent Truly, then he basically warned us against Truly."

Val looked around the room. Her smile disappeared, and her eyebrows dipped in the middle. Then she took a pen and notebook from her purse and wrote on it. "Did he mention this?" She held up the note so both he and Lucinda could see it. *Cártel del Mundo*.

"Well, not while he was here. But shortly after he left, a server delivered a coffee cart just like that one with this stuck under a saucer." He held up the piece of paper. "Then the guy down in room service said he had no idea who delivered the cart."

Val stood and started snooping around the room, opening drawers and looking under tables and lampshades.

Lucinda watched her intently. "Wait. You think we're—"

Val held her finger to her lips and shook her head. After several minutes of searching for a bug, she sat back down. "Have you said that out loud in here?"

"Well. Yeah," Brandon said. "Is that a problem?"

"Could be. Look. The governor is scared."

"What makes you think that?"

"He sent Talbot to you. He wouldn't have sent his best on such an errand if he wasn't afraid. And even Bruce knows that."

"So, I give up. Is this Talbot a good guy or bad guy? And, I must say, I've never seen a congresswoman sweep a room."

"Talbot is the best. The governor clearly wants him on your team. But you have to understand, Talbot's entire life has been about black ops. He's suspicious of everybody, and very few people really know him. The fact that he just came in here and spoke to you guys says someone has briefed him and he trusts you more than most. He must be a bit of a fan, too."

Brandon smiled. "Right."

"So, do you have any idea what the governor is afraid of?" Lucinda asked.

Val held up her notebook, revealing what she had written earlier.

"Oh. Of course. So now what?"

"First thing we need to do is get you moved out of this room."

"Wait. How would anyone who matters know that we were coming out here and for what reason? That's craziness," Brandon said.

"I have no idea. But if Bruce was here and did this," she held up the note, "anything is possible. Is your guy, Sonny, coming out to help?"

"What? How do you even know about Sonny? Why does everyone out here know Sonny?"

CHAPTER 7

Sonny arrived at a private residence in the foothills of the Sierra Nevada Mountains east of Sacramento. He had driven from Kansas in the limousine after deciding not to fly out and rent one. When he arrived, there were guards stationed at the front gate. Brandon emerged from the front door and motioned for them to let Sonny through. He drove up to the garage door and stopped.

"Hey, man. Glad you're here," Brandon said.

"Me, too. But where the heck are we?"

"Oh, a congresswoman that Beecher set me up with thought we'd be safer here. It's one of her Airbnb rental properties."

"Safer? Were you guys in some kind of danger? Does all this have something to do with Bruce Talbot?"

"In a way. But no. Apparently, we aren't on anyone's radar. Not yet. Did you learn anything about Talbot?"

"Oh, yeah. Clyde has worked with him several times before. He had the same opinion that I got when I was in training with him. One of the best of the best."

"Yes. That's the impression Val gave us."

"Val?"

"The congresswoman. I guess she and Talbot are both going to be here shortly."

"Ah. So, I get to see Bruce again."

"He's actually a likable guy, which is why this is all so weird."

"Hey there, Sonny!"

"Lucy! Hey! How are you enjoying your honeymoon vacation?"

"Yeah. Right." She gave him a hug. "I'm so glad you're finally here. Safe trip?"

"Yeah. It was all pretty uneventful."

"Good. Hungry?"

"No. Susan loaded me up with half the diner. She thought you all might enjoy some food from home." He opened the back door.

Brandon and Lucinda both dropped their jaws. "What in the world is that girl thinking?" Lucinda laughed at all of the large brown bags lined up across the back seat.

Brandon shook his head and reached in to pick up a handful. "Well, let's get it in the house. Crazy kid."

They stored the food in the kitchen. Then, the three of them walked out onto the back patio that overlooked the oak-covered foothills, stretching as far as the eye could see.

"I take it the congresswoman likes her privacy," Sonny said.

"I guess so," Brandon said. "She doesn't live here anymore. But she used to. She told me she had the house swept and had some of her security folks clear a perimeter a few miles around the house."

"Are you serious?"

"Yeah. I'm getting the impression Val Strickland isn't your ordinary congresswoman. She's sweet as can be, though."

One of the agents stuck his head out the back door. "Mr. McStocker, Congresswoman Strickland and her friend are coming up the driveway now."

"Thanks. We'll be right out." The agent closed the door. "Well, I guess this is it. Let's go try to learn what's going on."

Just as they walked into the living room, through the massive picture window that overlooked the green valley and the modest skyline of Sacramento, they could see the black SUV coming up the driveway. They went onto the front porch to greet the arriving visitors.

"Hey there, Brandon," Val said as she got out of the back seat. "I see everyone's here."

"Hello, Val. Good to see you. And Mr. Talbot. We meet again."

"Hey, Mr. McStocker. Yes, I want to apologize for all the mystery I left you with last time. I just got a little paranoid standing in a strange hotel room."

"Well, thanks for the coffee. Unfortunately, we chose not to drink it after we read your note."

"Sorry. I assumed you would track down the meaning. I just wanted to get away from that hotel. Public places like that make me nervous."

"I guess I understand. You remember my wife, Lucinda."

"Of course. Hi, Mrs. McStocker. Good to see you again."

"And this is my friend and security advisor, Sonny Langston. He just arrived as well."

Talbot reached out his hand. "Hey, Mr. Langston. I thought I recognized that name. It's been a long time. I've heard a lot of good things about you. Now it makes sense."

"Thanks. Good to see you. Please, call me Sonny. I wouldn't know how to act being called Mr. Langston."

"You got it."

"And you heard these good things, how?" Sonny asked.

"Oh, your buddy Clyde Baldwin called me this morning. Quite the blast from the past. He told me you were there checking up on me."

"Well, we can't be too careful now, can we?"

"No, we can't. I appreciate your due diligence."

Brandon interrupted. "So, Bruce, are you here representing the governor, or is this something different?"

"Why don't we all go inside?" Val said. "My sinuses are starting to flare up." She opened the door and walked in as if it were still her home.

"Can I get you two something to drink or a bite to eat?" Lucinda asked. "I have some iced tea in the fridge."

"I bet it's sweet tea, isn't it?" Talbot said.

"Well, actually, it is. Can I get you a glass?"

"I haven't had good ol' sweet tea in years. Yes. Please."

"Coming right up. Val?"

"Just water for me, please. Thank you."

Lucinda disappeared into the kitchen while the others sat around the empty gigantic stone fireplace. After several minutes, she returned with a tray full of glasses and pitchers.

"Sorry, I'm late," she chuckled.

"Nonsense. We haven't said anything important," Val said as Lucinda sat on a couch next to Brandon.

"So, after we last spoke, I looked up Bruce, and we discussed his brief visit with you guys. As I suspected, the governor sent him to you for a very specific reason. He is, indeed, running scared."

Talbot nodded at Val in agreement. "Yes. I wasn't quite clear of the purpose of your visit, but the governor is afraid of something. I have to assume it has something to do with Cártel del Mundo since he asked me to be his liaison."

"How so?" Sonny asked.

"Well, I've been following the activity of this cartel for quite some time. They seem to have been making small, imperceptible excursions into the U.S. for quite a few years now. They've managed to maintain a very low profile, but I can't help but believe it's part of something bigger."

"And you just let these guys hang out here in the U.S.?" Brandon asked.

"The DEA heads up a Special Operations Division for the Department of Justice. They're trying to get at the highest levels of these cartels to take them down. They'll never do that if they stop the trafficking at the lowest levels. Unfortunately, sometimes these lower-level bosses try to build their own empire and stir up crap the drug lords never intended."

"So, at what level is the cartel attempting to infiltrate the federal government?" Brandon asked.

"What do you mean?"

"Look, Bruce. The whole time we were planning and building Kéntro, people were dying because somebody didn't like us messing with the corruption established in D.C. My gut tells me that lobbyists weren't sophisticated enough to try and stop all that. Threats were thrown around on several occasions. Hell, somebody killed my best friend trying to stop that project. The feds thought the effort was dead when they arrested some local politicians. But what I've seen since then makes me believe those guys were just pawns."

"They also killed his first wife," Lucinda said. "A Secret Service agent pulled the trigger, but these thugs did the murdering."

Sonny and Brandon looked at each other then stared at the floor. After several seconds of silence, Sonny finally spoke up. "And I had to shoot a friend just inches from another friend because these monsters turned him into something he wasn't."

"Wait," Talbot said. "Are you sure this was all attributed to this cartel?"

"You mean, you don't know?" Brandon asked. "It's what the FBI reported to the president."

"Jeez, you guys. I am so sorry," Talbot said.

"I'm sorry," Val echoed. "I had no idea you guys were going through all that."

Brandon looked around the room, thinking. "You know . . . I bet all that has more to do with the president sending me out here than my project management expertise. It's starting to make sense now."

"What is?" Talbot asked. "What do you mean, project management expertise? What project did you think you were coming out here to manage?"

Brandon stood and paced across the sitting area, his hard shoes clicking across the hardwood floor. He turned and looked at Sonny, then looked around at the others.

"Brandon?" Lucinda said. "You okay, Honey?"

"I . . . uh . . . I need to make a call." He walked through the kitchen and out to the patio. He leaned against the handrail and took the cell phone from his pocket. He sent a text message to Senator Beecher.

I'm going to try to get through to the president.

After a few long minutes, Beecher finally replied.

What's up?

I need his permission to bring a couple of people in. Can I get your support? Maybe give him a heads up?

In?

Please.

Okay. On it.

Brandon put the phone back in his pocket and gazed into the brush behind the house. Sonny came out onto the patio.

"You okay, Boss?"

Brandon continued to stare at nothing. "Why did they come after us?"

"What do you mean?"

"Sonny, have you ever wondered why a cartel with the power of del Mundo would come after us? I mean, why target a little engineering firm in Virginia? Granted, Bob ended up getting us the most significant contract in history, but we were never driving the bus on it."

"I guess I never really thought about it."

"None of us did. I never really believed that it went any deeper than a few corrupt senators in D.C."

"Well, I knew that bus left the station when the former director of the Secret Service turned on the president."

"Yeah. That pretty much sealed it." Brandon's phone vibrated in his pocket. He looked and saw that it was the Central House switchboard. "Sorry, man. I need to take this privately."

Sonny drew his eyebrows together and slanted his head. "Uh . . . okay. I'll just step back inside."

"This is Brandon McStocker."

"Mr. McStocker, can you hold for the president, please?"

"Of course."

"Brandon! How is it going out there?"

"Not quite as expected, Mr. President."

"Senator Beecher sounded like this call might be a bit urgent. What can we do for you?"

"Sir, I think we know which cartel we're dealing with, and I think they're trying to get to Truly."

"What makes you think that?"

"Sir, he's scared. I'm almost certain that's why he wanted our help. He's petrified and doesn't know where to turn."

"And the political climate? What's happening in Frisco?"

"It's hard to tell if that many residents want change or if it's the cartel spinning that up as well."

"Well, I can't help but believe it's time to give them what they want."

"Yes, sir. That's why I wanted to speak to you. I need to bring a couple of people in on this."

"Brandon, you know we need to keep your real reason for being there under wraps."

"I know, sir. But the governor has assigned his security chief to help me investigate. Then, Senator Beecher put me in touch with a congresswoman out here to have inside assistance. She has put us up in a safe house."

"A safe house? Whatever for?"

"That's just it. They seem to think we're in danger—apparently just because we're out here."

"The cartel?"

"Yes, sir. Cártel del Mundo. These folks are acting very paranoid, and I don't think they even know why. I think I should tell them about the secession talks."

"Okay, listen. I'm going to get some secure communications equipment out to you. We can't do it this way."

"Fine, sir. But, all due respect; this is nuts."

"What's that?"

"Mr. President, I'm an engineer. I run a project management firm. Lucinda is an MBA. What are we doing?"

"Brandon, look. I'll get you some help from the DEA and perhaps even the CIA. I assume they're tracking this Cártel del Mundo anyway. But times are changing, and this is going to call for unprecedented measures. I don't expect you to take on these cartels. I just want you to be there to oversee the transition. I want it to be an amicable departure. You're the only one I can trust to make it happen without some under-the-table agenda."

"Does anyone in Congress even know how to cut a state loose? Won't that take years of wrangling and bureaucratic red tape?"

"I have some people looking into it. I still think most everyone here will be happy to see them go."

"Well, sir. I don't think it's going to be a wholesale, border-to-border departure. Most of the residents in the valley and the northern end of the state aren't going to want to stay with a newly established ultra-liberal nation. The state will likely need to be split vertically. But we'll engage some political scientists in a Genius Pod to figure all that out. In any case, I need to bring these folks onto our team."

"Okay, Brandon. Send me their names and affiliations, and I'll get them cleared. Go ahead and let them in on it. I trust your judgment. Just make sure they understand the critical nature of this and the importance of confidentiality. Do you want me to get Mr. Langston back onboard the Secret Service?"

"No, sir. I don't think that'll be necessary. I think he likes our arrangement."

"Hell, I'll read him into the CIA if you want me to."

"No. He's fine. I'll send you the information on these two and will bring them up to speed. Thank you, sir."

"Okay, Brandon. You be careful out there."

"Yes, sir."

Brandon disconnected the call and returned the phone to his pocket. He scanned the hills one more time and went back inside the house. Sonny was standing in the kitchen, just inside the back door.

"Everything okay, Boss? I've never known you to turn me away like that."

"I'm sorry, Sonny. Things are just getting a little freaky for me. Won't happen again."

They joined the others in the living room, and Brandon returned to his spot on the couch next to Lucinda. "Is there anyone in the house besides us?"

"No," Val said. "The security guys are all outside now. Why?"

"I need to bring you guys in on something. But, please keep it to yourselves. Completely confidential."

"Okay." Talbot leaned back in his chair.

"Beecher warned me there might be more to this," Val said.

"Look," Brandon said. "The president sent us out here to help Truly split California off from the U.S."

"What!" Val and Talbot shouted at the same time.

Val stood and paced to the window. "How can that be?"

"When we started the conversation, the president didn't know how much the cartel had infiltrated the state. I have to assume it explains the fear you see in the governor." Brandon stood. "Everybody, just calm down. Obviously, the president needs to keep this quiet for now."

"Obviously," Talbot said. "I've been working this cartel problem for a long time. But I haven't seen any indication that they are behind any bid to secede."

"No, I don't think they're spearheading it. But I wouldn't put it past them to find a way to capitalize on it. The split is being perpetrated by the radical left, which obviously has become a majority of California."

"What stops other blue states from following suit?" Val asked.

"I'm certainly not the guy to answer that. But I doubt that any other state is seriously considering such a move."

"You do know that there are a lot of folks in this state who would never want to leave the U.S.," Val said.

"I know. I know. That's what's going to make this so complicated. In any case, I need the governor to ask for my help. I can't come out here throwing the president's weight around to bully him into anything. But I really do think he wants to lead this state out of the Union."

"Does this have anything to do with all that Civil War II crap in the paper?" Talbot asked.

"I guess it kinda does. San Francisco is just the epicenter. The push to secede is reaching critical mass. If it gets on the ballot again this year, it's going to pass."

"But they can't just secede," Sonny said.

"No, they can't." Brandon turned to face him. "At a minimum, there would have to be some kind of Constitutional amendment to allow it. There is no legal process right now for a state to do it."

"Brandon, how did the southern states do it during the Civil War . . . or Civil War I, as it were," Lucinda asked.

"Oh, don't start," he grinned. "I'm no Constitutional scholar, but many would argue that the move by the South was completely illegal. Any permanent status change on their part would've rendered the Constitution useless. It wouldn't have been worth the paper it was written on."

"So, why does the president think he can make it happen now?" Val asked.

"The mood of the rest of the citizens. They've lost patience with California's attempts to drive politics for the rest of the country. If the rest of the country wants California to go, and the State of California wants to leave, it seems to me that they can figure out a way to make it happen. I would anticipate that even a Constitutional amendment would be fast-tracked."

"This is all getting a bit crazy if you ask me," Talbot said.

"Bruce, we just need you to stay focused on the cartel and see if they're trying to get to the governor as you suggest. Maybe you and Val can help me get him to actually ask for my help."

Lucinda placed her glass of tea on the end table. "We still need to deal with the residents of the state who don't want to leave. Heaven forbid we should have a mass exodus from California."

"Well, that's already kinda started," Brandon said.

"That's true, I guess," Val said. "Some of these farmers who have tried to operate thousands of acres that have been in their families for generations are being forced to sell off to developers and pack it all in, moving out of the state lock, stock, and barrel. Hell, the dairymen don't stand a chance with all the new environmental regulations they're forced to comply with. It never stops."

Talbot sat back down and leaned forward with his elbows on his knees, rubbing his face. He looked up at Brandon. "So, who gets to figure all this stuff out?"

CHAPTER 8

"Genius Pods!" Olivia shouted. "We need to pull the Legislative Genius Pod together as soon as possible."

"Uh. Okay. On it," Trevor said, looking up from his desk. "Are you okay?"

"Sorry, Trev. I'm just freaking out here."

"Ya think?"

"I just got off the phone with Daddy. We need to lay out a plan for California to leave the Union."

"Wait. What? Not only are you freaking out, you're cracking up."

"No. Really. We might want to bring both the Legislative and the Technology pods together to figure this out."

"You're serious? Like take-a-star-off-the-flag serious?"

"When can you get them together?"

"I'll try for next week," Trevor said.

"This week. It's gotta be this week."

"Or, I'll try for later this week."

"Thanks, Trev. I knew you could do it. Let me know when you have meetings set up. Gotta run."

The Genius Pods were Olivia's brainchild—teams of leading-edge technology experts from various industries around the country, recruited and formed at the beginning of the Kéntro Project. Brandon employed them to make sure the city was designed with the best that technology had to offer.

Olivia sped out of Trevor's office and past Mena's desk.

"Liv, Honey, you need to slow down. You're going to pop a cork."

"You mean, blow a gasket."

"Whatever. You are doing a good job."

"Will you follow me into my office, please."

Mena picked up her legal pad and a pen and followed behind Olivia into her office, closing the door behind her.

Olivia sat at her desk and put her face in her hands. "You know about California, right?"

Mena sat in one of the two chairs in front of Olivia's desk. "I've heard talk. Can't say I've been briefed. I sort of knew why your dad and Lucy went out there."

"He's out there because the president wants him to help Governor Truly secede from the Union."

"Oh, jeez. I was getting that impression but didn't want to push it."

"Weird, huh?"

"Well, weird. Yeah. But why doesn't the president have one of his political henchmen out there doing his dirty work?"

"I don't know. Daddy has a way, you know."

"Oh, I know."

"Politicians are too . . . well . . . too political to pull this off. These days, they don't want to put their political career in jeopardy to do what's right."

"So, what's right?"

"Huh?"

"Do we turn it all over to Mexico, or do we make it an independent territory of Canada? Perhaps dig a moat around it and make it an island unto itself." Mena kept a straight face while Olivia smiled in shock. Then they both erupted into laughter.

"Okay. Okay. I get it." Olivia shook her head and leaned back in her chair.

"Breathe, girl. Breathe. Really. You're doing great running this place. Brandon will be proud of you."

"I suppose. I just don't understand how he gets roped into these ridiculously complex projects."

"You know, when you think about it, when the country was first formed, it was put together by a bunch of really smart civilians. Not career politicians. Maybe that's why the president doesn't trust something this big to politicians with an agenda."

"You may be right. Anyway, Daddy wants me to try to get in with the president to talk about this cartel and to get some guidance for the Genius Pods. Can you set up a meeting?"

"Sure. I'll give the Central House a call."

"And, please let Susan know I'll be down for lunch."

"You got it," Mena said as she stood and walked to the door. "Open or closed?"

"You can close it, please, Mena. Thanks."

Before the door was even closed, Olivia picked up her cell phone and called Brandon. "Hey, Daddy."

"Hey there, Sweetheart. How are things going since the last time we spoke . . . fifteen minutes ago?"

"Oh, couldn't be better."

"Well, that's good to hear, half-hearted as it sounded."

"Lying. I'm dying here. Sorry to keep bugging you."

Brandon laughed. "What are you talking about? I'm sure you're doing just fine."

"Mena is setting up a meeting now with President Richland to talk about the mission and the work of the Genius Pods. I'm having a tough time coming up with ideas for them to discuss."

"And therein lies the problem," Brandon said.

"What do you mean?"

"Liv, you don't need to come up with answers for those guys. Just questions. You can even stay quiet if you want and let *them* come up with the questions. You know how that works."

"Yeah, I know. So, how did your meeting go?"

"Strange. I brought a couple of new folks into the conversation. Congresswoman Val Strickland and the governor's security director, Bruce Talbot."

"Mm. Is there any thread of a direction you can give me that might help Trevor get these pods engaged?"

"Well, California can't just leave. It would be illegal. So, we have two major leads to follow. One is, how can the state secede legally and peacefully."

"And the other?"

"How can we keep Truly safe from the cartel?"

"So, now we're bringing in the Legal pod?"

"No. Leave it to Technology first. See what they come up with. Between them and Legislative, I hope they can solve this thing, at least in theory."

"Let's hope. I'm planning to have lunch with Susan today. Any words of wisdom for her?"

Brandon chuckled. "Tell her thanks for all the groceries."

"Groceries?"

"Good grief, Liv. You should've seen all the food she loaded Sonny down with when he came out here. I'm surprised they had any supplies left in the kitchen."

"That's my sis. You know she just loves you guys, right?"

"Well, we love her too."

"I'll let her know. Call if you need anything." She disconnected the call.

"Hey, Liv," Mena said on the intercom. "Tim is on one."

"Thanks, Mena." Olivia put her cell phone aside and pushed the speaker button on the desk phone. "Hey, you. A call from the governor's office of the great state of Kansas. To what do we owe the pleasure?"

"Hope you're not busy. Do you have plans for dinner?"

"So, this isn't business, then?" Olivia smiled.

"I don't even know the last time I called you for state business," Tim chuckled.

"No plans. What do you have in mind?"

"It's a surprise. I'll pick you up at seven?"

"Well, okay. Sounds fun!"

"See you then. Love you. Bye."

"Okay. Love you, too. Tim? Hello . . . Tim?" She smiled and shook her head. Olivia picked up her briefcase and walked out into the hallway.

"He seemed awfully chipper today," Mena said as Olivia walked by.

"Unusually so. I'm headed down to Barney's. I'll be back sometime later. Call if you need anything."

"Will do. Enjoy. Tell Suze, hey!"

After a reflective two-hour drive from K.D. down to Barney's Diner on the north end of Manhattan, Olivia pulled into the parking lot, turned off the car, closed her eyes, and calmed herself down. After emptying her mind for several minutes, she began to pray.

"Mom, you know Daddy better than anyone. How can I help him right now?" She smiled, opened her eyes, and got out of the car.

"Hey, Sis!" She shouted when she walked through the door, looking up at the ringing bell.

"Hey, Liv! Table's clear. Go on back. I'll get your BLT and onion rings."

"Hey there, preacher," Olivia said, patting Pastor Emmet on the back as she walked by him sitting at the counter.

"Hey, Liv. Good to see you. Have you heard from the newlyweds?"

"Oh, yeah. They're doing great. Having a blast."

"Good to hear."

She sat at the usual table in the corner of the dining room, and Susan followed her carrying a glass of sweet tea. She put it on the table and whispered over Olivia's shoulder as she sat.

"You aren't lying to the preacher now, are you?"

"Shut up," Olivia whispered, and they both giggled.

Susan sat across the table and leaned forward. "So, what are they doing out there?"

"Sis, you know if I told you, I'd have to shoot you."

"Come on. It can't be that big a deal."

"You'll know soon enough. You just need to stay clear of it. You know—plausible deniability."

"I suppose. I'll be right back." Susan raced across the dining room, then behind the counter, and disappeared into the kitchen. Olivia met Pastor Emmet's smile and shook her head; then she took the phone from her pocket to check for messages. Susan returned with two BLTs and a mountain of onion rings on a huge plate. "Put that phone away."

"Why?"

"I want to hear about you and Tim."

"What about me and Tim?"

"Is it serious?" Susan took a bite of an onion ring.

Olivia stared at Susan and took a big bite of her BLT, leaving a piece of lettuce dangling from the corner of her mouth.

"Oh, come on. Why don't you want to talk about it?"

Olivia kept chewing, gazed around the diner, and back down at her sandwich.

"Seriously?" Susan said.

Olivia took a drink of her tea. "Sister, you really need to get a life. You've been living like a nun since you came back from Nashville. I know that whole recording contract thing didn't pan out, but you can't just hide out in this diner. You'll end up an old maid."

"Meh. Nothing wrong with that."

"Oh, please." Olivia's phone vibrated, and she turned it over to see who it was. "Hmm. Wonder what he wants." She pressed the speaker button. "Hey, Joe. What's up?"

Joe Russo was the construction foreman that Brandon had hired at the beginning of the Kéntro

Project. He was a trusted member of the team on the front lines.

"Hey, Boss. Got a sec?"

"I'm here eating lunch with Susan. She can hear you, so don't say all that bad stuff about her."

Susan bobbled her head with a fake smile.

Joe chuckled. "I'll be easy on her. Listen, I'm out here on the airport expansion project. We were doing a concrete pour when security shut the whole place down."

Olivia was stunned. "The airport is closed?"

Amelia Earhart International Airport was built just east of Lebanon, K.D. to serve the new nation's capital, replacing the services historically provided by Andrews Air Force Base, Dulles, and Reagan International in the Washington D.C. area.

"Yeah, 'fraid so. If I can't get these trucks offloaded, this is going to be a mess."

"You're the foreman. Why can't you just make it happen?"

"Liv. Come on. It's the airport."

"Yeah. I know. I know. I'll see what I can find out. I'll call you back."

"Thanks, Boss."

She disconnected the call. "Why in the hell would the airport be shut down?"

The phone vibrated again. "Hey, Mena. What's up?"

"Hey, Liv. I just got a call from a reporter friend of mine, wants to know why the airport was closed down. Do you know anything?"

"Not a thing. Joe just called and told me about it. Get the airport manager to call me . . . wait. Never mind. He's calling me now. I'll call you back."

"Okay."

"Rick. I just heard. What's going on out there?"

"Liv, since your people designed the systems, you may need to get some of them out here. ATC has had a major computer shut down. The FAA has its IT crew on it, but they're baffled. This has some pretty wide implications."

"I don't understand. We turned that system over a long time ago. Do you think it's a design problem after all this time?"

"At this point, we have to take all precautions."

"Air Force One?"

"We've given them verbal clearance to get in the air and move to the alternate site. They're taking Marine One over to the Central House, just in case."

"This is weird. Okay, Rick. I'll send a team over to help out. I assume TSA and airport security have been alerted."

"Oh, yeah. They're going nuts."

"Okay, Rick. Keep us posted."

"Wait. Hang on, Liv. They just told me they think someone has hacked into the system."

"What? How in the world does someone hack into the FAA's air traffic control system? You can't be serious."

"We're notifying the FBI. I don't want to take any chances."

"I understand. I'll get my team on their way."

"Thanks, Liv. Talk soon."

Olivia pressed some more numbers. "Hey, Trev. Liv. We need to get some of our top IT guys over to the airport."

"What on earth for?"

"Apparently, the FAA's ATC system has been hacked, and they've shut down the airport."

"Okay. But how is that on us?"

"Well, it isn't. At first, I thought it might be a design problem, so I agreed to help. The FBI will be there, so who knows who they might pull in."

"Right. Okay, I'll gather up the right folks and get them headed that way."

"Thanks, Trev." She disconnected the call and placed the phone on the table, facedown.

"Eat," Susan said.

"Yeah. Yeah. I'm eating."

"So, you seem to be handling all this okay."

"You mean Daddy being gone? It scares the bejesus out of me."

"Sis, you've got this. You clearly have that situation at the airport under control."

"Maybe. It just doesn't feel right."

"What do you mean?"

"You can't just hack into the FAA's computers. That's ridiculous. Too many lives at stake."

"Well, you can't just fly planes into the World Trade Center either."

"Good point. Crap . . . Joe."

Olivia called her construction foreman back.

"Hey, Joe. Liv."

"Hey, Boss."

"Listen, you better send those trucks back to be redirected. This isn't going to end any time soon."

"Well, crap. Okay. It sucks, but I'll get them out of here."

"Thanks, Joe." She placed the phone back on the table.

"Hey, Liv," Pastor Emmet said. "You girls might want to come see this."

Olivia and Susan stood and walked over to the counter. Susan picked up the remote control to turn up the volume on the TV. There was airport file video showing as the anchor reported.

"Shortly after the Amelia Earhart closure in Lebanon, K.D. due to an unexplained computer glitch, Chicago's O'Hare Airport was also shut down. Authorities aren't saying yet what the problem might be. Flights are backing up all across the country. So, travelers, keep an eye on those schedules."

"What in the world?" Olivia said. She heard her phone vibrating on their table and hurried back across the room to answer it.

"Hey, Daddy."

"Olivia, what in the world is going on?"

"I don't know yet. I spoke to Rick at the airport, and they're spinning everyone up to work the problem. Trevor is sending a team over to see if they can help."

"Good idea."

"Daddy, any chance this could be some of your cartel's handiwork?"

"Well, normally I'd say they aren't that sophisticated. But now, I wouldn't put anything past them. Honey, you may be hearing from the president to go over there sooner than expected. Technically, this has nothing to do with us, but he knows that I'm out here and why. So, he just might want a local source of information."

"Won't he be getting reports from his advisors?"

"He will. But he knows they bend things to suit their own agenda. Hang on; I've got another call coming in," Brandon said.

"Okay."

After several seconds, Brandon returned to the call.

"Hey, it's Josh. I put a call in to him a little bit ago."

"You mean, Josh, as in your FBI buddy, Josh Bixby?"

"Yes. Hang on. I'll get us on a three-way call."

A few seconds passed. "Okay. We're all on."

"Hey, Agent Bixby. Fancy meeting you here."

"Hi, Liv. Great to hear from you again."

"So, Daddy. What's going on?"

"Honey, I just learned from Josh that they finally got him relocated to K.D."

"Really!"

"Yeah, Liv. I'm right here," Josh said. "I just heard about the excitement at the airport. Where are you now?"

"I'm eating lunch with my sister."

"At the diner?"

"Well, yes. Why?"

"Stay put. I'm up in K.D., but I'll head that way. In the meantime, I'll see who they put on this from the bureau and try to get more info."

"Uh. Okay. I'll wait here."

"Thanks, Josh," Brandon said. "Sounds like you two have it under control, so I'll get back to my team out here. Liv, keep me posted."

"Will do, Daddy." She turned her phone face down on the table again and tossed a cold onion ring into her mouth.

Susan sat back down. "What's going on?"

"Josh lives here now. He's on his way down from K.D."

"Josh Bixby?"

"Yep."

"Wow. Didn't see that coming," Susan said.

"Tell me about it. Hey, I think he's single."

"Don't start."

"Suze! You've got to get a life."

The two picked at their food and chatted for a while before hearing the bell ringing over the front door. They turned to see Josh walking in. Olivia waved. "We're back here."

"Hello, ladies."

"Agent Bixby," Susan said, blushing. "Excuse me, I need to get to work. Something to eat?"

"Oh, no. I'm good."

Susan stood, gathered the dishes, and vanished into the kitchen.

Olivia grinned and shook her head. "So, Agent Bixby, the FBI moved you out here."

"First of all, call me Josh. And yes, I was relocated a few months ago."

"Of course. What's going on at the airports?" Olivia asked. "Seems a bit odd that two major hubs would be down at the same time."

"Yeah. It is definitely odd. Your dad tells me he's working on some project in California. What can you tell me about that?"

"Oh, he and Lucinda are out there for vacation. Their honeymoon, actually. Why weren't you at the wedding, by the way? They were married right here in the diner."

"I bet it was nice."

"It was beautiful. But then they had to rush off."

"Your dad invited me, but I just couldn't get away on such short notice."

"Yes. It *was* that."

"Doesn't sound like he's just out there on a honeymoon, Liv."

She hesitated and stared at the ice cubes in her empty glass. "No. The president sent him out there to help the governor."

"With what?"

"I guess all of that stuff going on in San Francisco."

"Wait. The president sent my buddy, Brandon, out to California to help the governor with his political problems. Brandon? The project manager, Brandon? How does that work?"

"Frankly, I'm not completely sure what the president is thinking. So, were you able to find out who's working the problem at the airport?"

"Yeah. There's a whole team of investigators over there now. So, you sent a team over there too?"

"Yeah. Just in case their IT folks can use some design help. They built a pretty impregnable backbone around the city, but the FAA has their own system."

"I gather. Probably vulnerable?"

"Well, I wouldn't have thought so."

Josh pulled the vibrating phone from his coat pocket. "Excuse me. I need to take this."

Olivia nodded.

"This is Agent Bixby. Yeah . . . are you kidding? That's crazy. Okay . . . thanks."

He placed the phone back in his coat and hung his head.

"Josh, what is it?"

"LAX is down. The president has ordered the FAA to ground all aircraft over U.S. airspace and territorial waters."

"I don't get it. Who's capable of this?"

Olivia's phone vibrated on the table.

"This is Olivia."

"Ms. McStocker?"

"Uh . . . yes. Speaking."

"Hi. This is the Central House calling. Do you have some time to meet with President Richland this afternoon?"

She looked at Josh as he looked at his phone with shock on his face.

"What?" she whispered to him.

"It's happening."

"What is?"

"It's San Francisco," Josh said.

"Ms. McStocker, are you there?"

"I'm sorry. Yes, I'm here. Yes. Of course, I can meet with the president. What time?"

"Can you come now?"

"Now?"

"If you can."

"Uh. Of course. I can be there in a couple of hours. I'm in Manhattan."

"Good. I'll let the president know."

CHAPTER 9

Brandon woke up and turned to see that Lucinda was already out of bed. He went to look for her. She was right where he thought she would be—in the kitchen making coffee.

"Good morning, Beautiful."

"Hey there, sleepyhead. It's almost ready. Have you heard from Liv?"

"No. Not since she went to see the president yesterday."

"I bet she was a nervous wreck."

"Oh, I don't know. She can handle herself."

"True. But I don't think she knows that," Lucinda said with a smile.

Brandon's phone vibrated in his pajama pants pocket.

"Already?" Lucinda said.

"It's from Josh. He said the airports are back online. Someone hacked in and planted a virus of some sort. An investigation is underway. But I guess they got the problem isolated and fixed. He said planes started flying early this morning."

"Well, that doesn't sound good."

"No. It doesn't." Brandon said. "I can't figure out why I haven't heard from Olivia."

Lucinda walked across the kitchen to sit at the table.

"Damn it!" Brandon shouted.

Lucinda jumped. "What, Honey?"

"He said the feds are moving troops in around San Francisco."

"You don't suppose there's a connection between those FAA outages and the cartel issue, do you?"

"Jeez, I don't know. At this point, why wouldn't there be?" His phone vibrated again. "It's Talbot."

Lucinda slid the pot back into the coffeemaker. "What the hell!"

"Good morning, Bruce. What's up?"

"Sorry to bug you so early. Are you guys awake?"

"Barely."

"Can I stop by?"

"When?"

"It may be an hour."

"Yeah. Come on in. We'll have breakfast ready by then." He looked at Lucinda. She smiled and nodded.

"Okay. See you in a bit," Bruce said.

Brandon disconnected the call and threw the phone on the kitchen table.

"What in the world does he want this early in the morning?" Lucinda asked.

"Beats me. Maybe something to do with San Francisco. I'm going to jump in the shower."

"I'll get breakfast on."

Brandon picked his phone up and texted Olivia. *What gives?*

He threw the phone back down, went into the bathroom, and turned on the shower, quickly steaming up the entire room. When he had finished and started back into the kitchen, he caught a glimpse of movement in the living room. He turned and saw, out of the large picture window, a caravan of black sedans coming up the driveway.

"Uh . . . Honey!" He shouted. "I think maybe Bruce is here."

"What do you mean, you think?" Lucinda followed Brandon's voice into the living room. "Holy crap."

"Exactly," Brandon said.

"I think I better get dressed."

"Good idea."

Lucinda disappeared into the bedroom as Brandon continued to watch the parade coming up the driveway. He opened the front door and walked out into the brisk morning air. The first car stopped, and Talbot emerged from the back seat.

"Hey, Brandon. Sorry about this, man. I didn't want to tell you over the phone, you know."

"Uh, okay."

Talbot jogged to the third car and opened the back door. Brandon's jaw dropped when the passenger got out. He raced to greet him.

"Governor Truly! What a surprise to see you here . . . so early in the morning . . . or anytime . . . sir."

"Sorry, Brandon. But we need to talk." They shook hands and turned to enter the house.

"Of course, sir. We can talk over breakfast if you like."

"That won't be necessary. Coffee is fine, but you all enjoy."

Brandon walked through the front door with the governor, and Talbot was close behind. Lucinda was walking out of the bedroom and into the kitchen just as they entered.

"Good morning, Mrs. McStocker. It's good to see you again."

Lucinda froze and jerked her head around. "Uh . . . Governor! What a nice surprise." She poked Brandon in the ribs as he walked by her. "Why don't you guys get comfortable in the living room, and I'll let you know when breakfast is ready."

"Uh, please wait," the governor said. "Can you join us first for just a minute?"

Lucinda stopped and pivoted to enter the living room instead of the kitchen. "Of course, sir." They all sat around the fireplace.

"I really am sorry to interrupt you both. I asked Mr. Talbot to bring me to you, but I didn't tell him why." He looked across the coffee table at Talbot. "Sorry."

Talbot shook his head slightly and looked at Brandon. The governor continued.

"Look, I know I got a bit defensive at our first meeting, and I'm sorry. Here's the thing. I could really use the president's help to get this state out of the Union. Hell, he's already flexing his muscles in San Francisco anyway. I know there is currently no way to leave the Union legally, but most of the residents of this state want out as badly as the rest of the country wants us out."

"Governor, we suspected that might be the case, but we made a conscious decision to wait until you asked, so as not to appear to be bullying you into anything."

"I understand, and I appreciate that."

"But you know, sir, the implications are enormous. What about your national and financial security?"

"Brandon, I know your role here cannot be as some political hack. It is no secret that you are one that gets things done. Can you take this project on?"

"Yes, sir. I'll confirm it with the president, and then we'll need to find some office space near the Capitol."

"Of course. I can get my people to help with the logistics."

"So, do you have a timeframe in mind?"

"Well, we'll get it on the ballot for next November, but the legislature will need to figure out the procedures."

"Governor, are you okay?" Brandon asked. "You seem a little tense."

Talbot looked at the governor and then glared at Brandon, indicating his discomfort with the question.

"I'm fine, Brandon. Can you please speak to the president and get this moving?"

"Of course, sir. My daughter is handling that end of the project these days. I haven't heard from her yet this morning, but we'll get right on it."

There was a tap on the door, and Sonny walked in. "Pardon the intrusion. Everything okay—Oh! Excuse me, Governor Truly. I didn't realize this was your caravan outside, sir."

"Relax, Sonny," Brandon said. "Come in and have a seat. How was the bed out there in the mother-in-law quarters?"

"Oh, suitable for any mother-in-law, I suppose."

They all chuckled. Governor Truly rose to his feet. "I think I better get back down the hill and leave you folks to your day."

"Of course, sir," Talbot said. "Hey Brandon, can I catch a ride from you back into Sacramento later on? I'd like to hang out here to discuss some things."

Brandon looked at Sonny.

"Yeah, Boss. We can do that."

"Thanks, Sonny," Talbot said. He stood and escorted the governor to the door and out onto the front porch. Brandon and Sonny followed them while Lucinda made her way into the kitchen.

"Thanks for the visit, Governor," Brandon said. "As soon as I hear from my daughter, we'll get to work on some preliminary plans, and I'll get back to you."

"Thanks, Brandon." Talbot walked the governor to his car and then walked up to speak to the driver of the car he arrived in. He tapped on the door, and the driver closed his window and drove around the house to exit the property. The other drivers, including the governor's, followed close behind.

"Okay. Now I'm hungry," Talbot said as he returned to Brandon on the porch.

Brandon smiled, and they both walked back into the house where Sonny had joined Lucinda in the kitchen.

"We're back," Brandon said.

"Do tell," Lucinda chuckled. "Are you all finished distracting me from cooking this breakfast?"

"So, Bruce," Brandon said. "Did you have anything to do with that?"

"What?"

"Getting the governor to admit he wants our help."

"I might have said something. But you sensed correctly earlier. He's nervous as a cat in a room full of rocking chairs. I don't get it. When LAX went down yesterday, I thought he was going to have a nervous breakdown. Now, he's hellbent on getting on with this secession."

Brandon's phone vibrated on the table. He turned it over to see that it was Olivia texting him. "It's about time," he said.

Airport is open.
I heard. How did your meeting go yesterday?
Prez was nervous. Josh went with.
Good. Call later to discuss. Governor asked for our help.
Really! Time to get to work, I guess.
Yep. Talk later.
K. Luv U.
You too.

He placed his phone back on the table.

"How can I help?" Sonny asked Lucinda.

"Well, I guess you can set the table."

Sonny opened and closed a couple of cabinet doors before he found the plates. Lucinda pulled the silverware drawer open that was right next to her as she stood in front of the stove. Sonny took out the silverware and slid it all across the table, crashing like a noisy diner.

Lucinda looked over at the mess Sonny made. She picked up a roll of paper towels and threw it, hitting him on the side of the head. It bounced into Brandon's hands.

"Nice bank shot," Brandon giggled. The three of them laughed while Bruce sat quietly.

"Sorry, Mr. Talbot," Lucinda said. "I forgot we had a guest. This bunch isn't much on scruples."

He smiled. "No problem at all. It makes me homesick."

"Where's home?" Brandon asked.

"San Diego. East of there, actually. A little town up in the mountains."

"Ah. So, you're a California boy from the get-go."

"Yes, I am. But, as I'm sure you know, this isn't the California I grew up in. I miss that California."

"I bet it's been hard to watch," Lucinda said.

"That, it has, ma'am. You know, Governor Truly knew that old California as well. I think he misses it too."

"You think that's why he finally admitted to wanting our help?" Brandon asked.

"Probably, something like that. Most of the folks along the coast think the changes have come as a result of the protests of the '60s—over fifty years ago. I think they're pretty proud of it, and that's why they get so passionate. But that isn't really it."

"Sounds like you have it figured out," Brandon said.

"Yes, I think I do. Over the last decade, the cartel has seen an opportunity to disrupt politics. Now, they see themselves as the great redeemers, taking back what they see as rightfully belonging to Mexico."

"So, you think this whole idea of secession is playing into their agenda?"

"Exactly," Talbot said. "Don't you?"

"Wait. Do you have some kind of proof? The president needs to know what's happening here."

Talbot chuckled. "Does one need proof that the wind blows? I think all the president needs to do now is acknowledge that it's too late to salvage California. He was right to pull the checkpoints in from the border to the state line as the president ordered."

"Yeah. It was the right thing to do," Brandon said. "With the previous governor's attitude toward controlling the border, illegals, and even other foreign nationals were flooding into this country. Richland had to do something with the checkpoints."

Lucinda delivered a bowl of eggs and a plate of bacon to the table. "So, we're supposed to roll over and allow California to become a state of sanctioned illegal drugs and human trafficking?"

"Absolutely not. That's what has gotten the governor's back up against the wall. He knows he has to stop it. But he also knows he has lost the state," Talbot said.

"That's a little harsh, don't you think?" Sonny said.

"Not really. Look at what's going on. The whole country thinks Civil War II is about to ignite in San Francisco."

"Jeez. There's that term again. I said that one time, half-jokingly, in a meeting back home. Now it's biting me in the butt everywhere I turn."

"Maybe it's just a coincidence," Sonny said.

"Maybe. So, you're saying that San Francisco could be the present-day Fort Sumter?"

"Exactly," Talbot said. "But I'm afraid that if it blows, it'll be much less organized and a lot more like a riot spreading across the countryside. There are far too many people in the Midwest that are becoming sympathetic to the antigovernment antics on the West Coast."

Talbot's phone vibrated in his pocket. "Excuse me. I have to take this," he said after looking at the screen. He stood and walked into the living room.

"I don't know about you guys, but I'm having a hard time wrapping my mind around all this," Lucinda said.

"What are we supposed to do with it?" Sonny asked.

Brandon loaded up his plate with food while Lucinda brought a plate of buttered toast to the table.

"All I can think of at the moment is that the president is going to get Congress to come up with some consensus on how to proceed. This can't turn into years of debates and ballot boxes."

Brandon took a drink of coffee and stared out of the kitchen window into the foothills. "There has to be something we can do."

Talbot returned to the table and sat, spooning scrambled eggs onto his plate. "That was Congresswoman Strickland. She's on her way up here. Wants to talk about some more permanent digs for the team."

"Team?" Brandon looked up from his plate.

"You're the project manager, man. You need to figure out a way to execute all this."

"Yeah, right."

"Brandon, he's right," Lucinda said. "We need to figure out a way to apply what we know to all this. What is the end result the president would like to see?"

"I'd like to think he wants to see a peaceful end to all this."

"Exactly. A happy, healthy nation of California and a forty-nine-state Union content with the results."

"So, that's our deliverable?" Brandon asked.

"Bingo!" she said.

"No pressure there," Sonny chuckled.

Lucinda sat down. "But we can't turn it over to the cartel. We just can't."

"I'm pretty sure that's not why we're here," Brandon said. "That's too easy." He picked up his phone and began tapping out a text message.

"What are you doing?" Lucinda asked. "I see that look."

"I'm sending a message to Liv and Trevor. I want them to engage the Genius Pods to see if there might be a technology-based solution for rendering the cartel powerless out here."

"Really?" Talbot said. "How in the hell are you going to do that?"

"Not for me to figure out. I trust my team, and I know those guys in the Pods love a good challenge."

"So, what's the deal with these Genius Pods anyway? What is that?"

Sonny snickered and shook his head while filling his fork. "Brother, I'm not sure you even want to know."

Talbot gazed at Sonny then turned, waiting for an answer from Brandon.

"It was actually my daughter's idea. Maybe it was my previous deputy, Debbie. Or, maybe it was both. I guess I don't really remember. Anyway, they decided that with a project as big as Kéntro, we should get more experts involved from around the country. Once we decided to run with it, they tracked down the best of the best in all of the disciplines of leading-edge research. We pulled together the top engineers and scientists in telecommunications, networks, security systems, social engineering, lawyers, government affairs, building systems; you name it, we made a team for it."

"Sounds ambitious."

"To say the least. But when we asked people who are driven by a challenge like that to help restart their country, you'd be surprised how willing they were to jump in. For them to be recognized as the top in their fields didn't hurt matters. Trevor Marshall is my guy heading all that up now. Heck of a banjo player, too."

"What?"

"Never mind."

Lucinda shook her head. Brandon pressed Send and placed his phone face down on the table next to his plate.

They heard a knock on the front door. Val entered with her security guard. "Hello!" she shouted.

They all looked at each other, then Lucinda shouted back, "In here, Val."

She walked into the kitchen as her security guard went back outside.

"Sorry about that. I guess I'm too used to just going and coming as I please in this place."

"No problem," Lucinda said. "Grab a plate and join us."

"Oh, no. Maybe just coffee."

"Suit yourself."

"So, do you have news?" Brandon asked.

Val poured herself a cup of coffee and took a piece of toast from a plate on the stove. "I do. I found a small office space that is somewhat secluded, considering that it's downtown. It's vacant, so I think it'll be ideal. It'll be more comfortable for you and closer to the governor."

"Great," Talbot said. "I'll get my guys to sweep it before the furniture people get in there."

"I'll give you a hand with that," Sonny said.

"Slow down," Brandon said. "We haven't even seen it yet."

"What about a sign?" Lucinda said.

Brandon looked up from his plate. "A sign?"

"Well, you have to call it something. You can't just sit in a building being all mysterious."

"She has a point," Val said.

"It's just a project management office," Brandon said. "A PMO. That's it."

"How about just *West Coast Engineering Services*?" Sonny asked. "I don't think that would attract too much attention."

Val smiled. "Unless you want to get cutesy and call it something like B&L Engineering Services."

"B&L?" Brandon said. "What's that?"

Lucinda chuckled. "Come on, goober. It's Brandon and Lucinda."

"Oh! Well, pardon my ignorance." He chuckled. "West Coast will be fine."

"Ah, you're no fun," Val said.

"When can we get in there to see it?" Brandon asked.

"All I have to do is call the property management agency, and they'll meet us there to unlock everything."

Brandon's phone vibrated. He answered. "Hey there, Sweetie. What's up?"

"Hey, Daddy. I've got Trevor in here with me. You're on speaker."

"Okay. We're just wrapping up breakfast here." Lucinda looked at him inquisitively. He dropped the phone from his mouth. "It's Liv."

Talbot stood and carried his plate to the sink. "Don't trip over any of those Genius Pods," he shouted.

They all quietly chuckled.

"I heard that," Olivia said. "Who was that?"

"Oh, that was Bruce Talbot from the governor's office. I explained Genius Pods to him a minute ago. He's just being silly."

"Hey, Boss," Trevor shouted.

"Hey, Trev. So, what are you learning?"

"I've placed several phone calls, and the majority of the Tech Pod can be here tomorrow. So, do you have anything specific in mind for them?"

"Not really. I guess the question to answer is, how do we stop the cartel from overtaking the State of California? Even if the state left the Union tomorrow, the governor is going to need security support from us."

"Okay. I'll get them going on it. It may end up being more than technology, but I'll let you know."

"Yeah, I understand. Thanks, Trev. So, Liv. Everything going good for you there?"

"I don't know, Daddy. You may have thrown me in over my head."

"Don't let her kid you, Brandon," Trevor said. "She's doing great. She has the respect of everyone in this place."

"I'm sure she does. And the meeting with the president?"

"I'll jump out here, Boss, and head back to my office."

"Okay. Thanks, Trev. I'll be in touch."

Brandon heard Olivia's office door close. "So, the president?"

"Uh . . . well . . . I guess it went as expected. He was apparently doing some confidence building. He wanted to be sure you and I were communicating regularly."

"Well, he's a little nervous. It doesn't mean he lacks trust."

"Oh, I understand."

"Listen, Honey. Apparently, we're going to be moving into an office building to set up a base of operations. Get ready to send out some of our IT guys to set up a remote node on your network."

"My network?"

"You know."

"Oh. That. Yes, I'll have them design something and bring it out."

"I think the governor's office will be setting up the infrastructure, but I want something separate to talk to you on."

"I understand," Olivia said.

A flash of light lit the kitchen and then disappeared.

"What was that?" Talbot asked, looking out of the kitchen window.

"I saw that flickering, too," Sonny said.

They both jumped to their feet and ran out onto the back patio.

"What's going on, Daddy?"

"Sweetheart, let me call you back."

"Daddy?"

CHAPTER 10

Sonny ran off of the patio and into the back yard looking out over the scrub-covered foothills. "I think I saw someone running up there."

"What was that flash?" Talbot asked.

"Maybe the sun reflecting off of something." Sonny stood still and continued to scan the area.

Brandon joined Lucinda and Talbot on the patio. "Does he see something?"

"He thought he did," Lucinda said. "Liv okay?"

"She's fine. She's going to send some guys out to help us get the new PMO squared away."

"That'll be good. No telling what kind of support we would get from the state."

"Good point. Hey, Bruce."

He turned to face Brandon and Lucinda. "Yeah."

"Do you trust the support organizations at the State Capitol?"

"You mean, do we have a deep state out here?"

"Something like that."

"I've never had trouble trusting anyone there in the past. Why do you ask?"

"I don't know. As we build out the PMO in that new facility, do you think we can do a periodic sweep?"

"You mean for bugs?"

"And anything else that might compromise the operation. Not only am I wondering about the state employees; I don't know how sophisticated this cartel has gotten."

"I understand. I'll talk to Sonny and see what we can do. With your buddy in the FBI and his connections with the Secret Service, surely, we can figure out something. Who knows, we might need some of those SEAL Team tactics."

Brandon smiled. "You heard about that, eh?"

"Who hasn't heard about the president and the first lady being kidnapped at the White House in the middle of the night and swept off to their new home in Kansas without the country knowing about it? It's legendary."

"It does seem to be the standard by which all covert operations are measured these days," Sonny said as he walked up the steps onto the patio.

"Really," Brandon said. "I had no idea."

"That kind of cross-pollination was unheard of before that," Talbot said. "It'll be in textbooks and field manuals everywhere before you know it."

Brandon looked at Lucinda and shook his head. "Oh, please. That's crazy."

"No, sir. That's genius." Talbot walked back into the kitchen. "I need more coffee."

The others followed. Val was still sitting at the kitchen table thumbing through messages on her phone. "Find anything?" she asked.

"Nope. It could've just been an animal of some sort," Talbot said.

"Probably so. I've been texting the property management folks, and they can meet us any time."

Brandon looked around at everyone. "Well, let's go."

"Let me get this kitchen cleaned up," Lucinda said.

Sonny started picking plates up from the table. "I'll help."

"Yeah, me too," Talbot said.

After the kitchen was back in order, they climbed into their separate cars and headed down the hill toward Sacramento. When they arrived, they followed Val into the parking lot of their new offices. They got out and gathered behind Val's car.

"So, this is it, eh?" Brandon said.

"This is it," Val said.

Lucinda wrapped her arm around Brandon's. "Well, it's unassuming; that's for sure."

Sonny smiled. "Low key. That's a good thing."

"I'm glad I'm not going to be living here," Talbot chuckled.

"Well, let's go check it out." Val started walking across the parking lot.

Brandon looked around the neighborhood as he and Lucinda walked arm in arm.

Sonny noticed him from behind. "Not many high places, Boss. Is that what you're looking for?"

"Yeah. What do you think about it?"

"I think we'll be fine."

They walked around the corner to the front door. An agent from the property management company was waiting, keys in hand. "Welcome. Come on in. Let me show you around."

When they walked in and saw the reception area and the digital phone switch, Brandon stopped. "How many offices are in there?"

"Six, sir. They're all down the hall there in the back."

"Is something wrong, Brandon?" Val asked.

"Not really. It just hit that we're going to have to think through the administration of the team. Are we going to have to hire a receptionist?"

Lucinda cleared her throat. "Why risk bringing an outsider in? I can be your receptionist, office manager, project coordinator; you name it."

"Come on, Lucy," Brandon said. "I can't ask you to do that."

"You don't have to ask. I just volunteered."

Brandon looked at Sonny. Sonny smiled, shrugged his shoulders, and walked back into the dark hallway.

"Well, okay," Brandon said. They all followed Sonny.

"Do you know what you're going to need on your team, Brandon?" Val asked.

"Not yet. I haven't fully wrapped my head around this as a project . . . as opposed to an insurrection."

"I understand," Val said.

"I think I have to have a more formal kickoff meeting with the sponsor," Brandon said.

"The sponsor?"

"The governor."

"Oh. As in project sponsor."

"Right."

"I can make that happen," Talbot said.

"Who gets to furnish this place?" Lucinda asked.

"Let's just do it out of our own budget," Brandon said. "No sense in getting the state and the feds wrapped around the axle on who gets the bill."

"We have a budget?" Lucinda chuckled.

"We'll have to create one. The president will make it right, I'm sure." Brandon walked into the large office at the end of the hall. "Not much, but I guess I like the sweeping view of the parking lot and the alley full of dumpsters behind that restaurant over there. I'll take this one."

Lucinda texted Mena.

Can you find me a good office furnishings contractor and office supplies place here in Sacramento?

On it.

"So, this is it, then?" Val asked.

"Works for me," Brandon said, looking around at the others. Everyone nodded.

Lucinda sat at the receptionist's desk and took a legal pad and pen from her bag.

"Uh, you don't have to start answering the phone yet," Brandon chuckled.

"Shut up. I'm just starting a list of what we're going to need in here."

Brandon noticed Sonny looking around the rooms and out the windows. "What do you think? Can you work with it?"

"Oh, yeah. We'll be fine here. I'm going to miss eating at Barney's, though. Even if I do eat mostly in the parking lot."

"Tell me about it. Once we get settled in, we'll check out a few of the eateries around here. Maybe we can find a place . . . you know . . . trustworthy."

"That would be good. Hopefully, with a nice table in an out-of-the-way corner."

"Right. What do you think, Bruce? I know you aren't actually moving in here with us, but is there anything you might need?"

"Maybe just a place to sit in case I need to be onsite for any significant length of time."

"We'll just assign that office there to you." Brandon pointed to the dark room next to his office.

"The crappiest room in the place?"

"Of course."

"That's fine. I'll get our telecommunications guys from the Capitol out here to check out this phone system so they can update it and improve your security. Maybe they can find a good network to put you on."

"Encrypted?"

"Maybe. Might even be best to get everyone on a VPN system. The backbone is pretty good here in the city."

"Well, folks. This is where we part ways," Val said. "I need to get back to my own job. My people need me, you know."

"Wait," Brandon said. "That's it?"

"I'm here if you need me," Val said. "Just reach out. I hope Senator Beecher didn't think I was going to be able to support your team full-time."

"No. No. I'm sure he didn't expect that at all. I'm sorry. Of course you have a job to do. Thank you for all of your help."

"My pleasure. And you'll handle the lease with the agency?"

"Of course." Brandon looked at the agent, and he nodded.

Val walked out the front door as the agent pulled the contract from his briefcase and put it on the receptionist's desk next to Lucinda.

"You want me to take care of this?" she asked.

"Sure, Luce. If you don't mind. How are we going to furnish this place?"

"Mena just texted me a few places to call. I'll get on that now if you guys want to go do something to get out of my hair."

"Wow! That was fast," Brandon said. "Uh, yeah. We can walk around some. Maybe grab some coffee?" The three men nodded at each other and turned away from the desk and toward the front door. The agent smiled, taking the keys from his pocket and placing them on the counter next to the contract.

"You don't mind if we get all the locks rekeyed, do you?" Sonny asked.

"Oh. No, sir. Of course not. We'll just need the new keys when the lease is up."

"Of course."

Brandon left the building with Sonny and Bruce trailing behind. They followed him across the street and down a couple of blocks to a small diner. "You ever been in here, Bruce?" Brandon asked.

"Never seen it in my life."

"We'll get some coffee here, but I really want to check out the restaurant behind our new place."

Sonny smiled. "Sounds good to me."

They sat in the dark, empty diner and waited for someone to serve them. There was what seemed to be a server behind the counter, but he was too busy staring at his phone to realize they were there. Then Brandon noticed coffee cup rings and crumbs on the table where they sat. He curled his mouth down and shook his head while looking at the other two. They all slid their chairs away from the table and started toward the door.

"You guys don't want anything?" the man behind the counter finally asked.

"Not today, friend," Brandon said.

"Whatever."

They walked out the door and down the sidewalk. "Well, we can cross that one off our list," Sonny said.

Brandon pointed across the street. "Yep. Let's just go ahead and check that place out over there."

They went back across the street and walked toward their building and went into the restaurant that backed up to Brandon's new office.

A voice immediately came from across the room. "Hello, gentlemen. Have a seat anywhere, and I'll be right with you as soon as I'm done serving these fine folks here."

Brandon turned and looked at Sonny and Bruce. They all smiled and found a table in the corner of the dining room. After serving the couple across the room, the waitress came to their table as promised.

"I don't recall seeing you gentlemen in here before. First time?"

"Yes, ma'am," Sonny said.

"Well, I'm Gloria. I own the place. So, welcome."

"Thank you, Gloria," Brandon said. "It's a pleasure to meet you."

"So, what brings you fellas to this part of town?"

"We just leased the office building next door," Brandon said. "We hope to be moving in soon."

"Oh, the old Slidell Building. I'm glad they finally got somebody in there. It'll be nice to have good neighbors for a change."

"For a change?"

"Well, yeah. The company that was in there before wanted to buy up this whole block and tear everything down. Their tactics weren't very nice. Luckily, nobody sold to them, so I guess they decided it wasn't worth hanging around. It's been empty for almost a year."

"Really? It seems to be in pretty good shape."

"That's good to know. So, what can I get for you gents?"

"Coffee for me," Brandon said. He looked around the table, and the others nodded.

"Three coffees coming right up," Gloria said.

After she walked away, Brandon smiled at Sonny. "Now, if her food is any good, we've got our place."

"I take it a good restaurant is important for you guys," Talbot said.

"Oh, yes," Sonny chuckled. "This man here gets his best work done in a diner."

"Is that right?"

Brandon smiled. "My younger daughter took over a diner back home a while back. It's kind of a natural thing to eat there or just to meet people to discuss things. It's a nice little escape."

"I can appreciate that."

Brandon's phone vibrated.

I'll finish this ordering later. Where are you guys?

"It's Lucy." He texted back.

In the restaurant next door.

"Sorry, Miss," Brandon said. "I didn't notice a sign when we walked in. What's the name of this place?"

"Gloria's Place," the waitress said from behind the counter.

"Oh, duh," he said.

The other two chuckled.

It's called Gloria's Place, he texted.

On my way. I'll lock up here.

Gloria brought a tray with three cups and a container of coffee to their table then disappeared into the kitchen. They chatted for several minutes before Gloria returned with a plate full of hot food.

"What's this?" Brandon asked. "We haven't ordered anything."

"This is just a specialty of mine. A plate of cinnamon bites fresh out of the oven. On the house."

"What? Are you serious?" Brandon could hardly contain his excitement.

"Here are some napkins and forks. Enjoy!"

She went back to the kitchen, and the men started eating the pastry.

"Mmm. So good," Talbot mumbled.

"I wonder where Luc—"

They heard four loud pops in quick succession.

"What the . . ." Brandon jumped from his seat and ran to the door. The others followed close behind. Gloria ran out of the kitchen and peered out of the large window at the front of the diner.

When Brandon got outside, Lucinda was lying face down in a puddle of blood that that had already begun running off the edge of the sidewalk.

"Lucy!" Brandon screamed.

Sonny turned and yelled through the window at Gloria. "Call 9-1-1!"

Gloria ran to the phone next to the cash register and made the call.

"Lucy!" Brandon shouted again and fell to his knees next to her. He lifted her head into his lap. "Lucy! Come on, Luce. Talk to me."

She looked up at him, barely able to hold her eyes open. "Brandon," she whispered.

"Come on, Lucy. Stay with me."

"They're on their way," Talbot shouted from the front door of the diner while Sonny looked in all directions to see if he could see anyone running.

Brandon heard the sirens in the distance and continued talking to Lucinda. "Honey, come on. You stay with us now, you hear?"

Then everything became eerily calm and quiet. Brandon looked up at Sonny, then back down at Lucinda and began to cry. "Come on, Baby. Hang in there. I can't do any of this without you. Stay with me."

The sirens continued to get closer until Brandon saw an ambulance turn the corner near their new office complex.

"They're here, Honey. You hang on. They're here. Help is here."

She tried to open her eyes again, but her eyelids only quivered. The ambulance stopped on the street next to them, and the EMTs jumped out with armloads of equipment and immediately fell to their knees and attempted to resuscitate Lucinda. One started CPR while the other prepared to get her vital signs. She pulled the radio from her belt and called the local emergency room to report the incident.

"Sir, you need to move back, okay?"

"God, don't let her die."

"Sir. Please."

Brandon carefully lowered her head to the sidewalk and slid back away from her. "Come on, Boss," Sonny said as he helped Brandon to his feet.

"God, not again. I can't do this again." His thoughts flashed back to the day his first wife, Cassandra, was murdered inside their house. He shuddered with fear.

"Is she okay?" he asked the EMTs.

"There's still a heartbeat. Sinus rhythm is elevated." The EMTs continued to work on Lucinda and reported her vital signs to the hospital ER. "Two bullet wounds and only one exit wound that we can see. Prepping for transport."

Sonny wrapped his enormous arm around Brandon's shoulders. "You go with them, Boss. I'll stay back and call the girls; then I'll help Bruce and his guys comb the area. He has already called for support."

"Oh, God. The girls."

"It's okay, man. They'll be fine. We'll take care of everything here."

The two EMTs loaded Lucinda on a gurney into the back of the ambulance. Brandon climbed in behind them. He sat on the bench near her head and took her hand in his. "Please, Lucy. Stay with me."

The ambulance sped off with the siren blaring. Two police patrol cars arrived on the scene. One stopped where Sonny and Talbot were standing, and the other officer turned on his siren and fell in behind the ambulance.

"Mercy General, two-six, patient is in defib. Prepping paddles. Sir, you'll need to lean back out of the way, now. Hey Tony, I'm using the AED," the EMT shouted to the driver.

"Oh, God, no," Brandon cried.

"Charged. Clear!"

Lucinda's lifeless body jumped from the three-thousand-volt surge. The EMT immediately started CPR.

"Is there anything I can do to help?" Brandon said.

"Just relax and stay out of the way, sir. She has a heartbeat."

"Thank God."

They arrived at the emergency room entrance where the ER staff waited. The back door of the ambulance flew open, and they pulled the gurney out onto the ground and quickly rolled it through the automatic doors. "Get her into triage one!" someone shouted. As soon as they rolled the gurney into the assigned room, they transferred Lucinda onto the operating table. "On my count! One-two-three!"

"Sir, you'll have to wait outside. There's a waiting room right down the hall."

Brandon backed out of the emergency room, staring through the glass at the chaos of those trying to save his wife.

"God, no. Please, no. Don't do this again." He dropped his head and gazed at the floor. He turned and slowly walked down the corridor to the waiting area where there were a number of empty chairs adjacent to a nurse's station. He sat and dropped his face into his hands.

Who? He thought. *Who would have done this?*

He remembered the fear he had felt when he first heard that Cassandra had been shot. He trembled at the memory of watching Jimmy, one of his managers, holding a gun to Susan's head. Had it not been for Sonny, she would be dead. Why Lucy? Why now? What do these people want from me? Why don't they just kill me?

He sat up and leaned his head back against the stanchion behind the chair.

Maybe this is all just a bad dream, and I'll wake up, and it'll all be over. He was exhausted and fell asleep.

CHAPTER 11

Brandon dreamt that he was being held down to the ground by some force. Something grabbed his feet and started shaking them. The shaking turned into punching.

Why would something be punching my feet? Wait. It's kicking. Something is kicking my feet.

"Hey, Boss."

Who is this kicking my feet?

"Hey, man. Wake up."

"What?" Brandon shouted. He opened his eyes, startled, and sat straight up. "Lucy!"

"No, Boss. It's Sonny."

Brandon rubbed his eyes. "Jesus. How long have I been out?" Then he remembered where he was and looked at the clock above the nurse's station.

"Lucy? How is Lucy?" He finally looked up at Sonny.

"She's in surgery, Boss."

"She's still alive, then?"

"She's hanging in there."

"Thank God." Brandon looked around the room until he realized that Talbot was sitting next to him, and Val was sitting across from him.

"Brandon. I'm really sorry about this. We're here to help with anything you need," Val said.

Talbot twisted around and put his hand on Brandon's arm. "Look, buddy. The governor sends his regrets and wants me to do whatever it takes to find the asshole who did this. Sorry. My words, not his."

"Is it related to anything we're doing?" Brandon asked.

"I don't know. But something else is happening, and I think you need to get to the president as soon as possible."

"God. Now what?"

"More lives."

"Oh, no. San Francisco?"

"Yes."

Brandon looked up at Sonny and saw a look in his eyes he hadn't seen in a long time. "What's going on?"

"Boss, we think the cartel has built a bunker somewhere in the Bay Area. They've wiped out a considerable number of local law enforcement officers. The governor called on the National Guard. There have been heavy firefights. But so far, nobody has been able to pinpoint the location of the bunker."

"So, this is it, then?"

"It would appear so. They even have surface-to-air missiles and have already taken out two Air National Guard jets."

"Are you kidding me? What the heck! I haven't been out that long!"

"It was actually going on before we even got here to the hospital," Sonny said.

"Is the governor asking for more help?" Brandon asked, looking at Talbot.

"He is. Swift and decisive action. But we still don't know what the prime target is."

"A rough area?"

"Rough, yes. East Bay Area, in the hills."

"Damn it. Uh . . . Sonny, contact Mena and . . . wait. Do the girls know what's going on with Lucy?"

"They do. Of course, they're all freaking out."

"Oh, jeez. Okay, get with Mena and get the contact info for Lucy's dad, Kevin Reagan. He wouldn't get into any details about what he does, but something tells me he can help us. I'll have to tell him what happened to Lucy, but surely he'll want to help when he knows."

Brandon took the phone out of his pocket and called the Central House.

"Hello, this is Brandon McStocker for the president. Please let him know it's urgent."

"Of course, Mr. McStocker. Please hold."

Brandon looked around the room and rubbed his face with his free hand. Val and Talbot both stood and stared down at him in disbelief.

"Brandon. What in the world is going on?" the president shouted. "Are you okay?"

"I'm okay. I see it's hitting the fan, Mr. President. I'm watching it on the news reports here in the waiting room."

"It's awful out there. Uh . . . waiting room?"

"Sir, Lucy was shot."

"Oh, my God. What?"

"We were downtown checking into our new offices, and she was shot on her way to meet us in a restaurant."

"Brandon, how is she?"

"She's in surgery. Still hanging in there, but touch and go from what I can tell."

"I am so sorry. Does this have anything to do with what's going on in the Bay Area?"

"I don't know, sir. Investigators are working on it. But, sir, there's something else. The governor wants your support in San Francisco."

"What? What kind of support?"

"Apparently, it's Cártel del Mundo that set up that base of operations in the hills east of the city. They're obviously using some pretty heavy firepower. With the body count climbing the way it is, the governor wants it taken out quickly."

"Oh, my God. Does he know what he's asking?"

"I think he knows exactly what he's asking, sir."

"Do we have a target?"

"Not precisely, sir. I'd like to activate Mr. Reagan, Lucy's dad."

"Kevin?"

"Yes, sir. Do you know him?"

"Of course. How did you know what he does?"

"I can't say that I do, Mr. President. Not really. I was planning to give him a call to let him know about Lucy and ask if he can support the governor."

"Yes, he can support the governor. After you tell him about his daughter, you tell him to call in for a code. I think he's in the process of moving his operation out here to Manhattan. But he should be able to move quickly. He never lets his guard down too far. He just needs a code."

"Sir?"

"He'll know what to do."

"Of course, sir. I'll tell him."

"Brandon, I'm going to call the governor," President Richland said. "We need to understand what we're doing. I also need to notify Congress."

"I understand, sir."

"I hope you do, Brandon. May God be with us all."

Brandon's phone vibrated. Mena texted a phone number for Kevin Reagan.

"I'll call Mr. Reagan now, sir."

"Okay, Brandon. Keep in touch."

Brandon disconnected the call. "You guys, I'm going to need to make this call outside. Excuse me." He walked down the hall and out onto a patio. He paced back and forth looking into the sky and then down on the street. How do you tell someone his daughter has been shot? he thought. He started to punch in the numbers, but his hands began to shake, and tears welled in his eyes. "Oh, God."

He took in several deep breaths and called the number.

"Reagan."

"Mr. Reagan, sir, this is Brandon McStocker."

"Brandon? I didn't expect to hear from you anytime soon. How are you two doing on your honeymoon? And it's Kevin."

"Kevin, sorry. Sir, I don't know any other way to say this. Lucy has been shot."

"Oh, my God. How can that be? Is she okay?"

"They tell me she's in surgery, and it's critical, but everyone is hopeful."

"Jesus. I can be out there in a few hours. Do I need to come now?"

"No, sir. Not now. I'll let you know if that changes. But I do need your help with something. Have you been watching the news?"

"That mess in San Francisco? Yes, I have it on in the background. I was wondering how close you guys are to all that. Is that what happened to Lucy?"

"No, sir. At least I don't think so. Maybe. I'm just not sure. In any case, we aren't near there."

"Then what is it, Brandon?"

"Kevin, that city is under attack in a big way by a drug cartel that has entrenched themselves in a bunker somewhere east of the bay. They've managed to get SAMs down there and are already taking out aircraft."

"Damn! Drones?"

"Not yet. All manned aircraft from the Air National Guard. But I think we can use your help to pinpoint that bunker. The president is speaking to the governor now. He wants it stopped."

"I'll need to get clearance to fly out there."

"You have it."

"Pardon me?"

"I just spoke to the president, and you have it. He told me to have you call in for a code."

"Are you kidding me?"

"I'm afraid not, sir. I wish I were."

"I'm sure this will be a six-hour or less alert mission. I don't suppose he told you who's scrambling?"

"Scrambling?"

"Never mind. Probably NAS Lemoore."

"Kevin, I don't think I completely understand what's happening. Do you?"

"Brandon, I need to go. Keep me posted with any updates on Lucinda."

"Of course, sir."

The line fell silent. Brandon looked at his phone then pressed the End button. Brandon looked into the sky for a minute, then turned and walked back into the hospital corridor and down to the emergency room waiting area.

"Boss, you look like you've seen a ghost," Sonny said.

"No. No ghost. But I feel like I'm in a James Bond movie."

"Boss?"

"Never mind. Something is about to happen, and I can't quite put my finger on it."

Val's phone began to emit an eerily loud tone. She grabbed it up to read the alert. "Uh, I need to call in. I'll be right back." She rushed down the hallway, almost reaching a full run, and disappeared out of sight.

Brandon looked at Talbot. "You know, don't you?"

He nodded. "I spoke to the governor while you were outside."

"So, you know what's about to happen? 'Cause frankly, I don't."

"I'm sorry, Brandon. All I can say now is history is about to be made."

"Crap. Civil War II?"

"Well, not exactly. I sure hope not anyway."

Brandon noticed the silence, and then a collective gasp came over everyone in the waiting area.

"Will you turn that up, please?" Talbot asked the nurse behind the counter. She looked up to see *Breaking News* emblazoned across the TV screen. She quickly picked up the remote control and turned it up.

A national news station had interrupted regular programming to air a live video feed looking out over the hills, east of San Francisco above Black Hawk Ridge. Streaks of smoke were coming from the cliffs as rockets were being fired toward the jets flying in the area.

A reporter started speaking. "We interrupt this broadcast to bring you breaking news from the San Francisco Bay Area. We have reporters on the ground near this firefight that have witnessed many people being killed in an apparent attempt by a militant group of some sort to take over the area. Blocks and blocks of homes below the ridge are on fire. Secondary fires are beginning to overwhelm the heavily forested areas. We still aren't clear who this militant group is."

Brandon looked at the clock. Lucinda had been in surgery for over two hours. He sat back down and began to wring his hands. He continued to watch the action on the TV as more people gathered around the nurse's station. Another two hours had passed before he realized it.

"You okay, Boss?" Sonny asked.

Brandon looked down at his vibrating phone and slanted his head, confused by the caller ID. He answered the call. "Liv?"

"Daddy. Are you okay?"

"Fine, Honey. What's going on?"

"Are you watching this?"

"Of course. Why?"

"Daddy, the president is here."

"At our offices?" Brandon asked.

"Yes."

"Why?"

"It's hard to explain. I don't even understand it, but Lucy's dad is having targeting data shipped back here to the third-floor computer center, and two of our Genius Pods are in there processing data and shipping it back to the Navy."

"That's nuts, Liv. What are you talking about? The Navy? Why?"

"Wait. Here's President Richland."

"Brandon?"

"Mr. President. What's going on?"

Everyone in the waiting area fell silent. Val and Talbot jerked their heads around when they heard who Brandon was speaking to. Brandon covered his mouth and quickly walked to the corner of the waiting area.

"Brandon. Listen. I've brought some NSA and CIA personnel with me to your offices to use your systems. I was informed that someone has been trying to hack into our systems, and these folks didn't want to take a chance on this operation failing."

"The airport?"

"For starters. Yes."

"So, what's the status, sir?"

"Kevin will have his drones staged near San Jose and ready to launch in a couple of hours."

"Are these armed drones, sir?"

"No. This is strictly a locating and targeting mission. I don't know what these monsters are capable of."

"What about the Navy, sir? What's that all about?"

"I've briefed the Joint Chiefs, and they activated a couple of attack squadrons from NAS Lemoore."

"So that's what Kevin was talking about."

"He's been around the horn a few times," the president said.

"Sir?"

"Never mind. Not important."

"What about the surrounding area, Mr. President? What about the civilians?"

"The Navy will be using laser-guided munitions. They assure me there will be no collateral damage."

"Okay, sir."

"Look, the media is all over this," President Richland said. "It's not like we can keep this covert as if it were on the other side of the world. You'll be able to watch it on the news in real time. I doubt that you'll see the drones, but you'll certainly see what the drones enabled. Brandon, I need to run. Here's Liv."

"Thank you, sir."

"Daddy?"

"Honey, are you okay?"

"Not really. We're worried sick about Lucy."

"I know, Sweetheart. She's strong. You know that."

"I know."

"Listen, I'm going to go. If you start feeling overwhelmed, you call me, okay?"

"I will. I promise," Olivia said.

"You've got this, Honey. Just give the president the support he needs."

"Of course, Daddy. Love you."

"Love you too, Sweetie. I'll let you know the second she wakes up."

"Bye, Daddy."

Brandon placed the phone back in his pocket and made his way through the crowd to the nurse's station.

"Excuse me, do you have any updates on Mrs. McStocker's surgery?"

"No, sir. I'm sorry. Nothing new yet. I'll let you know as soon as we hear something."

"Okay. Thank you." He turned, hanging his head, and returned to his seat. He could see the TV monitor over the heads of the crowd.

Again, Brandon, surprised he had fallen asleep, awoke to Sonny tapping his knee. "You'll want to see this, Boss."

Brandon looked at the clock. Another two hours had passed. "What's happening?"

"The news reporters have picked up a squadron of F/A-18s coming into the area from the east. They look like they're in some kind of holding pattern."

"Lucy?"

"We haven't heard anything. Val and Bruce had to leave. They didn't want to wake you."

Brandon's phone vibrated. He looked down and saw Olivia's text message.

You watching this?
Yes
Lucy?
No change yet
The president is about to turn them loose.
k
A SEAL Team is there on the ground to take out the SAM site.

He put the phone on his knee. "This is it," he said to Sonny. "We're about to attack an enemy on our own soil. God, I hate this."

"I know, Boss. I know. Me too."

They both stared at the large TV monitor as the camera locked on to what appeared to be the lead F/A-18. The wings leveled, and another jet joined up in formation as they went into a dive from the north side of the city. The news station went to a split-screen to show another camera aimed at a spot in the mountains east of the city. Gunfire and smoke began to stream from the rocks.

Two surface-to-air missiles were launched, and the camera operator tracked them past the incoming F/A-18s. Then there was an explosion on the ground where they landed after missing their targets. Then the jets turned in together, wingtip to wingtip, approaching the bunker at high speed. Two missiles were fired from the wings of the aircraft and streaked to the ground. There was a massive explosion on impact. The jets split and flew in opposite directions while releasing their load of bombs on the target. The cameras shook when the shock of the enormous blast reached them.

The gasps and muffled comments were nonstop from those who had gathered around the TV. The reporters had fallen silent, obviously speechless with what they were witnessing on location. The aircraft rejoined to the west and flew north to where they started the run. After circling for several minutes, the two joined up with the rest of the squadron and flew east until they were out of sight.

What's happening? Brandon texted Olivia.
SEALS going back in to clean up.
He leaned over and showed her message to Sonny and smiled. Sonny returned the smile with a thumbs-up.
Are there other encampments?
Don't know, Olivia answered. *Prez is federalizing the California National Guard to begin sweeping the area.*
You okay?
Nervous wreck.

You're my hero.
I miss you, Daddy.

"Mr. McStocker," a nurse shouted.

Brandon stood and rushed to the nurse's station. "Yes?"

"Sir, the surgery has been completed. The doctor will be out shortly."

"Is she okay?"

"Sir, I don't know. You'll have to wait for the doctor."

"Thank you." He looked up at the TV, then turned and paced around to the back part of the waiting area before eventually making his way back to his seat.

CHAPTER 12

Val and Bruce returned to the waiting room, briefly looked at the TV monitor, and sat in the seats across from Brandon.

"Mr. McStocker?"

Brandon looked up at a tall black man in a white coat. He jumped to his feet.

"Are you the doctor? What's happening? How is my wife?" The others stood and closed in around him as he spoke to the doctor.

"Mr. McStocker, I'm the attending on duty. Lucinda is still back in the OR. She has a bullet wound to the chest, which is quite serious, but it barely missed her heart. She has another, more superficial wound to the leg—her upper thigh, actually."

"Is she going to make it, Doc? Why is it taking so long?"

"It's a complicated surgery. It's looking good, but we won't know for sure until she comes out of the OR. The surgeon will be down to see you then."

"Thanks, Doc." Brandon turned and paced around the waiting area rubbing the back of his head.

"Can we get you something?" Sonny asked. "Coffee?"

Brandon looked at the clock again. "Jeez, it's six already? Yeah, coffee would be good."

"Sonny, you stay here," Val said. "I'll go get it. Are you hungry, Brandon? Do you want some supper?"

"No, thanks. Coffee is fine."

She hurried down the hallway, out of sight.

"The girls. Now that the dust has settled some, we need to update Liv and Susan on Lucy. It probably hasn't sunk in yet."

"I contacted them," Sonny said. "They were shocked, of course, but they're fine. Liv left the president with Trevor and went to stay with Susan at her apartment. They were going to wait there to hear from you."

"Okay. You know what? I'm going to go outside and give them a call."

"Good idea, Boss."

Brandon took the phone from his coat pocket and walked toward the patio. After he went out through the large automatic glass doors, he walked across the patio and sat on a secluded concrete bench behind several tall potted plants and made the call.

"Daddy!"

"Hey, Sweetheart."

"Daddy, are you okay?" Olivia asked. "Now that I have time to think straight, I'm worried sick about you guys. Hang on; I'm putting you on speaker."

"Daddy, how are you?" Susan asked. "How is Lucy?"

"I'm fine. I'm fine. Luce is in surgery. She took a shot to her leg and one through her chest, but the doctor said it missed her heart."

"Daddy, I'm scared," Susan said.

"Honey, we're going to figure this out. I don't think you guys are in any danger. My gut is telling me this is strictly a California issue."

"Daddy, I spoke to the president," Olivia said, "and told him what happened when he was here at the office."

"I'm not sure that was necessary. I had already told him about it."

"Sorry. I didn't know what else to do. I had to do something."

"I understand. It's fine. What did he say?"

"He was horrified. After the airstrike, he told me to do whatever it takes to get protection for you guys. He's getting the Secret Service involved. Who knows who else? I called Josh. He's on his way over."

"Oh, good. I'm glad you did that. I think we're going to need him sooner than we thought. Listen, girls, I need to run. If anything changes, I'll let you know. I love you both so much."

"We love you too, Daddy. We're glad you called," Olivia said.

"Bye, Daddy," Susan said. "Give Lucy our love when she wakes up."

"Okay, girls."

"Daddy."

"Yeah, Liv."

"She *is* going to wake up. We're praying for her."

"I know, Sweetheart. We'll talk soon." Brandon returned the phone to his coat pocket and sat motionless, staring at the concrete between his feet for several minutes. He heard birds singing above him. He looked up and saw a pair of doves sitting on the edge of a gutter on the corner of the building. He lowered his face into his hands and began to cry.

"Brandon?"

He wiped his face and looked up. "Oh. Hey, Val."

"You okay?"

"Not really." He managed a faint smile.

"Sorry to bother you. Here's your coffee."

"Thanks, Val."

"Mind if I have a seat?"

"Sure, go ahead."

She sat next to him and cupped her coffee between her hands. "Listen, I'm going back to K.D. tomorrow. Congress is going back in session."

"Have fun with that."

"Yeah, really. But I'm going to start talking to them about all this junk that's going on out here. I also have some friends in Homeland. Surely, we can come up with legislation to help us get a handle on it."

"Val, what would that even look like?"

"Honestly? I have no idea. But there's got to be something we can do to remove this scourge from the state."

"If you come up with something, shoot me a text. And just so you know, my daughter has the Genius Pods at the firm working on technology solutions."

"I keep hearing those folks can do amazing things."

"Yes. It's impressive. Maybe if we marry up the technology with your legislation, we can finally get something done. Just make sure they get focused on this secession."

"Well, my friend, here's to hope." She lifted her coffee cup to meet his. "I'm going back in. I'll leave you alone."

"Thanks, Val. I'll be along shortly."

She disappeared through the sliding doors, and Brandon was once again alone on the patio. He looked up, and the doves had gone. He took a sip of his coffee and stood to pace around, looking over the edge of the handrails into the parking lot below. He noticed a small diner across the street and smiled. It reminded him of Barney's and the day he and Lucinda were married. He stared into the clouds.

"Dear God. Why is this country in such a mess? I thought we did a good thing by moving out of D.C. What do you want me to do here in California, Lord? Why am I here?"

The two doves came back and flew a few hundred feet in front of him, dancing together in the sky. Then they landed together on a brace of a pole beneath the sign at the diner. He grinned through his tears when he saw the sign, and he read it aloud.

"Hope's Diner."

He looked back into the clouds and chuckled. "Funny. Thanks, Lord."

He took a drink of coffee and threw the cup in the trash as he walked back into the hospital. He proceeded down the hall and into the waiting area where the others were sitting quietly.

"She's going to be okay, you guys. Lighten up."

They looked up at him. "Of course, she is," Val said.

Sonny stood and walked closer to Brandon. "Hey, Boss. I got a call from Clyde. He had just heard from the Central House. Apparently, the president has directed the Secret Service to give us whatever we need."

"Really? Liv told me she spoke to him. I guess he was serious. Something tells me she didn't tell me the whole story."

"Of course, she didn't, Boss."

"She did tell me that Josh was going over to Susan's apartment to meet with them."

"I hope they can come up with some kind of plan out there."

"Hey, Brandon." Talbot was staring at his phone.

"What is it?"

Talbot continued to read silently.

"Bruce? What is it?"

"They found the rifle."

"What?"

"They found it just a few blocks from Gloria's in a dumpster."

"Anything on the owner?"

"They're processing it now."

"It's a start, Boss," Sonny said.

"Yeah, it's a start."

Sonny took his phone from his pocket. "It's a text from Clyde."

"What does it say?"

Sonny read the text. "SS credentials reinstated. Are you armed?"

"What the heck!" Brandon said. "What does that even mean?

"Right?" Sonny said.

"They're bringing you back into the Secret Service?"

"Apparently so."

"Well, are you?" Brandon asked.

"What!"

"Armed."

"Boss, California is really goofy with that kind of stuff." Sonny looked back down at his phone and continued to read aloud. "Overnighting badge and interstate permits. Where are you staying?"

"What in the world is going on? So, you're back in?"

"Apparently, the president thinks you're worthy of Secret Service protection, and I'm the easiest solution."

"That's crazy. I didn't think he was going to do that," Brandon said.

"Boss. What isn't crazy right now?"

Everyone turned to look at a person walking toward them. It was an older man, obviously a doctor, draped in a surgical gown, a blue skullcap tied around his head, and a face mask dangling loosely around his neck. He looked around the waiting area.

"Mr. McStocker?"

"Yes, sir. Right here."

They shook hands. "Mr. McStocker, your wife is out of surgery and is doing well."

They all dropped their heads and exhaled, relieved at the good news.

"Oh, God. Thank you, Doctor," Brandon said. "Can I see her?"

"Not yet. She'll be out of it for a while, but as soon as she's able, someone will come out to get you. It won't be long."

"Thank you so much," Brandon said with a grin. Everyone behind Brandon nodded at the surgeon. He smiled and walked back down the hall and out of sight.

Everyone breathed another sigh of relief and took turns hugging Brandon.

"And, on that note, I need to hit the road," Val said. "Early flight tomorrow."

"Yeah, I need to run, too," Talbot said.

"Thank you, guys, so much for hanging around," Brandon said. "Even though you don't know us well, you've been good friends."

They nodded and smiled, then patted him on the back and left together. Brandon sat back down and took the phone from his coat.

Luce out of surgery. Going to be fine.

Thank God, Daddy, Olivia replied. *Pods starting full-throttle first thing in the morning. Josh joining us.*

Good work. I'll be in touch. Get some rest.

Will do, Olivia replied.

Sonny sat next to him and leaned back in the chair. "Letting the girls know?"

"Yeah. Those two are amazing."

"Yes, they are. You are a blessed man."

"In so many ways, Sonny. In so many ways."

"Mr. McStocker?"

Brandon jumped to his feet. "Yes."

"You can come on back, sir. Lucinda is waking up."

Brandon started walking toward the nurse then turned back and saw Sonny bend over and drop his face into his hands.

"You okay, Buddy?"

"I'll be fine, Brandon. You go ahead. Give her a hug for me."

"You sure?"

"Yep. Go."

Brandon followed the nurse down the darkened hallway through a set of double doors and past two more nurses' stations.

"This is recovery in here. She's over there in two."

"Thank you so much," Brandon said.

He strolled into the room where Lucinda lay with her head sunken into a pillow and wires coming out from under the blanket that covered her. He followed the wires with his gaze into the equipment that surrounded her. Then he went to her side and stared into her face.

She apparently sensed his presence and slowly opened her eyes.

"Hey there," came a raspy voice.

Brandon slid a chair next to the bed and sat down, not taking his gaze from her. Then he held her hand and lowered his head onto her arm and began to weep.

"Hey. Hey. I'm okay," she said. "I'm here. I'm fine. Sore as hell, but I'm fine."

He looked up at her and smiled. "Luce, you scared the crap out of me. All of us. We thought we lost you."

She smiled through her grogginess. "You aren't losing me that easy."

"Nothing easy about it."

"My mouth is so dry. Is there any water?"

"Yes. Right here." He picked up a Styrofoam cup from the table and helped her get the straw into her mouth. After she had taken a sip, he wet his finger and rubbed some water onto her lips.

"Mm. That feels good," she said.

"Do you remember what happened?" Brandon asked.

"Not really. They told me I was shot. I remember locking up the new office and walking toward the restaurant, but that's it."

"Well, that's when you were shot."

"Do you know who did it?"

"No, but the local police just found the rifle they used. At least, they're pretty sure."

"This is unbelievable. Hell, we're just getting started."

"Honey, when you're up and around, I think we need to get you back to Kansas."

"Oh, hell no!" Lucinda shouted as best she could.

"What?"

She tried to sit up but cringed in pain and lowered herself back to the bed. "Don't you dare go there. I'm staying right here with you, and we're going to finish what we started . . . together."

"But, Honey."

"No, no. Don't you 'but Honey' me. It's not going to happen. End of discussion."

A nurse ran in the door. "Is everything okay in here?"

"Fine. Why?" Lucinda asked.

"Sorry to interrupt. We just saw a spike in your pulse rate and blood pressure out here."

"I'm fine. Really. My husband just gave me some really good news." Lucinda smiled.

Brandon nodded toward the nurse and forced a smile as well.

"Okay, then. Press the button there if you need anything."

"Will do. Thank you," Lucinda said.

As soon as the nurse left the room, Brandon dropped his head back down on Lucinda's arm. "This is nuts."

"Just leave it alone, Brandon. Nothing changes. I'll be fine."

"Okay. Okay." He kissed her. "I love you more than you will ever know."

"Oh, I know more than you think."

Lucinda closed her eyes, and Brandon leaned back in the chair and closed his. After several minutes, the nurse returned.

"I'm sorry to disturb you, but I'm at the end of my shift, and visiting hours are almost over."

"Nurse, I'm just going to stay here tonight if it's okay."

"I'll check with the doctor. In any case, they're coming in to take your wife to her regular room. She doesn't need to stay here in recovery."

"Oh, okay." Brandon touched Lucinda's hand, and she opened her eyes. "They're coming to move you."

"Oh, man, I feel rough," Lucinda said.

"That's to be expected," the nurse said as she began to disconnect Lucinda from all of the monitors.

Brandon moved the table and chair back away from the bed when the orderly came in to move her.

The orderly quickly kicked off the wheel locks and flipped up the safety rails. "Here we go, ma'am."

The nurse pushed the bed from the head position and grabbed the IV stand, rolling it along behind them. Brandon fell in behind the hospital staff and followed them to Lucinda's new room. It felt to Brandon like it was down miles of hallways.

"Okay. Here we are," the orderly said. "We'll get you set up here, and I'll get out of your way."

The nurse placed her IV stand behind the head of the bed and connected the blood pressure and heart rate monitors. Brandon sat in the chair in the corner of the room, out of the way, and texted Sonny.

We're in room 406 if you want to come up.
I guess I will. Need anything?
No. All good.
On my way.

"Okay, Mr. McStocker," the nurse said. "The doctor should be making his rounds shortly, and he'll check in with you then."

"Thank you," he said.

"But first, Lucinda, what's your pain level, one to ten?"

"Oh, maybe a seven."

"We'll get you something for it."

"Thanks, nurse," she said.

"Seven?" Brandon said after the nurse left.

"I think the good stuff is wearing off."

Brandon paced around the room and then stopped to stare out of the window down into the city streets.

"You've been staring at that an awfully long time. Everything okay out there?"

"I'm sure it's all fine. I just can't help but believe this is about me in some way."

"What do you mean?" Lucinda asked.

"Why are they coming after the people I care about?"

"They, who?"

"The cartel."

"You think the cartel did this?"

"Cártel del Mundo. Yes. I do."

"Dang. Sweetheart, relax. Why would they even know who you are? Or care? Don't get yourself wrapped around the axle on this. We have work to do."

"I'm sorry. I know we do," Brandon said.

"We're going to whip this thing, Honey. Trust me. I know you. And I know your kids and your friends who love you. You're going to whip this thing."

"I just don't think I can keep putting the people I love at risk like this."

"You aren't, Brandon. We are. We are putting ourselves at risk. We do it because we believe in you. We believe in what you're doing. With the exception of California, this country has never been this united, and that's on you. You did all this, Brandon."

"But, I—"

"But nothing. Stop it!"

"Everything okay in here?" A fourth-floor nurse walked into the room with Sonny following behind her.

"You all need a referee?" Sonny chuckled as he threw a white teddy bear across the room at Lucinda.

"Hey! Injured person here!" she shouted and caught it before it landed on her chest. "Aw. Thank you, Sonny. It's adorable."

"You're welcome. They told me it's guaranteed to make you feel better."

"Well, okay, then. Hear that, nurse? We've got this."

"Oh, I'm sure you do."

"That is if this one doesn't throw in the towel." Lucinda looked at Brandon with a smirk.

"Nope. Ain't gonna happen," Sonny said. "He ain't throwin' in nothin'."

"Fine. Fine," Brandon said. "But if you guys get in trouble, it isn't on me. Just remember, I wanted to turn this off."

CHAPTER 13

"This is Olivia McStocker."

"Miss McStocker, this is Mary Solice from the WRHF News. Got a sec?"

"I suppose. How can I help you?"

"Can you tell us why your father is in California?"

"Uh . . . he's there on business."

"What kind of business? His wife of not more than a week has been shot. Did that have anything to do with the business he's conducting?"

"No. Why are you asking me this?"

"Miss McStocker, your father became something of a legend when he uncovered the plot to stop President Richland's plan to move the federal government. He seemed to be the president's right-hand man when he oversaw the building of an entire city in the middle of nowhere. It's no secret that Brandon McStocker is one who gets things done for the president. Olivia, why is your father in California?"

"You know what? No freakin' comment." She slammed the phone down.

"Liv, I don't think you can talk to the media that way," Mena said.

"Why the interest in Daddy all of a sudden?"

"Well, I wouldn't say it's all of a sudden. He's done some pretty amazing things for this country—highly visible things, I might add."

"Do you think they're trying to tear him down? Why would they do that?"

"I wouldn't assume that yet, Liv. I would almost think the opposite."

"What do you mean?"

"I think maybe the country is beginning to learn more about him and is falling in love with him."

"Why don't I believe that?"

"Well, something to think about. But now that everyone knows he's in California on business, you have to admit, it raises the question, *why*. Why would the president's right-hand man—the one who led the biggest construction project on the planet—the man who moved the whole federal government—be in California?"

"I don't know what we're going to do with all this. I don't want to talk to him about it yet. Not until Lucy is back on her feet. I really think he expected his presence out there to be low key."

"I don't know. We'll have to wait and see. I'm going back out to my desk, but if I hear anything else, I'll let you know."

"Thanks, Mena."

"Open or closed?"

"You can leave it open."

"Hey, Liv?"

"Yes. What's up, Trev?" she said, answering the intercom.

"We're all gathered here in the third-floor conference room. You ready to join us?"

"Be right down." Olivia walked out of her office and past Mena's desk. "I'll be down on three with the Genius Pod. I have no idea how long it'll be before they cut me loose."

"Good luck. It's always fun being in a room full of engineers."

"Right?" Olivia chuckled. "Not to mention the top minds in the country."

"Only in Mac and Mac land. Have fun."

"Oh, I will," Olivia said.

She walked into the conference room as Trevor was wrapping up his housekeeping brief on the facility and the local area.

"Oh, and here is our host and senior executive project manager, Miss Olivia McStocker."

All twenty heads turned in unison to see her standing in the back of the room. Some stood as she walked to the front to meet Trevor.

"No. Please. Have a seat. We aren't big on formality around here. You can relax." She shook Trevor's hand, and he sat in a chair against the wall behind her.

"Thanks, Trev." She turned to face the attendees. "It's wonderful to see that the female engineers and scientists in this country are well represented here today. Welcome to you all. Let me begin by saying that those of you who have been with these Genius Pods from the beginning have been an invaluable asset to the country. What you've done to create the model infrastructure in this town is nothing short of astonishing. I want to personally thank you. My father and the entire company, not to mention the President of the United States, are all eternally grateful for your hard work.

"Today, I'm going to ask you to take on something completely different and completely unprecedented. We asked you to sign those nondisclosure agreements when you got here because this really needs to stay under wraps. You probably noticed the language was a little stronger than usual. If you've ever been exposed to Lockheed's Skunk Works, you understand the concept. You've agreed to work for the president, so we have to be responsible. Ready?"

They all nodded and looked around the room at each other, then back at her. Olivia turned and smiled at Trevor, then she began to pace across the front of the room, back and forth, as if in deep thought.

"So, you're all familiar with the resistance we've experienced during the building of K.D. We've learned that most of that resistance, while not necessarily a direct effort of the drug cartels, was undoubtedly shaped by them. The cartels have a lot of money and influence. Most of the corruption in our government can be traced back to the drug lords that lead these organizations. It's that infiltration of corruption that keeps our law enforcement agencies from doing their jobs effectively.

"All of them: the CIA, DEA, FBI, NSA, the entire Homeland Security umbrella, are being frustrated by the actions of the cartels. Their financial standing is what makes them so hard to defeat. The flow of cash from drugs and human trafficking must stop, or this country is doomed. That's how bad it has gotten.

"So, here's the word of the day: disruption. How in the hell do we disrupt this malignant disease at its very core? How do we fight it from the inside out? Too many of our undercover agents go native from so much exposure to the dark innerworkings of these organizations. It's just too big. And the granddaddy of them all is the organization called Cártel del Mundo. If we can rattle their foundation, the house of cards just might fall.

"The nation has been so focused on al-Qaeda for so long, we've largely ignored the threat of the cartels. Again, it has to stop. Before I say anything further, I want to make sure you understand the threat. Please. Ask any questions you might have."

All of the pod members looked at each other shaking their heads. Their gazes all came back to Olivia. She had them mesmerized. But one of the engineers sitting toward the front finally raised his hand.

"Yes," Olivia said, smiling.

"Miss McStocker, what—"

"Nope. Stop."

His eyes grew large with her interruption.

"Sorry. Call me Liv. Everybody okay with that? Just call me Liv."

They all nodded their heads and smiled as the engineer continued his question.

"Uh, I'm Dave Mathers, by the way, from CynTech."

"Welcome, Dave."

"Thank you . . . Liv. What does this have to do with us? What does a drug cartel have to do with a bunch of engineers and scientists?"

"Boom!" she shouted, slamming her hand down on the table, startling everyone in the room, including

Trevor. "And there it is! This has everything to do with you. You know why? Because nobody else has been able to get it done. That's why. The very reason we came up with these Genius Pods to begin with is to make the impossible possible."

She turned to see Trevor smiling when he saw everyone in the room sit up a little straighter. He looked at her and nodded. He knew she had them.

"Technological Saturation Enforcement."

Everyone around the table tilted their heads and squinted their eyes.

"You wanted to ask how, right?"

They all nodded.

"Technological Saturation Enforcement. Hell, I'm not even sure what that means yet. Call it what you want," she said, smiling.

The room erupted in laughter as she released the tension.

"TSE is just something that's been on my mind. The point is, if we can bring together every available database related to the activities of the cartels, we can start building on it. We start identifying every single member and start tracking every move they make. Every credit card charge, every phone call, every Uber or Lyft trip. Everything. Of course, the privacy advocates are going to scream bloody murder. But going overboard to protect everyone's privacy is what led us to this underground world to begin with."

"So, how do we get around the laws associated with all that?" one of the members asked.

"That part, you'll have to let me deal with. I want you guys to design a system assuming there are no laws. No restrictions. Everything is on the table. Maybe you link together every camera on the internet and merge the links into a secure system. Maybe we link to every credit card company on the planet. Maybe we embed GPS trackers on the vehicles of every cartel member we identify. I don't know. Everything is game."

A hand went up in the back of the room.

"Yes, ma'am."

"Does this all have anything to do with California?"

"Pardon me?" Olivia said.

"California. Does any of this have to do with California? We know your father is out there, and we know his new wife was shot. Sorry, by the way. Then the bombing runs the Navy did. Is this related?"

Olivia turned and looked at Trevor. He shook his head slightly and tried to hide his cringing. She paused and stared out the window across the city. She took a deep breath.

She looked at the young scientist in the back. "Thank you for that." She scanned the room and continued. "Well . . . we have to go into this knowing that we are building a national asset. But having said that, yes, my father is dealing with some unprecedented issues in California. And yes, we may have to turn this tool, whatever it becomes, to quickly test it out west. I remind you that you have all been read into the project, so I'm going to share some things that have to stay in this room. Understood?"

They all nodded as Olivia looked at each one of them, one by one, acknowledging their commitment.

"Okay. Trev, would you lock the doors and turn on the white noise, please?"

"Of course." He walked to the back of the room and did as she asked. They stared at each other as he walked back to the front and returned to his chair behind her.

"Okay. We all know what kind of turmoil California has been in of late. To the rest of the country, they seem to have lost their way. Their decisions at the highest levels seem to be so radical as to threaten their very existence. The problem is that now, they seem to want to start making decisions on behalf of the entire country. Yes. You have a question?"

"Not so much a question," the man said. "My firm is based in California, near Sunnyvale. And—"

"Okay. Hang on. Anyone else here from California?"

Six members raised their hands.

"I mean no disrespect to you whatsoever. Do any of you disagree with what I've said so far? Show of hands."

All six lowered their hands and smiled, shaking their heads.

"Okay. Go ahead, sir. Sorry to interrupt."

"Well, I just wanted to say that what you describe is true. Over the years, the state has really gotten derailed. Even the disagreements within the state run so deep they wanted to get splitting the state on the ballot. Many of the extremists wanted to break up into two or three states."

"I hear that one of the biggest riffs out there is the farmers against the conservationists."

"Oh, yeah. Many would just as soon see all the farmers pack up and leave. The regulations they have to deal with daily are absurd."

"I understand," Olivia said. "But I think one thing that has never been acknowledged is the part cartels play in all the chaos going on out there. With so much confusion in local and state government, they have the anonymity they need to set deep roots in the state. We're afraid we've reached a point of no return. And, frankly, so is the governor."

"So, it's happening, then?"

Olivia looked where the voice came from in the back of the room. Everyone turned to look at her.

"What's that?"

"Secession. It's happening?"

Olivia rolled a chair from against the wall up to the table and sat down, then motioned for Trevor to join her there. He rolled himself up to the table next to her.

She quieted herself and the room by looking around at each of their faces, saying nothing. Then she looked down at the table and took a deep breath.

"Yes. It's happening," she said, quickly looking around the room as everyone gasped, looking at each other as a roar of chatter erupted.

"Hang on. Hang on," she said, trying to regain their attention. "Hey!"

Trevor stood and started knocking on the table. "People. People. Let's quiet down. Come on."

Olivia put her hand on Trevor's arm to calm him. The room quieted, and he sat back down.

"It isn't a done deal yet, but my dad did go out there at the president's request to see if Governor Truly wants his help."

"And does he?" someone asked.

"Of course he does," someone else said.

"Well, that remains to be seen. At first, definitely not. But with everything going on now, I think his mood may be changing. My dad thinks he might be warming up to the idea. The governor is the one who asked for help with eliminating the immediate threat east of San Francisco the other day. So, you can see the importance of neutralizing the cartels, especially in the U.S. While they are the ones who have twisted the minds of the residents out there, we can't just turn an entire state over to them. If we let California go now, that's exactly what's going to happen, and that's what the governor is afraid of. We need this technology."

"Liv, there are still a lot of Conservatives in California, especially among the farming community in the valley and the eastern side of the state. What about them?"

"Well, that won't be part of our technical solution, but they'll definitely have to address it on the political front. I don't think they'll be ignored."

"Yes, Ron. You have a question?" Trevor asked, acknowledging the hand at the side of the table.

"Uh, yes. Ron Sievert from Global Geo-Systems. Will we have access to satellites to make all this happen?"

"Yes," Olivia said. "Trevor will be coordinating all of your national resources. So yes, I will be able to get that approved."

They looked at each other, seemingly in awe that this woman could wield that kind of influence. Olivia stood and slowly paced toward the back of the room as everyone's eyes followed her. "What I would like to do now is give you time to brainstorm some ideas—gather the collective thoughts that you might already have. I know you haven't had time to digest any of this, but my guess is your minds are reeling."

They smiled and chuckled, nodding their heads.

"We're going to try this the old-fashioned way." Trevor took a stack of Post-It Note pads from his briefcase and walked to the large whiteboard in the front of the room. There was a collective moan from the room.

"Seriously?" Someone said. "That kind of brainstorming? Can't we just project some mind-mapping software?"

"You might eventually get to that," Olivia said. "But for now, let's keep it organic. Throw your thoughts, ideas, and questions out so Trevor can capture them and stick them on the board. Those notes will undoubtedly plant the seed for other notes. You've all done this before, right?"

She noticed some blank faces around the table.

"Okay. Who has never done this before?"

Several younger members raised their hands.

"Okay, then. Trevor is going to explain the finer points of Post-It Note brainstorming. I will leave you all to it. I'll come back in a couple of days, and we'll see how things are going. Of course, Trevor will be reporting your progress to me regularly, but I promise not to do any backroom micromanaging. This is on you guys. Okay?"

Everyone nodded and stood as Olivia walked toward the door. She stopped and smiled at them. "Will you guys stop doing that?"

They all laughed as she left the room and closed the door behind her. She went to the elevator and up one floor to return to her office.

"Well, how did it go?" Mena asked.

"Actually, not too bad. Pretty astute crowd."

"Well, that's why you pay them the big bucks."

"Right. I'll be in here if you need me."

"Brandon called, but he didn't want to interrupt you. Said it wasn't anything urgent."

"Okay. I'll check in with him," Olivia said.

She went into her office and sat at her desk, taking a deep breath. She looked at her phone and noticed that Susan had sent her a text.

I'm coming up to do some training in the cafeteria. Lunch?

Sounds like a plan, Olivia answered.

She punched in the numbers for Brandon's phone.

"Hey, Sweetheart. How did your meeting go?"

"It went very well. You called earlier?"

"I did, but I didn't need anything. Just checking in."

"I'm glad you did. I got a call from a reporter this morning wanting me to answer some questions about you."

"About me? Whatever for?"

"She didn't say, but Mena seems to think they want to make you a hero."

Brandon laughed. "Yeah, right."

"I blew her off. But what if she calls back?"

"Well, I trust your judgment, Honey. I certainly have nothing to hide; well, except for maybe this California thing."

"I think the cat may be out of the bag on that, Daddy. How's Lucy doing?"

"She's doing well. They've got her in rehab for a while and hope to release her in a few days."

"That's great, Daddy. She sure put a scare in us. How awful for you to have to go through that again."

"Oh, I know. That's all I could think about."

The line fell silent.

"Sweetie, are you still there?"

"I'm here . . . Daddy?"

"What is it, Honey?"

"Daddy, do you think Mom is looking out for us?"

"I do now, Sweetie. I do now."

"Me too."

"I need to run," Brandon said. "Talbot, from the governor's office, is trying to call. Hey, was Josh at your meeting?"

"No. He called and told us he couldn't make it."

"Okay. But you need to get him engaged with that Genius Pod activity."

"Okay, Daddy. I will. Talk to you later."

"Love you, Sweetie."

CHAPTER 14

"Hey, Bruce. What's up?"

"Hey, man. I've been trying to get in touch for a while, but no answer. You okay?"

"All is well. I was on the phone with my daughter, Olivia."

"Ah, okay. How is Lucy doing?"

"She'll be able to go back up to the house tomorrow. She's planning to be at the office Monday to help get things set up."

"Seriously? Are you going to let her do that so soon?"

"First off, I don't *let* Lucy do anything. She is definitely her own woman. Secondly, I really need her help to get organized."

"Okay. Okay. I get it. Listen, can you pay a visit to the governor? I think he's ready to talk."

"Sure. When do you want me there?"

"The sooner, the better. He told me he has a clear schedule this afternoon."

Brandon looked at Lucinda. She smiled and nodded, knowing that he was being called away to something. "Go. I'll be fine."

"Okay. I've got to go back up the hill to get a shower and change clothes. I can be there around two if that'll work."

"I'll let him know."

"Okay. I'll text you when I'm on my way."

"I'll meet you on the front steps."

Brandon put the phone in his pocket. "I guess the governor wants to talk."

"It's about time," Sonny said. "So, do you want me to take you up to the house?"

"No. You stay here with Lucy."

"Brandon, no," she said. "I'll be just fine by myself."

"Stop. Not gonna happen. We have no idea what kind of lunatics are lurking around here, let alone what they're after. You're not staying alone."

"It's fine, Boss. I'll stay here and watch her take her first steps," Sonny said. "It'll be fun. She might actually learn a thing or two."

"Shut up." Lucinda laughed and threw the pillow at him from behind her head.

"Well, okay then," Brandon said through his chuckling. "I'm outta here."

Sonny threw Brandon the keys to the rental car and told him where it was parked. Brandon went to the parking garage and drove away in the tiny car.

How did Sonny even fit in here, he thought.

When he had driven out of the city and into the foothills, Brandon started thinking about who may have shot Lucinda and why. Was it a random drive by? He noticed a blue sedan in his rearview mirror but didn't think much about it. But after several turns on smaller and smaller roads leading to the safe house, he couldn't help but believe he was being followed. He called Sonny.

"She's fine, Boss," Sonny said when he answered the call.

"No. I'm sure she is. Hey, I think I'm being followed. Can you get the guys from the house to come down and meet me at the end of the driveway?"

"Sure thing. Can you describe the car?"

"Wait."

"Boss. You okay?"

"They turned off." Brandon took a deep breath.

"False alarm?" Sonny asked.

"Maybe. Just have the guys keep a close lookout. I have an uneasy feeling about this."

"No problem. I'll give them a call."

"Okay, I'll let you know when I'm headed back down the hill."

"Roger."

Brandon turned into the gravel driveway and drove slowly up the hill to minimize the dust that would inevitably billow up from beneath the car. When he arrived at the house, a few of Sonny's guards were walking around, looking into the hills behind the house. He parked the car and got out, pulling his briefcase out behind him.

"You guys seeing something?"

"I don't know, sir. Agent Finley thought he saw something flash up there, like metal reflecting the sun. It's probably nothing."

"Okay. I won't be here long. I need to get back into town."

"Yes, sir. Would you like one of us to escort you? Agent Langston told us we might expect that."

"Oh, he did, did he? No. I'll be fine . . . for now, anyway."

"Of course, sir."

Brandon entered the house and went straight to the master bedroom where he took some clothes from the chest of drawers. He then went into the bathroom and took a shower. Once dressed, he went to the kitchen and prepared a sandwich to eat on the drive back. He stood at the sink, washing the knife he had used. A flash caught his attention. He froze and peered into the hills through the window over the sink.

Seeing nothing more, Brandon picked up his briefcase in one hand and the sandwich in the other. He put the sandwich in his mouth between his teeth as he walked out onto the porch and across the yard to open the car door. Then he took a bite and looked at the guard he had previously spoken to.

"Hey, I saw that flash too," he said, mumbling through his full mouth. "Something is up there."

"We'll check it out, sir. We're going to put a small drone up."

"Really?"

"Yes, sir. We have a couple in the trunk." He motioned to the black sedan parked to the side of the driveway.

"Sorry, I can't stay to watch. Let us know if you come up with anything."

"Of course, sir."

Brandon got in the car, texted Talbot, and raced back down the hill, anxious to get to the State Capitol. He kept looking in his rearview mirror but noticed nothing suspicious. When he arrived, Talbot was waiting on the front steps.

"Hey! You're here," Brandon said when he stepped out of the car.

"As promised. This gentleman here will take your car and park it."

"Well, okay." Brandon pulled his briefcase out of the car and joined Talbot on the steps, and they walked in together.

"So, what does the governor want to discuss?" Brandon asked.

"You mean, you don't know?"

"Ah. So, he's ready, huh?"

"Indeed, he is. So, Lucy's doing well?"

"Very well, actually. She's one strong woman."

"Haha. She's never left a doubt with me in that regard." They chuckled and walked to the governor's office.

"Go right in. He's waiting for you," the secretary said as they walked by her desk.

Talbot opened the door for Brandon to enter.

"Mr. McStocker. Come in. Come in."

"Governor Truly. It's good to see you again, sir. Please, Brandon is fine."

"You as well. Mr. Talbot, good to see you. Please, you two come over and have a seat. How is your wife, Brandon? I was so sorry to hear about the shooting."

"She's doing fine, sir. I think she'll be back to work before any of us thinks she should."

"Good to hear. If there's anything the state can do to make things easier for her, just ask."

"Thank you, sir."

"Brandon, I want to apologize for my attitude at our first meeting. I was rude, and it wasn't called for. Then for leaving so quickly when I was up at the house."

"No harm, sir. These are stressful times."

"Damn right. I keep hearing the phrase Civil War II being bantered about."

"Well, sir. I think that's probably an exaggeration."

"Frankly, I don't think it's far off. Especially after what we had to do in San Francisco."

Brandon and Talbot sat up straighter and listened closer to what the governor had to say.

"Sir?"

"Brandon, I know the president and I think differently, but I never thought California would get to the place where we don't even have the same goals as the rest of the country. One of those things where you just wake up one day, and the train has gone too far to back up."

Brandon and Talbot listened intently, knowing the governor was speaking from his heart and not a political platform.

"I do think it's time for California to step out on its own, but I damn sure don't want to go to war over it. I feel like there is a movement growing to do just that. If something major doesn't happen soon, I'm afraid Civil War II is a reality. Do you understand?"

"Uh, yes, sir. I do. But for what it's worth, we don't think this is necessarily a grassroots movement. While I agree it's probably gone too far, this may all be instigated at the hands of Cártel del Mundo."

"So, you agree the drug lords are planting instigators out there?"

"Mercenaries is more like it, I'm afraid," Brandon said.

The governor lowered his head, and silence filled the room. Brandon and Talbot looked at each other and waited for the governor to think through it.

"Well . . . I guess I have two problems, then. I need to figure out how to get this state out of the Union peacefully, and I need to do it in a way that I'm not just turning it over to Mexico and a damn drug cartel. Can you imagine having an entire nation based on drug money and human trafficking? I can't have that hanging over me, gentlemen. I just can't."

Brandon caught the governor's gaze and looked him solemnly in the eye. "Sir?"

"Okay, Brandon. I don't know any other way. Can I count on the president's support to make this happen peacefully?"

"Yes, sir. You can." Brandon and Talbot exhaled. "I already have a team working on the cartel problem. The president will have to get his cabinet working on the secession issue since there is currently no constitutional way to make it happen."

"You mean Richland gets another amendment?"

"I don't really know, sir. That may be the only way. Do you still have the allegiance of the National Guard?"

"Oh, of course."

"We may have to mobilize them again, but let's not rush to that. I'll consult with the president as to when it might become necessary."

"Okay. But you're right. It may just fan the flames."

"I'll alert the CHP when the time is right," Talbot said.

"I'll contact the president as soon as we leave here," Brandon said. "This is the conversation he's been waiting for."

"Oh, I'm sure it is." The governor rubbed his face and looked around at the pictures hanging on the walls in his office—images of famous sites around the state. "I'm sure it is."

"What next for us, Governor?" Talbot asked.

"I need to call a special session of the state senate."

"Of course, sir."

"Go ahead and give the CHP chief a heads-up as well. No special action. Just notification."

"Yes, sir."

"Anything else you can think of, Brandon?"

"No, sir. I think that's enough for now."

"Indeed," the governor said.

"If I learn anything more from the president, I'll let you know. But I suspect he will be calling you directly for a verbal handshake."

"Good idea."

"Thank you, Governor. We'll leave you to your day," Talbot said.

Brandon and Talbot left the governor's office and walked back to the front door together.

"So, this is happening, then," Talbot said.

"It would appear so." When they arrived at the front steps, Brandon turned and shook Talbot's hand. "I'll be in touch."

"Let me know if you guys need anything," Talbot said.

"Will do." Brandon drove away from the Capitol toward Mercy Hospital, only a few blocks away. When he arrived, he parked in the garage and went up to Lucinda's room on the fourth floor.

"That was fast," Sonny said. "How did it go?"

"We're on," Brandon said.

Lucinda smiled. "It's official?"

"It's official!"

"Well, okay. Here we go," she said.

"No. No. You calm down. You rest first. Focus on getting better before you worry your pretty little head about all this stuff."

She smirked and wrinkled her nose. "You know I won't sleep if I'm not working on this with you."

"We'll see. If you have to keep yourself doing something, fine-tune your thoughts on how to set up the new offices. We need to get in there."

"Okay. I'll check with the office furniture place tomorrow and see when they can deliver."

"Perfect. I need to go find a quiet place to see if I can speak to the president."

He texted Mena. *Can you set up a call with the prez?*
On it. I'll let you know.
Perfect. He's expecting me.

"Mena's going to set it up. It was pretty quiet out there on that back patio. I'll check that out."

Brandon walked back out of the room and down the hall to the rear of the hospital to the garden patio. Just as he approached the bench where he and Val had spoken, his phone vibrated.

You'll be getting a call shortly.
Thanks, Mena.

He sat on the concrete bench and looked up to see if the doves were still around. He didn't see them. His phone vibrated.

"This is Brandon McStocker."

"Mr. McStocker, this is the Central House. Please hold for the president."

"Of course."

"Brandon! How are you?"

"Doing well, Mr. President."

"How is your wife doing? What a shock that was."

"That, it was, sir. She's recovering well."

"I'm really sorry. I know she didn't bargain for that."

"No, sir. I don't think that was part of the deal. But she's a trooper—raring to get back to work."

"I would expect nothing less from her. So, you met with the governor?"

"I did, sir. He's onboard. He officially asked for your help and is calling a special session of his state senate to discuss next steps."

"Do you think he'll get their support?"

"I can't tell for sure, Mr. President. But he was very convincing to me. He wants to avoid Civil War II as badly as you do . . . as we all do."

"Yeah, I get that. Boy, that term sure grew legs in a hurry."

"That, it did, sir."

"So, you found some office space?"

"Yes, sir. Senator Beecher put us in contact with Congresswoman Strickland out here, and she's been invaluable. We're staying in one of her houses, and she found an office for us downtown, not far from the Capitol. Apparently, the state is picking up the tab on that."

"That's great. I'll send her a note of appreciation."

"That would be nice, sir. Thank you."

"So, I guess the ball is in my court, then. We need to spin up a committee to determine how to make this work without thumbing our collective noses at the Constitution."

"Yes, sir. But the word committee always makes me nervous, especially when it comes to the federal government. No offense, of course."

"Of course. Maybe when we get things going, I can have you back out here to testify on behalf of the governor to see if we can expedite things."

"I can do that, sir. I'm not sure how much influence I'll have."

"I don't know, Brandon. I've seen your name coming up quite a bit in the news. You're becoming a topic of discussion in the halls around here as well. Don't sell yourself short."

"I think that's just idle chatter, Mr. President. Sounds like everyone is getting bored."

"Well, bored or not, you're becoming a force to be reckoned with, and everybody knows it. We need to talk more about that sometime in the future. But for now, let's stay focused on the task at hand."

"Yes, sir. Let's."

"Can I get your daughter's support out here to pull all this together? I hate to say it, but it's so much easier to work with you folks than dealing with the red tape around here."

"Of course, sir. I'll let her know your office may be calling on her. But you might want to work on that red tape problem as well, sir. There has to be a better way to get things done."

"True. But for right now, I have this GSA waiver to short circuit the bid and proposal process to get things done with you. I don't take that lightly, and I want to take advantage of it, if you know what I mean."

"I get it, sir. No problem."

"I'll let you go, Brandon. Good talking to you. Glad you've got everything in control out there and that Lucy is doing well."

"Thanks, Mr. President. We'll be in touch."

Brandon put the phone in his coat pocket and stood to walk across the patio. He looked up just in time to see the two doves flying from a pine tree across the yard, landing on the corner of the building's gutter. "There you are," he muttered.

"Hey!"

He turned to see who the voice was calling behind him. "Well, hey! What are you doing out here?"

"The doc wanted her to take a short walk," Sonny said.

Lucinda ambled across the patio holding onto the IV stand, wheeling it along beside her.

"You need help?" Brandon asked.

"Nope. I'm good. I'm just tickled to be outside."

"Yeah, I get that. How are you feeling?"

"Still sore as hell. But besides that, I feel pretty good."

"Well, the president sends his regards and is glad things turned out okay."

"So, what's happening on that front?" Lucinda asked.

"Well, now that the governor is on board, he's going to gather up his advisors to see what it will take to give the governor what he wants."

"And what exactly is that?"

"Departure from the Union without Civil War II."

Brandon's phone vibrated in his hand.

"Susan! Hey, Sweetie. Everything okay?"

"Hi, Daddy. Yeah. All good. How's Lucy?"

He smiled at Lucinda. She nodded.

"She's doing great, Honey. They have her up and walking around a little bit."

"Really? That was fast."

"Yes, it was. But she's handling it really well. I'm standing here watching her right now."

"God, I love that woman," Susan said.

"Yeah, me too. Shall we keep her?"

"You damn well better," she said chuckling. "Hey, do you know the press is out digging up stories about you?"

"I keep getting the hint. They've approached your sister as well."

"Well, they're here in the diner right now asking questions. I came into the kitchen to call you because I wasn't exactly sure how to handle it. Should I talk to them?"

"Honey, you know I have nothing to hide. If they're asking you reasonable questions and you're comfortable with it, go ahead and talk to them. I think you're smart enough to know if they start trying to build some bogus story about me."

"Yeah, I know how that is. They certainly love to do that in Nashville."

"Oh, I'm sure. But for security reasons, if they start asking about why I'm in California, don't even go there."

"Well, I have no idea what that's about anyway. Liv keeps shutting me down every time I try to talk to her about what you're doing."

"Right, Sweetie. We're leaving you out of it on purpose. Don't take it personally. It's for your own safety."

"And you have nothing to hide?" She giggled. "Right. Plausible deniability."

"Exactly. At least this way, you're free to be our ambassador."

"Well, alrighty then. Here I go!"

CHAPTER 15

Susan walked out of the kitchen, nervously smiling at the reporter sitting at the counter. "Okay. We can talk now. Let's move where it's a little more private. Is that all right?"

"Of course," the reporter said.

"Hey, Barney. I'm taking a break," Susan shouted through the order window into the kitchen.

"Okay, Suze."

The reporter picked up her handbag and followed Susan to the corner table. When they arrived, she began spreading out her tools.

"I hope you don't mind if I record this."

"Uh. I guess that'll be fine," Susan said. "You say your name is Gladys?"

"Yes. I'm Gladys Turnbull from KGLG Radio here in Manhattan."

"I think I've heard of it. Talk Radio?"

"Yep. That's us. The plains' voice of reason."

"O—kay." Susan sat with her back against the wall in her dad's chair. "So, what is this about?"

"Look, we've heard about your dad and what he has done here in North Central Kansas. We just want to give our listeners a chance to get to know him a little, you know. A little more intimately."

"Okay. Why?"

"He's an important guy, your dad."

"He is? I mean, of course, he is . . . to us," Susan said.

"Let's get started, shall we? So, Miss McStocker, you're Brandon McStocker's daughter."

"Yes—the youngest of two. And God, please call me Susan."

"Of course, Susan. I thought you worked with your dad. Yet, you're here in this diner. What happened?"

"That's my older sister, Olivia. She's my dad's partner. Some would tell you she's the actual brains in the firm."

Gladys smiled. "Really? And you're just a waitress. How does that work?"

Susan twisted her head and squinted at the reporter. "Is this going to be that kind of interview? Are you really going to be that person?"

"No. No. I'm sorry. I mean, it seems like such an odd thing for a daughter of Brandon McStocker."

"Look. I own this place. I bought it from Barney several years ago. I bought it because I love it. I love the people that come in here. I love that we play music in here every Friday night."

"President Richland once said that when the new city was being built, most of the big decisions were made here," Gladys said. "Is that true?"

Susan relaxed her shoulders. "It is. Right here at this very table, as a matter of fact."

"Are you kidding me? That's amazing."

"Well, I hadn't really thought about it that way, but I guess it kinda is."

"Have you always lived here in Manhattan?"

"No, we were raised in Virginia. That's where my dad first became a partner in the firm. He worked for Bob McClellan in Fairfax. That's where Liv and I grew up. I went to Nashville for a while, but that didn't pan out. That's when I bought this place."

"What about your mom? I know your dad was just married here. Is your mom still in Virginia?"

"U-h-h-h. My mom died like twenty years ago."

"Oh. Susan, I am so sorry. I didn't know. I'll strike that."

"No. Please. Leave it in."

"Okay. I will. Is Mr. McClellan still a partner?"

"No, he has passed as well. His widow, Anne McClellan, recently turned the entire firm over to my dad and my sister. It used to be called McClellan and McStocker Engineering Services. Now it's McStocker and McStocker Enterprises."

"Wow. Very cool," Gladys said.

"We thought so."

"So, no rivalry between you and your sister?"

"Olivia? Heavens no. We were always close, but when Mom died, we became inseparable. Well, except for that stint in Nashville. We're two very different people, of course, but she's the best. And she is so good for my dad at work. The things she does are amazing."

"So, where is your dad now? Do you think I might get an interview with him?"

"Uh . . . No. Not likely. No time soon, anyway. He's out of town on an important project."

"Another big one?"

"Uh . . . well . . . you could say that. So, why all the interest in my family?"

"Like I said. People want to get to know him better. He seems like a pretty cool dad. I did find some information about him being a heavy drinker at one time."

"What the hell!"

"I'm sorry. You can tell me if it isn't true."

Susan cooled herself off before continuing. "That was a long time ago. Yes, after Mom passed, there was a period of time when he lost his way. But he got through it. We don't even think about it anymore. Is there really any need to go there?"

"Well, it will probably come up if he . . ."

"If he what?"

"Well . . . Susan . . . uh . . ."

Susan chuckled. "Spit it out, woman."

Gladys smiled. "Uh . . . is there any chance that your dad will run for president next year?"

"What! Are you kidding me right now? That's what this is about?" Susan turned her head and looked out the window around the parking lot. She shook her head until her anger slowly began to turn to laughter. She looked back at Gladys. "You mean President of the United States? That kind of president?"

"Well, yes."

"Now, that's funny. If you said that to his face, he'd probably laugh you right out of this place."

"Why?" Gladys asked.

"He hates politics. The more he gets sucked up in it, the more he hates it. A lot of people have lost their lives while he tried to build K.D. It just about killed him. Why would you even think such a thing?"

"Susan. He gets stuff done. He has worked side-by-side with President Richland all these years. Why wouldn't he?"

"Sorry. I can't see it. I probably won't sleep tonight thinking about it. Thanks for that. But I just can't see it."

"I could even see you as his campaign manager. You're quite the no-nonsense gal."

"Now, I know you're high on something," Susan said. "Let's get back to the question. No. There is no chance my dad will run for president next year."

"I've spoken with a few people in the halls of Congress, and some think he would make an outstanding candidate. One of them told me even the president thought he should run."

"Come on. That's craziness. You want a cup of coffee or something?"

Gladys chuckled. "Come on. You have to admit; it would be pretty cool to be the president's daughter."

Susan gazed at the scratches in the table for several seconds then looked up at Gladys. "Sorry. Doesn't put stars in my eyes. I'm just afraid this place might turn into a nuthouse."

"Why? You probably wouldn't even have to work here anymore."

"Work here? Girl, I don't work here. This is my life. What part of 'I love this place' didn't you understand?"

"Okay. Okay. I get it. It's just that President Richland has done so much to bring this country back together . . . well, except maybe for California. It just seems like Brandon McStocker would be a great guy to carry that torch."

Susan dropped her head to break her connection with Gladys. *Damn*, she thought. *Not now.*

"Susan. You okay?"

"Uh, I'm fine. I'm fine."

"Look. I need to wrap this up. You think we can talk again sometime?"

"Well, I suppose. I'm usually right here."

"And, I'd love to talk to your dad when he's back in town. Can you arrange that?"

"I'll talk to him, but no guarantees."

"I understand. Thanks for your time." Gladys stood and stuffed everything back in her bag. "Great place, by the way. I'd love to come back here to eat and hang out sometime."

"You should. And you should bring your friends. You'll have fun."

"I'll take you up on that. I promise."

Susan stayed seated, turning her gaze back to the table while Gladys made her way to the front door. The bell ringing above Gladys's head shook Susan from her trance. She took the phone from her pocket and texted Brandon.

You got a few to talk?
Sure. Done with the interview?
Yep. You're not gonna believe this.
Give me a call. I'm sitting with Luce.
She called his number.

"Hey, Sweetheart. So, you're all done, eh?"

"All done," Susan said.

"So, what am I not going to believe?"

After a few seconds of silence, Brandon could only hear her breath turn to chuckling.

"Suze?"

"I can't, Daddy. This is too good."

"Susan, where are you?"

"At the diner, sitting in your spot," she said, almost unable to speak through her laughter.

"Are you okay?"

"I'm sorry, Daddy. I'm sorry." She worked to regain her composure.

"What in the world is so funny?"

"Daddy, they want to know if you're going to run for president next year."

Brandon paused, then shouted, "Oh, hell no!"

Susan burst into laughter again. "You're so predictable!"

"Are you kidding me? That's what she wanted to talk to you about?"

"Oh, it gets even better. She wants to interview you when you get back home."

"You didn't tell her where I was, did you?"

"Oh, no. Of course not. But we were getting dangerously close to the subject before I steered the conversation away."

"Good girl."

Susan heard Brandon tell Lucinda what the discussion was about and then heard Lucinda laughing in the background.

"Now, just wait a minute here," Brandon chuckled. "What is so funny about me running for president?"

"Daddy. Seriously?"

"Stranger things have happened," he said.

"Uh. No. They haven't. Is she still laughing? Is she allowed to laugh like that in her condition?"

"She's holding her chest. Hang on. Hey . . . Susan thinks you should stop laughing."

Susan heard Lucinda laughing even harder.

"Will you stop?" Brandon said.

"Put her on the phone," Susan said.

Lucinda was still laughing. "Susan, Sweetheart, that was the funniest thing I've ever heard. You should've seen the look on your dad's face. It was priceless."

Then Susan got tickled again and began laughing with Lucinda over the phone.

"But seriously. Stop laughing, Lucy. You're going to break something."

"Okay. Okay. So, was it a friendly interview, or was the reporter pushy, or what?"

"She was actually really nice. I thought for a second there that I was going to have to take her out, but I think she realized the tone of her question and backed off."

"Who was it?"

"Gladys Turnbull from KGLG. Heard of her?"

"That talk radio station?"

"Right."

"I've heard of the station. I may have listened from time to time. I don't know. Never heard of her, though."

"I actually kinda like her. I invited her to bring her friends in for a meal."

"Well, stay close to the enemy. That's what I've always heard," Lucinda said.

"I got the feeling that she *wants* Daddy to run."

"Really? I wonder where all this is coming from."

"Beats me. Listen, I need to get back to work. Tell Daddy I'll call later."

"Okay, Suze. Don't work too hard. Love you, babe."

"Not a chance. Love you, too.

Susan put the phone back in her pocket and walked behind the counter. "It's pretty dead out here, Barn. I think I'll take the afternoon off and go do that training up in K.D. Call one of the others if things get crazy."

"Okay, Boss. Enjoy."

Susan took off her apron, went out to her tiny car, and drove out of the parking lot. When she arrived at the Mac and Mac offices, she texted Olivia.

I'm here.
Going to the cafeteria? Olivia replied.
Yes. I'll start the training.
Let me know when you're ready for lunch.
Will do. Big news!
Really? You're going to do that to me?
:-)

Susan walked into the kitchen of Cass's Place Cafeteria carrying a cardboard carton full of printed material for the training session she regularly did for the foodservice staff.

"Hey, everyone. Can you drop what you're doing as soon as you can and come on out? Have a seat at one of the tables. This shouldn't take long." She looked at the clock on the wall. "What, do we have, like an hour before the line opens?"

"That's right. 'Bout an hour," the supervisor said. Miss Sadie was a large elderly black woman who had run the cafeteria from the time it opened. Susan loved her dearly. Her caring nature was everything Susan hoped to be someday.

The kitchen staff gathered around one of the tables and began to take their seats as Susan handed out the workbooks.

"Everybody grab one, and I'll get through this as fast as I can."

"Y'all know this is state law stuff, right?" Miss Sadie said.

Everyone nodded and opened the cover of their books.

"You might want to write your name at the top, just in case," Susan said. "I have some pens here if you need one."

Susan spent the next fifty minutes covering food safety regulations before everyone had to get back into the kitchen to prepare the line for lunch.

"Good job, everyone. I'll be hanging around for lunch with my sis, so let me know if you have any questions." She cleaned the extra papers and booklets from the table and put them back in her case and carried it to the corner table of the cafeteria. She sat and texted Olivia.

All done. Line is about to open.

On my way, Olivia replied.

Susan smiled and took a deep breath while looking around the large room. There were pictures hanging on the walls depicting the evolution of the company. Her dad was in most of them. There were a few with her dad standing with Bob McClellan. That made her smile. There was even one with both Brandon and Cassandra standing with Bob and Anne. Tears welled up in her eyes.

She began to walk around to look at the pictures closer. There was one with her and Olivia as small children standing with their parents in front of the old office building in Fairfax, Virginia. *Dang*, she thought. *How long ago was that?*

"Hey, Sis!"

"Oh, hey, Liv."

"What are you doing?" Olivia asked.

"Have you looked at these pictures?" Susan asked. "It's like a Mac and Mac history exhibit in here."

Olivia chuckled. "I guess I haven't. Not closely anyway. Anything good?"

"This is great. I had almost forgotten what Mr. McClellan looked like."

"I just remember he was a really good man," Olivia said. "He always had a candy bar in his pocket for us."

"God, I remember that. It's a wonder we had any teeth at all. Used to make Mom a little crazy, though."

"That, it did. We were so little back then."

They were interrupted by the loud rattle of the serving window doors being rolled open.

"Okay, ladies," Miss Sadie shouted. "You girls come and eat now. I have special plates just for you two."

They smiled and made their way across the cafeteria as some other employees began to file in behind them.

"Well, hey there, Susan," Trevor said, walking toward the line. "Didn't know you were going to be here today."

"Hi, Trev. Come get in line with us. Yeah, we had some training here today."

"Yeah, Trevor," Olivia said. "Join us. Susan has us set up back in the corner."

"Of course. If you're sure you don't mind."

They picked up their trays and silverware, pushing them along the rail.

"Not at all. I'd love to hear how the Genius Pod is doing. Oh, and I guess my sister here has some news."

"News?" Susan asked. "Oh, news. Yes. I do. And, yes, Trev, you'll get a kick out of it as well."

They gathered their food and drinks while walking through the line, then made their way to the table in the corner. Once they were settled, Trevor held out his hands. It took Olivia and Susan by surprise, but they took his hands, and he led them in a prayer over the food.

"Amen. Well, that was nice," Susan said. "Unexpected, but nice."

"So, what is this news you've been teasing me about?" Olivia asked.

"Well, I had an interview this morning."

"Like a job interview?"

"No, goober. Like an interview with a reporter. A reporter for a talk radio station."

"Really? Whatever for?" Olivia asked.

"About Daddy."

"Daddy? What about Daddy?"

"They wanted to interview you about your dad?" Trevor asked. "This should be interesting."

"What in the world did they ask you about Daddy?" Olivia asked. "They aren't trying to get in his business in California, are they? Holy crap. That could be disastrous."

"No. No. Relax. We didn't get into that at all."

"What, then?"

"They want to know if Daddy is going to run for president next year."

"What!" Olivia shouted. Every head in the cafeteria turned to check out the ruckus at the corner table.

"Shhh. Keep it down. Yes. She was asking all these questions about me and you and Daddy. Then finally, she told me why."

"That's crazy. Daddy isn't going to run for president. Have you told him about this?"

"Yes, I told him about this. I called him right after she left the diner."

"And he said?"

"Exactly what you might imagine he would say."

"That's too funny," Trevor said.

"It is absolutely hysterical," Susan said.

Olivia lowered her head into her hands, rubbing her temples. "Oh, my God. I can see it."

"You can see Daddy becoming president?"

"No, but I can see why some might make that leap. Daddy has told me in the past that even the president has hinted at it. Look at all the time the president has spent with him. All the work they've done together. All the support he has given Daddy."

"You think the president has been grooming him?" Susan asked.

"I think it's entirely possible."

"No way," Trevor said. "That's freakin' huge."

"But Liv, there's no way Daddy's going to do this, right?"

"Well, I don't think so. But I guess stranger things have happened."

"No! No, they haven't! Listen to yourself!"

They all fell silent and gazed at their food, knowing it was getting cold. Then Trevor began to chuckle. Olivia turned to look at him and started snickering, her head bobbing up and down. She lifted her long blonde hair behind her shoulder and leaned back. Susan put her hands on each side of her head and pulled her hair. They all started laughing—not just any laugh, but a long, deep belly laugh that caught the attention of most of the people in the cafeteria.

"Stop!" Susan shouted. They continued to laugh. Tears ran down Susan's face. "Stop!"

CHAPTER 16

"Are you sure you're up to this?" Brandon asked as he unlocked the door to their new office building.

"I've never been surer of anything in my life," Lucinda said. "I've been looking forward to getting this place set up. It's all I've been able to think about. Well, except maybe for the bullet that went through my chest."

They walked in, and Lucinda looked around the room to see the progress. "Oh, my. Honey, this looks wonderful."

"I thought so. The furniture guys were here yesterday and got most everything put together."

They continued through the reception area and into the back hallway. She stuck her head in each of the offices and waved her hand in front of the motion detectors so the lights would come on. "Wow. This is really nice."

"Of course, it is. You're the one that picked it out."

"I know, but I was just looking at pictures. I did well."

"Yes, you did. Do you want to go grab some breakfast before we dig in?"

"Sounds good. Let's walk to that little restaurant I never got to see."

"Really? Honey, are you sure?"

"Yeah. Let's go."

They walked back out onto the sidewalk, and Brandon locked the door. Sonny was standing against the corner of the building, looking around the block.

"Those new sunglasses make you look pretty mysterious," Lucinda chuckled and put her arm through Brandon's for the walk.

Sonny smiled and started walking ahead of them. "Where are we going?"

"Just over to Gloria's Place."

Sonny stopped and turned to look at Brandon for confirmation. Brandon nodded and smiled. After they turned the corner and had walked most of the way to the front of the restaurant, Lucinda froze.

"Honey? What is it?" Brandon looked at her and saw her staring at the sidewalk ahead of them. He and Sonny both looked to see the bloodstain spread across two sections of the concrete.

"Damn," she said. "Looks like I bled out pretty badly."

"Honey, we can turn around."

"No. No. I'm fine. Just a little freaky to see, you know."

"Yeah. I'm feeling a bit nauseated myself. I don't know that I had ever been so scared in my life than when I saw you lying there in a pool of blood. Are you sure you want to do this?"

"Yeah, I'm hungry. Let's go."

Sonny shook his head and grinned, then turned back toward the restaurant. The other two followed, walking right over the bloodstain on the sidewalk. When they entered the restaurant, a shout came from behind the counter.

"Oh, my lord, look who it is coming back in here," Gloria shouted as she quickly came out to Lucinda. "Honey, I don't know you, but I just need to hug you. Is that okay?"

Lucinda smiled and fell into her arms. "Well, we almost met that day."

"Girl, you scared us all to death." She looked at Brandon. "Did they ever get the shooter?"

"Not yet."

"I'll be out front, Boss," Sonny said.

"You sure? Come eat with us," Lucinda said.

"I may be in shortly. You guys go ahead."

Brandon nodded. "Gloria, do you have any of those cinnamon bites?"

"Fresh out of the oven. I'll get you some . . . on the house!"

"Great. We'll have some coffee, too."

"Coming right up."

The two walked to the back of the dining room, where Brandon slid a chair out for Lucinda to sit.

"You mean you already have a table in the corner picked out?"

"Well . . . Yeah." He smiled and sat across from her. "Luce, are you sure you're okay with all this? We don't have to force it."

"Really, Sweetheart. I'm fine. I feel surprisingly calm."

Gloria walked up to them with a tray loaded with a carafe of coffee, two cups, and a large bowl full of piping hot cinnamon bites with white icing drizzled heavily over the top of them.

"Oh, my God," Lucinda said, her chin dropping in amazement.

"You're not going to believe these things," Brandon chuckled.

Lucinda looked up at Gloria and shook her head. "Well, they look incredible. Thank you. Cinnamon rolls are the way to this man's heart."

Brandon took the vibrating phone from his coat pocket.

"Sorry." He read the text and slid his chair away from the table. "I'll be right back."

"Brandon?"

"Really. This will just take a second." He rushed out of the restaurant onto the sidewalk and looked around for Sonny. "Hey, man. Go in and have some cinnamon bites with Lucy. I'll be back in a few minutes."

"Everything okay, Boss?"

"I'll fill you in when I get back."

"You sure, Brandon?"

"Go!"

Sonny walked into the restaurant, and Brandon ran back to the office. When he rounded the corner, he saw Talbot leaning against his black sedan parked on the curb at the front door.

"They got that son of a bitch?" Brandon asked as he approached him.

"Got him. The local police picked him up last night. Apparently, he couldn't handle all of his new-found money. One of the shop owners in town got suspicious with the way he was flashing money around while looking like a thug, and called it in."

"A hired hitman?"

"Well, I wouldn't give him the honor of such a title. A local hack would be more like it. He's been in interrogation all night."

"What's he saying?"

"Not much, really. Ramblings of a junkie. Hopefully, he'll come to his senses enough to tell us who hired him."

"I'm more interested in why."

"Yeah, I get that."

"Anything on the rifle you found?"

"It was stolen. Obviously, our meth-head buddy is a thief, too. Sorry to drag you away from your breakfast, but I thought you'd want to know."

"Yeah, thanks. I appreciate it. Let me know if he talks," Brandon said.

"We'll get to the bottom of it. I promise."

"Thanks, Bruce. Care to join us for a bite next door? You drove all the way down here."

"No thanks. I need to run to an appointment, but I wanted to tell you in person."

Brandon shook his hand, and Talbot got back in his sedan. Brandon turned and walked back toward Gloria's. When he walked in the front door, he saw Sonny sitting with Lucinda in the corner and smiled.

"Did you eat it all?" he asked, while sitting next to Lucinda.

"Hey. You bolted, man. More for us," Sonny said. "Where'd you go in such a hurry?"

"It was Bruce Talbot. He was over at the office. They found the guy."

"The guy who shot me?" Lucinda asked.

"Yes. They've been interrogating him all night, but I guess he's pretty pumped up on meth."

"So, he's not a pro, then," Sonny said.

"Apparently not. Do you guys want to order any real food?"

"This was plenty for me," Lucinda said.

"I'm good. I'll meet you guys back outside." Sonny stood and left the restaurant.

Gloria had seen Brandon come in and took another small bowl of cinnamon bites to their table.

"Well, thank you," Brandon said.

She nodded so as not to interrupt the conversation and walked back to the kitchen.

"So, what will they do now?" Lucinda asked.

"I don't really know," Brandon said. "I guess they'll try to get him cleaned up enough to talk. Maybe he can tell us something, but I have my doubts."

After they had finished their coffee and cinnamon bites, they bid farewell to Gloria and walked back to the office. Lucinda sat at her reception desk, and Brandon walked back to his office. Sonny resumed his position leaning against the corner of the building.

"You do know you aren't going to get any visitors off the street, right?" Brandon shouted down the hallway.

Lucinda chuckled. "I know. I know. I just like the view here—what the . . ."

"What is it, Luce?" He heard the door open and walked out of his office just in time to see Tim O'Neil and Olivia standing in front of Lucinda's desk.

Lucinda ran out from behind it and threw her arms around Olivia. "What are you guys doing here?"

"Honey? This is a surprise." Brandon shook Tim's hand. "Is everything okay?"

"Everything's great, Daddy."

"How did you even find this place?"

"A little birdie told me," she said, pointing her thumb over her shoulder to the outside.

"Ah, so this was kind of a planned surprise then."

"Something like that."

"You just missed breakfast. How long are you in town for?" Brandon asked.

"We have to leave. I need to get back to K.D."

"Well, what the heck. You just got here."

Tim smiled and nodded at Olivia. She raised her left hand toward Brandon and Lucinda to show off her new ring.

"We're getting married, and I didn't want to tell you over the phone."

Lucinda screamed and ran back into Olivia's arms. "Oh, my God!"

Brandon smiled and shook Tim's hand again. "Well, congratulations. This is great news." He turned and wrapped his arms around Olivia. "Honey, I'm so happy for you. This is awesome."

The room quieted, and a tear came to Olivia's eye. Lucinda put her hands on Olivia's shoulders.

"Liv, Honey, I know you miss your mom right now. She would be so proud of you and so happy for you. I know I can't replace her, but if there's anything I can do to help, you let me know, okay?"

Olivia smiled through her tears and fell into Lucinda's arms. Brandon fought to hold back his own tears. He squeezed Tim's shoulder and smiled.

Olivia pulled away from Lucinda and wiped her eyes. "Well, we have to go."

"Liv, I can't believe you have to just leave already," Brandon said.

"It was on a fluke, Daddy. I borrowed your company plane. I hope you don't mind. Your pilot made himself available, so we just went for it."

Brandon chuckled. "It's fine. It's fine." He looked outside and saw a taxi. "Is he waiting for you?"

"As a matter of fact, he is," Tim chuckled.

"Are you kidding me?" Brandon and Lucinda both laughed. "Okay. Well, you guys have a good flight back."

"Thanks, Daddy. Thank you, Lucy. I love you both so much. But, Daddy, before we go, I should tell you that the Genius Pod is working with the CIA. The tracking database we spoke about is becoming a reality. The system is going online as we speak, and it's basically populating itself. Almost five-hundred confirmed members of del Mundo are being actively tracked in real time."

"Seriously? That's great news, Honey. Keep up the good work. I'm so proud of you."

Tim shook Brandon's hand and hugged Lucinda before walking out the door. Brandon and Lucinda watched through the window as Olivia hugged Sonny and climbed into the back seat of the taxi with Tim and sped off. Sonny smiled and gave Brandon a thumbs-up through the window before leaning back against the building.

Lucinda turned and walked into Brandon's arms. "Well, that was pretty amazing."

"Yes. Yes, it was," he chuckled.

"Your girls love you, ya know."

"Oh, I know. I can't imagine what I would do without them."

"Well, I'm going to get back to work."

"Back? What are you working on already?"

"Mostly just brainstorming my way through what the State of California depends on the federal government for. You know, what services they would lose if they left the protection of the U.S."

"Hmm. Maybe we just make them a territory so we can provide some support to them."

"No. That's not the way it works," Lucinda said. "Territories were established as a pathway to statehood. Not the other way around. But it is ironic that Puerto Rico wants to become a state, and California wants out."

"Yeah, we need to sit with the governor to figure out what we're all asking for exactly. I'm sure if we talk to two thousand people on the street, we'll get two thousand answers."

"No doubt," Lucinda said.

"Let's see if we can get some time with the governor to work all this out."

"Okay. I'll give his office a call," Lucinda said.

Brandon kissed her on the forehead and walked down the hall to his office. He began to think through a project plan with the end goal of California being an independent nation. He began jotting down headings and bulleted lists on one of the two whiteboards that had been installed on his wall.

They both skipped lunch and worked late into the afternoon before finally asking Sonny to drive them to their temporary home in the foothills of the

Sierras. They locked up the building and drove out of the city into the tiny country roads that curved back and forth through the rocks and brush into the quiet darkness of the mountains. When they arrived at Val's safe house and pulled into the driveway, they saw two guards sitting on the front porch. The guards stood as soon as the car pulled in.

"Good evening, Mr. and Mrs. McStocker. Welcome home. We've just had a walk-down of the grounds, and all is quiet for your evening."

"Thank you, Agent," Brandon said.

Sonny nodded, acknowledging his report and closed the car doors behind Brandon and Lucinda. They walked into the house and went directly to the kitchen. Lucinda turned on the light and opened the refrigerator door.

"Anybody hungry?" she shouted. "We have some apple pie in here."

"Perfect," Brandon said. Sonny smiled and nodded, sitting at the small kitchen table.

She took the pie from the refrigerator and placed it on the countertop. "I'll put on some coffee, too."

A loud crack rang out in the back yard, and Sonny ran for the back door. "Get down!" As soon as he got out on the back patio, he saw one of the guards peering into the darkness toward the foothills.

"What is it?" Sonny shouted.

"There's somebody up there. I saw him with my goggles."

"That was you shooting?"

"I thought I could see a rifle in his hand."

"I didn't realize you guys had night vision goggles up here. Who are you working for?"

"You, right now."

Sonny walked back into the kitchen and closed the door.

"What was it?" Brandon asked.

"They thought they saw someone up in the hills."

"In this blackness?" Lucinda asked.

"That's just it. These guys have NVGs."

"That seems awfully sophisticated just to cover us," Brandon said.

"My thoughts exactly. Something's not right here."

"What do we do?" Lucinda asked.

"For now, let's eat pie and drink coffee. I think these guys will keep us alerted. I need to think through this." Sonny sat back down at the table and stared through the window over the sink into the darkness.

Lucinda served the coffee and pie, and they all sat quietly eating. Then they heard a car coming up the driveway and the guards running around the house to see who it was. Brandon, Lucinda, and Sonny walked through the living room and out onto the front porch to see what was going on.

"Val? What are you doing here?" Brandon asked. She and two of her security escorts got out of the car.

"Hi, Brandon. Hi, Lucy. I was in town, so I wanted to come up and see how things are going."

"Uh, we're fine," Lucinda said. "This is unexpected. I thought you were back in K.D."

"Oh, I was," Val said.

Brandon's phone vibrated in his pocket. He saw that the text was from Josh Bixby. *What in the world could he want?* he thought.

Val stared at Brandon nervously when he looked back down at his phone.

Hey Brandon. You around?
Yes. Long time, no see.
Liv told me you're staying at a safe house east of Sacto.
That's right. What's up?
Owned by CW Val Strickland?
Yes. Why?
Brother, you need to get out of there.
Why?
I got an uneasy feeling and had my people look into all this. It's a trap. Those are my guys planted there, but she is not your friend.

He looked up just as Val shouted at her two escorts. They pulled their guns and pointed them at Brandon and Lucinda. Sonny and the two guards drew their service weapons and targeted her.

"This craziness has to stop, Brandon!" Val shouted. "Do you really think anyone is going to let you take the whole damn State of California away from the U.S.? Are you so arrogant as to think you can pull this off?"

"Ms. Strickland!" one of the guards shouted. "Put the guns down."

"Val," Sonny said. "You know this isn't going to end well. Tell them to lower their weapons."

"You have no idea," Val said.

A shot was fired from the hills behind the house, and a plume of dirt flew up next to one of Brandon's guards. Everyone jumped to the ground except Congresswoman Strickland.

"You're all going back to the hell you came from!" she shouted. Then she yelled at one of her men. "Make sure you shoot to kill this time. That useless meth-head you hired didn't do what I asked!"

"Wait. Val, that was you? Brandon shouted. "Why? Why Lucinda?"

"I wanted you gone, Brandon. It was supposed to be you. That kid this idiot hired decided to take things into his own hands. He decided to be creative."

Sonny pushed Brandon and Lucinda back into the house, and then he dove into the shrubs along the front wall out of the line of fire from the back of the house. Val ran as her two escorts began firing their pistols at the shrubs, hoping to hit him. Before they could succeed, an agent fired his gun, placing a round straight through the heart of one of the gunmen. Another one of Bixby's agents shot and killed the second gunman standing next to Val. She turned and ran down the driveway into the darkness.

Gunfire came from her direction. An agent lowered his NVGs and saw her shooting from the end of the driveway. He took aim through his sights and shot her in the head. She was dead before her body hit the ground.

Sonny went back into the house. He, along with Brandon and Lucinda, ran into the kitchen and turned off the lights, hunkering down to look out of the back windows.

"Stay down!" Sonny shouted.

The two agents flipped down their goggles, ran to their sedan on the side of the house, and took two rifles from the trunk before proceeding to the back yard. After they had taken up a position behind the steps to the patio, one pointed to his eyes and held up two fingers for the other agent to see. He had spotted two shooters.

The agent on the left aimed at the bright green glow on the left while the other agent aimed at the one on the right.

"Ready."

The other agent quickly raised his thumb.

"Three-two-one." Two shots rang out simultaneously, and the back yard fell silent. The agents stood and walked out from behind the steps. Sonny opened the back door. "Clear?"

"Clear."

One of the agents flipped his goggles back down and scanned the hillside. "Nobody else up there. You might want to give Agent Bixby a call, Mr. McStocker. Let him know what happened here. We'll call in our people to process this site and wrap it up."

"Of course," Brandon said. Thank you. He pulled the phone out of his pocket and made the call.

"Brandon. You okay?"

"Josh. We're fine. What the hell just happened?"

"Glad you're okay, Buddy. It was a setup from the beginning. Come to find out, Congresswoman Strickland was willing to do anything to stop this secession."

"So, this wasn't the cartel?"

"No, I don't think so. Not this time. She was completely on the other extreme."

"Yeah, I guess that's true."

"You might want to have my guys sweep your offices again, just to be sure," Agent Bixby said.

"I can't believe you snuck your agents in here. When did you know?"

"We started getting suspicious this morning. I had a couple of our guys act like they worked for the congresswoman and relieved a couple of her agents."

"And they just took them at their word?"
"Apparently."
"Are there more? Like Val, I mean?"
"I don't think so. At least we know that we're dealing with two sides of the same war, so we know what to look for now. I'll coordinate with the state. I think you guys will be okay to focus on the task at hand. I may be out in a few days, depending on what Liv comes up with. That new database she's working on is pretty amazing. Smart kid you have there."

"Yeah, you don't have to tell me," Brandon said.

"Hey, Boss," Sonny said. "We need to clear out of here."

"Josh, I need to run, my friend. Thank you so much for looking out for us."

"That's what we do. I'll be in touch," Agent Bixby said.

Brandon disconnected the call and put the phone back in his pocket.

"Clyde is going to send out a group from the Secret Service to clear a new place to live."

"An ex-SEAL Team?" Brandon asked.

Sonny chuckled. "Wouldn't surprise me."

CHAPTER 17

Brandon sat on the edge of Lucinda's desk in the reception area watching the news on the TV they had just installed. The death of Congresswoman Strickland was saturating the news cycle. The phone on Lucinda's desk rang. She pressed the speaker button.

"Lucinda Rea . . . uh, McStocker."

Brandon snickered.

"Hey, Lucinda. Senator Beecher here. Is Brandon around?"

"Yes, sir. He's here. I have you on speaker. You need me to hand him the phone?"

"No. It's fine. This apology is for both of you."

"Apology? What's up, Senator?"

"Hey, Brandon. I can't tell you both how sorry I am. It was me that hooked you up with Congresswoman Strickland. I had no idea she had gone off the deep end."

"Not your fault, Senator," Brandon said. "Apparently, she had a radical love for the old California that nobody knew about. Who knew she had become so extreme?"

"So, you don't think it had anything to do with the cartel, then?" Beecher asked.

"No, not really. We haven't been able to find any connections from phone records and such. We think she was all on her own."

"Well. At least there's that. I remember her as such a good woman. A real go-getter," Beecher said.

"We're sorry for the loss of your friend, Senator," Lucinda said.

"Thanks, Lucy. So, I assume you guys are out of her house?"

"Yes, sir," Brandon said. "We've been staying in a hotel here in town, close to the office. We've been checking out places to rent. Something small. Once we find something, Sonny has some guys ready to sweep it and secure it. We're kind of sensitive about location. I would just as soon not be surrounded by hills or tall buildings."

"I understand. Hey, you two, I need to jump off. Good luck in your new digs and call if you need anything. I know you're pretty much direct to the president on this one, but if I can help, let me know."

"Thanks, Senator."

Lucinda pressed the speaker off, and they returned their focus to the TV monitor and the news.

Brandon took the vibrating phone from his coat pocket. "Speak of the devil. It's Sonny texting."

I'm meeting with the agents Clyde sent. Any luck finding a place?

We've narrowed it down to two. I'll send the address, Brandon replied.

I'll let you know which one is safest.
That works.

All ok there?
Yep. Val still all over the news. It's been 3 days. Crazy. I'll be back by lunch.

"He's going to check out those two rental houses," Brandon said to Lucinda. "He'll us know which will be more secure."

"Sounds like a plan. You know, Brandon, we need to get with the governor and his staff to nail down the details of this withdrawal."

"Yeah, we do. Give his secretary a call and try to coordinate something. I have a hunch he'll give us priority."

"Probably. I'll give her a call. She's used to working with Mena. I hope I don't freak her out."

While Lucinda called the governor's office, Brandon turned down the TV and walked back to his desk. He started thinking about his daughters and all the music he was missing out on back home in Kansas. He leaned back in his chair and gazed through the window across the parking lot. *I miss my view of the city*, he thought.

He opened his laptop and began brainstorming the issues that might arise and ideas for their discussion with the governor. His phone vibrated.

"Brandon McStocker."

"Mr. McStocker, this is the Central House calling. Do you have a moment for the president, sir?"

"Uh . . . of course."

"Please hold for the president."

"Brandon! How are you doing today?"

"I'm doing great, Mr. President. And you, sir?"

"Couldn't be better. I wish we could say we miss you back here, but that daughter of yours is giving you a run for your money."

"Good to hear, sir. I never had a doubt."

"I hated to hear about that congresswoman. What a shock. Everybody's okay?"

"Yes, sir. It was quite sad, really. Scary when it was going down, but sad after the fact. Her heart was in the right place, and her love for the state was undeniable. Her passion just drove her over the edge."

"Sad indeed. Brandon, I just wanted to let you know that my staff and I have been meeting with Congress and each of the governors, individually, to talk about this withdrawal. I just wanted to take their temperature; you know?"

"I understand, sir. How is it going?"

"Frankly, you would be surprised at how much they are unanimously in favor of it. They have some good ideas that might help the transition go more smoothly. I've been pleasantly surprised."

"That's great news, Mr. President. Governor Truly also seems to be making headway with the state senate and his lawmakers. It'll take a while."

"Of course. But it's good that we've gotten the ball rolling. We just need to make sure everyone working on it understands the need for confidentiality."

"Yes, sir. I'm hoping to meet with the governor over the next few days to work out some details. I will reiterate the need to keep it close to our chests. There were two more deaths in San Francisco yesterday. Cartel hits, apparently. So, he may want to try to use the story as leverage."

"Yeah. I get it, but we can't have him going off like that."

"Yes, sir."

"Well, that's it, Brandon. The wheels of government don't turn quickly, I'm afraid. But I'd like to have this off my plate before this last term ends."

"It's been a long road, Mr. President."

"That, it has, Brandon. That, it has. I'll be in touch."

Brandon walked out to the reception area as he put his phone back in his coat pocket.

"Did I hear you talking to somebody?" Lucinda asked.

"It was the president."

"The president? What did he want?"

"Just giving me an update on his discussions related to the withdrawal."

"He's reporting to you now?" she chuckled. "That's interesting."

"Oh, stop. No. He was just catching up."

"If you say so. We're on with the governor tomorrow afternoon at two."

"Sounds good. I've been prepping back there."

Lucinda heard her phone chiming in her purse. "What the . . . it's Sonny. Why is he texting me?" She read his note aloud.

"How do you like the Chestnut house? It's the safest."

She looked up and smiled. "I'm okay with it."

"Works for me." Brandon winked and walked back toward his office.

The following morning, Brandon, Lucinda, and Sonny met with the property management agent at their new home on Chestnut Avenue. She unlocked the front door, and they followed her into the kitchen, where she placed the contract on the countertop for their review and signature.

"Can we do a quick walkthrough?" Lucinda asked. "I mean, we've seen it, but not with the eye of one actually living here."

"Of course, ma'am. Take your time."

Sonny walked back out onto the front porch while Brandon followed Lucinda through the house. She unlocked the sliding glass door in the master bedroom, and they walked out onto the covered patio.

"I really do love this deck," Lucinda said. "The pool. The picket fence. It's perfect. I'm glad Sonny landed on this one."

"I'm glad I did, too," Sonny said, startling them as he walked around the corner into the backyard. "We've checked in with all the neighbors, and they've been cleared. I don't think you'll have any trouble here. But Clyde told me that the president wants coverage on both of you."

"Secret Service? Again?"

"Sorry, Boss."

"Any idea who they're assigning to us?"

"I know him well."

"Really? Who is it?"

"Me."

"You?"

"Yep."

"I thought that assignment was temporary. You mean, you're back in full-time?"

"Yes, sir."

"You sure that's what you want?" Brandon asked.

"Under the circumstances, it's exactly what I want," Sonny said.

"Well, that's great, then. Congratulations."

"Congratulations, Sonny," Lucinda said. "That is so cool."

"They'll give me a partner. I just don't know who yet."

"Well, okay," Brandon said. "Let's do this."

They walked back into the house, and Lucinda locked the door behind them. They went into the kitchen.

"All ready?" the property agent asked.

"Let's do it," Lucinda said. She took the pen from the agent's hand and signed the lease agreement.

She handed the pen to Brandon, and he signed as well. "I hate to sign and run, but we need to get back to the office. We have an important meeting to get ready for."

"Of course. I understand," the agent said. "Here are your keys and a list of phone numbers for the services in this area. Congratulations on your new home. If there's ever anything we can do for you, please do not hesitate to call."

When they arrived back at the office, Sonny parked the car, and they all got out and walked around to the front of the building. There was a package leaning against the front door.

"Whoa," Sonny said, placing his arm in front of Lucinda. "You guys wait here." He walked slowly toward the door and tried to see if there were any markings on the large yellow envelope.

"Can you tell what it is?" Brandon asked.

"There's a label on it, but I can't tell what it says." Sonny walked back to Brandon and Lucinda while taking the phone from his back pocket. "I don't like this. I'm going to get our EOD guys out here."

"Wouldn't the local bomb squad be faster?"

"Maybe, but they'll come with sirens blasting. I want to keep this quiet in case it's nothing. You guys have a seat on that bench over there and relax."

After about thirty minutes, a black armored vehicle quietly rolled into the parking lot, and several agents jumped out and immediately went to work unloading and setting up equipment. One of them spoke to Sonny for several minutes.

Sonny walked back over to the bench. "They're going to run a robot over there to get some pictures. It won't take long."

As crowds began to gather on the sidewalk, the men removed the small machine on tracks from the vehicle and drove it around to the front of the building using the controller on the end of a long cable that extended behind the robot.

"I need you all to move back past that stop sign, please!" one of the agents shouted while pointing behind the crowd.

"So much for keeping a low profile," Sonny said.

The robot slowly crept up on the envelope and began taking pictures. The man operating the machine was looking at a small monitor and was relaying information to a woman standing next to him. Brandon saw her shaking her head. She motioned Sonny over to her.

The operator controlling the robot picked up the envelope with its claw and shook it. The woman, apparently in charge, continued to shake her head and was talking to Sonny about what they were discovering. The operator returned the robot to where they had set it up and took the envelope from the claw. He held it up to the sun. The woman then ran a wand over it and wiped it with a small cloth and placed it in a machine on the top of the robot.

Sonny smiled and waved Brandon and Lucinda over to them. When they got there, he shook his head. "Nothing here. Just a package."

Brandon exhaled. "Whew! I'm glad that's over."

"Here you go, sir," the woman said. "This package is safe."

"Glad to hear it. Can we go in now?"

"You're free to go, sir. Thank you. Good to see you, Sonny. Welcome back. Glad this was nothing."

"Thanks, Jo. Me too. I'll be in touch," Sonny said.

"You got it."

Sonny walked to the front door just as Lucinda was opening it to go in. Brandon stepped in behind them and placed the package on the reception counter.

"Okay, now. What the heck is this? Brandon asked. "There's no return address." He slowly opened the envelope and took out a folder full of papers.

"What is it, babe?" Lucinda asked.

"What the . . ."

"Boss? What is it?" Sonny asked.

"It says Federal Election Commission on the top of it." He looked inside the folder. "Apparently, it's the forms needed to file for candidacy."

"For what?" Lucinda asked.

He shook his head, then turned serious and looked her squarely in the eye. "President."

Sonny clapped his hands and leaned back in laughter. "Oh, man, you should see the look on your face right now."

Lucinda started laughing. "Honey, who would send you that?"

"I have no idea. But it's not funny," he said, pointing his finger at Sonny. "Shut it. Not funny."

Sonny and Lucinda laughed harder.

"I'm putting this back in my office, never to see the light of day again," Brandon said. "Come on. We need to get ready to see the governor."

"Okay. Okay." Lucinda walked behind her desk and gathered some of the files that were scattered around.

"I'll be out in the car," Sonny chuckled. "Oh, man."

"Brandon. Mrs. McStocker. Please, come in."

"Thank you, Governor. It's good to see you, sir."

"You as well. So, we're ready to get down to business?"

"Yes, sir. I think we have a plan sketched out," Brandon said.

"Good. Have a seat. This is my lieutenant governor, Allen Pinkerton, and the senior member of our state senate, Janice Martin."

They all shook hands and sat around the governor's conference table in a room off to the side of his office.

"So, Brandon, where is the president on all this?"

"He's having discussions with the other governors and Congress about your withdrawal. So far, everyone seems supportive."

"So, they aren't calling it a secession?"

"No, sir. I think we all know the images that brings to mind. This is what we're going to call an amicable withdrawal from the United States."

"Good. This talk of Civil War II is trying my patience."

"I understand, sir," Brandon said. "It's getting a little scary down there."

"And where is 'down there'?" Senator Martin asked.

"Well, San Francisco, ma'am."

"That's my district. I think if we let my constituents know what's going on, they'll calm down."

"No!" Governor Truly shouted. "Do not let these negotiations get out. Not yet."

"Sam, I don't understand the issue," Mr. Pinkerton said.

"Look, Allen, we've got the damn drug cartels nipping at our heels. The feds are trying to figure out a way to stop it, but if we let them know we're leaving the Union, they'll only see it as an invitation to waltz in here and take over. Hell, the rest of the country thinks we want to turn California back over to Mexico as it is."

"Okay. Okay. I get it," Senator Martin said. "No press releases."

"So, Governor," Brandon interrupted. "Are there any concerns that you want to get on the table? Besides the obvious, of course."

"Well, it'll take us a while to get our footing."

"Of course, sir. I don't think there is an expectation that this will be an overnight departure. California is a significant food supply for the whole nation. I think we need to include trade, in that regard."

"I agree. Perhaps we can trade commodities for security."

"Sir?"

"Hell, you don't think California has a standing army, do you? We're going to need protection. We've got Mexico and the whole damn Pacific Ocean to keep an eye on. I don't think the people that want out have thought any of that through."

"Oh, of course. Yes, sir," Brandon said. "That makes sense. We are making some progress on the Cártel del Mundo issue."

"How so?" Governor Truly asked.

"My firm is working on a more robust database for tracking each and every member of the group, including the drug lord himself."

"How is he still alive, anyway?"

"Well, sir. It's complicated," Lucinda said.

"Yeah, that's what my daughter keeps telling me about her boyfriend," the governor chuckled. "I still have no idea what that means."

Lucinda smiled. "Sir, I think that means you don't really want to know."

The governor smiled and shook his head. "Right. I imagine that's true."

"Governor, what else do you think the state might need from the president?" Brandon asked. "The border crossings at the state line will likely be beefed up, but if we can get the immigration traffic under control, we can probably ease up some."

"Like the Canadian border?" Lt. Governor Pinkerton asked.

"Hopefully. But again, the traffic coming *through* Mexico, not *from* Mexico is what we're worried about, as you well know."

"Yeah. All too well, I'm afraid," Pinkerton said.

The group continued negotiations for the remainder of the day and into the night. Some arguments made Brandon wonder again, why the president sent him into the firestorm. *I'm not a politician*, he thought, time after time.

They often stopped the discussion to remind themselves why they were there. The State of California wants to leave the United States, and they want to do it peacefully. They said it so often, Brandon finally wrote it in large letters on a whiteboard on the front wall of the conference room. Finally, at two A.M., they had nothing more to talk about.

"I think we've about got it," Brandon said.

"I believe you're right," Governor Truly said. "I can't think of any bridges we haven't crossed."

"I've been taking copious notes," Lucinda said. "I'll get a copy to everyone once I have them transcribed and cleaned up. Brandon and I will present this to the president tomorrow . . . or, I guess I mean, later today."

"Yes. Let's get out of here," the governor said.

They all stood and moved the coffee cups and glasses from the conference table to a tub on the service counter, then packed their briefcases and left. Brandon and Lucinda walked out the front door of the State Capitol and saw their car that Sonny had pulled off into the grass out of the way. But no Sonny.

Brandon smiled. "I bet I know where he is."

They continued down the steps and across the driveway. They approached the car and saw Sonny sunk down in the driver's seat, fast asleep.

"I hate to wake him up," Lucinda said.

"Yeah. Me too. But probably for a different reason. When I knock on the window, stand back."

"What? Why?"

"I've had to wake him up before. Let's just say I pity the poor sailors in Iraq that had to wake this guy up."

"Oh. One of those."

"Yep." Brandon tapped on the glass. As expected, Sonny jumped in his seat and reached for his gun. He quickly realized where he was and saw Brandon grinning outside the car. Sonny looked at his watch and opened his door.

"Dang, man. It took you guys long enough."

"Yeah, nobody said it was going to be easy. I sure wish Richland had sent a politician out here. Unbelievable."

"Let's just get back to the hotel," Lucinda said. "I can't wait to get moved into the house."

They loaded into the car, and Sonny drove them away from the Capitol building.

CHAPTER 18

"Mr. Speaker, the President of the United States," the House sergeant at arms announced as the House chamber erupted in shouts of approval and a standing ovation by all members of Congress. It seemed to go on forever. Brandon and Lucinda had returned to K.D. for the event and were seated in the gallery next to the first lady.

After several false starts due to the jubilant members of the Senate and the House, President Richland was finally able to speak.

"Thank you for your warm welcome. Today, I come to you to ask for your help in this most unsettled time. I am asking you to create laws that will allow for the unprecedented actions of the likes this nation has never had to experience.

"Tomorrow, a document will be delivered to each of your offices. This document contains a set of proposed agreements with the State of California to allow for their peaceful withdrawal from the Union."

After the message had sunk in, the members began to smile. Everyone turned and held up their hands in the direction of the representatives from California and began to applaud. Not out-of-control cheering, but a respectful acknowledgment of a peaceful gesture after all that had happened. The members returned to their seats.

"As you all know, our Constitution doesn't allow for such a departure. But I think we all agree that it is time to give California their independence. I know it will take time, but I need both houses of Congress to carefully consider what it will take to make this happen."

The chamber was completely silent. Every member wanted to hear exactly what the president was saying.

"As you know, my second term will be ending next year. It is my hope that we can gather here one more time before I leave office to announce the completion of this agreement. I really thought the crowning moment of my presidency would be the building of Lebanon, K.D. and the relocation of our federal government."

Every member in the chamber jumped to their feet in deafening applause. President Richland tried several times to quiet the members without success. The applause continued for over fifteen minutes. The members were laughing at the intensity, talking, and shaking hands. The representatives from California were crying from mixed emotions. They, too, were proud of what their president had been able to accomplish during his two terms in office.

"Please. Please. Have a seat. Please." The president continued trying to regain order in the chambers.

Finally, the Speaker of the House began to slam his gavel to get everyone's attention. After several more minutes, the chamber quieted, and the president was finally able to continue.

"Thank you. Thank you so much. Your support has been overwhelming. While we are focused on the task at hand, we can't forget that we have a severe threat to our security from the southern border. While many of us are concerned that this enemy will merely walk in and take over California, it is most definitely not what the governor and the citizens out there want.

"We have a focused effort underway to ensure it doesn't happen. And to that end, I would be remiss if I didn't acknowledge the efforts of Mr. Brandon McStocker and his team at McStocker and McStocker."

The chamber again erupted in a standing ovation. It was clear that they all knew Brandon and what he had accomplished. The president allowed the applause to continue for several minutes before turning and nodding at the Speaker to use his gavel.

"Thank you all." The president looked into the gallery where Brandon had been standing and acknowledging the members. "Thank you, Brandon. Your service to this country has been above and beyond anything we could have imagined."

The members jumped back to their feet as Brandon pointed straight up. Tears flowed down Lucinda's face knowing that he was tipping his hat to his friend, Bill McClellan, and Brandon's first wife, Cassandra. Finally, everyone returned to their seats. Lucinda wrapped her arm around Brandon's and laid her head on his shoulder.

"Thank you, Brandon. People have lost their lives to make K.D. happen—people who didn't even know what was going on. My own family was threatened. And come to find out, the enemy was not us. People in high places were being threatened and forced to commit unimaginable crimes against the country. But now, we know the source. We will get to the bottom of this at all costs, and we will stop it."

The members returned to their feet in loud approval. They seemed to understand that it was time for a new kind of lawmaking. The president's speech lasted for over an hour, but nobody noticed. Brandon looked around the chamber and knew the president had struck a chord with a nation that had lost its way before he took office. While previous administrations spoke of change, none was able to make it happen like this. Brandon smiled and put his arm around Lucinda. They were both in tears.

After his speech, during the deafening applause, the president made his way up the aisle, greeting members and shaking their hands. It was another thirty minutes before he made it to the chamber doors. When the chamber was emptied, Brandon and Lucinda made their way to the front door of the new U.S. Capitol in Lebanon, K.D.

"Brandon! Brandon!"

"Senator Beecher. It's really good to see you, sir."

"It's been too long. How are things out on the left coast?"

Before Brandon had time to answer, Senator Beecher continued. "Listen, I have someone I want you to meet." He held Brandon's arm and pulled him through the crowd. Brandon grabbed Lucinda's hand

and pulled her along behind them. She struggled to keep up.

"Brandon. This is Congressman Buddy Sanchez."

They shook hands. "Pleased to meet you, Congressman."

"Mr. McStocker, I've wanted to meet you for a long time."

"Please, call me Brandon."

"Brandon, you need to remember Congressman Sanchez," Beecher said.

"I'm sure I will, but why is that?"

"Congressman Sanchez is the party leader."

Lucinda looked up at Brandon and covered her mouth, trying to hide her giggling from the others. Brandon squeezed her hand, and she turned her head. Her laughter was becoming more difficult to hide.

"Mrs. McStocker, are you okay?" Beecher asked.

She nodded, still facing the opposite direction as if looking for someone. She finally regained her composure and rejoined the conversation.

"I'm so sorry, gentlemen. I thought I saw someone I knew." Another quick giggle slipped out, and Brandon looked at her with a smile.

"It's good to meet you, Congressman, but we really need to go."

"You as well, Brandon. Would you mind if I give you a call over the next few days?"

"Uh. No, of course not. Senator Beecher has my number."

As soon as they cleared the crowd and walked down the front steps, Lucinda began laughing again.

"What is the matter with you?"

"Oh, my God. Oh, my God. Oh, my God," she said.

"What?"

"You don't know?"

"Know what?" Brandon asked.

"Sweetheart, are you really that oblivious? They want you to run."

"What are you talking about? Run for what?"

"President, goober."

"Oh, please. That's ridiculous. That was all just some reporter's joke."

"Okay. I'll say nothing more. But you mark my words, mister."

Brandon shook his head, and they continued toward their limo. Sonny was leaning against the front fender with a newspaper open.

"Oh, hey, Boss. How'd it go?"

"I have to say, the whole thing was a pretty moving experience," Brandon said.

"It was a-ma-zing," Lucinda said. "They want this one to run for president."

Brandon jerked her arm and laughed. "Will you shut it?"

"What? It's true." She looked at Sonny. "They want him, and he can't stand it."

"Get in the car," Brandon said through his laughter.

As they traveled toward the hotel where they were staying, Brandon noticed that Sonny kept looking at him in the rearview mirror.

"Something on your mind, man?"

"Oh, nothing. It can wait," Sonny said.

"Well, now that I know there's an *it*, of course, it can't wait."

"Spill it!" Lucinda chuckled.

"Well, no big deal, really. I was just wondering if I might take tomorrow night off."

Brandon's jaw dropped. "Dude, I don't know that I've heard you ask for time off since I've known you. Of course, you can take it off. Take a few days if you want."

"No. No. I just wanted tomorrow night."

"What? Is it like a date?" Lucinda asked.

"Just hanging out with an old friend," Sonny blushed.

"Oh, my God! Sonny is going on a date," Lucinda said.

"Stop. Leave him alone. Is it anyone we know?" Brandon asked.

Sonny looked at them in the rearview mirror again but said nothing.

"Come on," Lucinda said. "Tell us!"

"Jeez," Sonny said. "Do you remember that EOD officer that responded to the bomb scare we called in when you got that package at the office?"

"Yeah," Brandon said. "Jo, was it?"

"Right. Jo Anderson. We used to work together and thought it might be fun to catch up."

"Wow. A date. Damn. Who knew!" Lucinda said.

"Come on, Boss. Really?"

"Sorry, man. I've just never seen you in this mode before. It suits you."

"Well, thanks . . . I think."

"You know what? Before we head back to Sacramento in the morning, you might want to stop by the diner to get Susan's approval," Brandon said.

Lucinda chuckled. "Oh, that's right. That girl adores you. It might break her heart."

"Oh, stop," Sonny said.

"I do remember some pretty touching times between you two," Lucinda said.

"Yeah, she's a cute kid. An old soul full of love. Pretty dingy sometimes."

They all laughed. "Let's go see her now," Lucinda said.

"Is she even working?" Sonny asked.

"That girl is always at that diner," Brandon said.

They had just passed the diner, so Sonny took the first turn he could find going into Manhattan on the north side. He turned around and went back.

"Yep. There's her car," Sonny said as he pulled into the parking lot.

All three walked in the front door as the bell rang over their heads. Susan turned to see who it was.

"Holy crap!" she shouted. "Is that Sonny I see walking into this diner? Has hell frozen over?"

"Oh, shut up and give me a hug." Susan walked quickly from behind the counter and straight into Sonny's arms.

"It is so good to see you." She turned to Brandon and Lucinda. "You guys too. Liv told me you would be here for the president's address, but I wasn't sure if you'd have time to stop in. I'm so glad you did. You two are looking mighty dapper."

"When's the last time you saw your sister?" Brandon asked.

She was in here for breakfast, as a matter of fact. I think she wanted to go to the speech, but apparently, she's up to her neck in alligators."

"Is she okay?" Lucinda asked.

"Oh, yeah. A little frazzled, maybe, but she's fine. She's been working some crazy hours."

"Yeah, I bet they're onto something," Brandon said.

"We should have stopped while we were up there," Lucinda said.

"No, if she's that busy, we would have been a distraction."

"Yeah, you're probably right."

"You guys want to eat? Your table is clean," Susan said.

They smiled and walked back in the corner and took a seat.

"I'm not that hungry," Brandon said. "Any cinnamon rolls left?"

"I just happen to have a few."

Lucinda looked at Sonny, and he nodded. She spun her finger over her head. "Cinnamon rolls all around."

"You got it," Susan said. "Coffee?" They all nodded.

After Susan heated the rolls and delivered everything to the table, Sonny slid out the extra chair. "Hey, Kiddo. You don't look busy. Have a seat."

She froze. "What?"

"You heard me. Sit."

She slapped his shoulder with the towel she had in her hand and sat next to him. "Fine. Why so serious?"

Brandon and Lucinda smiled and took a bite of their rolls.

"No big deal, really," Susan said. "But I have kind of a date tomorrow night."

"Shut up! With whom?"

"An old friend from the Service out in California."

"Are you kidding me? Dude, your hair is turning gray. Are you sure you can handle it?"

They all laughed.

"I can handle it," Sonny said.

She turned and punched his shoulder. "Buddy, that is awesome news!" She leaned into him and wrapped her arms around his neck.

"Wait. Are you crying?" Sonny asked.

She smiled through her tears. "I'm just so dang happy for you."

"Well, it's just a date. First date at that."

"I know, but my whole life, I was always afraid of you being lonely."

"Well, little buddy, ever since that first dinner we had with you when you were a kid, I knew I'd never be lonely."

"That night I asked you if you'd ever shot anybody?"

"Yeah, that night."

"That was a long time ago. What was I, like eight or something?"

Brandon chuckled. "Yeah, maybe."

"I bet you were the cutest kid," Lucinda said.

"Pain in the ass was more like it," Susan chuckled.

Brandon grinned and looked down at his food.

They all continued to laugh into the night.

Brandon walked into their newly leased home. Lucinda was cleaning and organizing the kitchen.

"Did you get by without me?" He asked.

"Oh, I managed. How's it going?"

"Did I mention I hate moving? It's exciting, but dang, it's a lot of work."

"I know. We've only been back a week. There's no rush to get this place together," Lucinda said.

"I know, but I want to get it done."

"Why don't you take a break and let's go somewhere nice for dinner. What do ya say?" she asked.

Sonny tapped on the front door and walked in.

"Hey, Sonny. How are you?" Lucinda asked.

"All good. You've got it looking nice in here. Doesn't even look like the same place."

"Thanks. It's been a chore."

The door opened again. Brandon and Lucinda froze. They were surprised to see Jo Anderson walk in behind Sonny.

"I'm sorry. I left my phone in the car and had to go back to get it." She curled her arm through Sonny's and smiled. "Hi. I'm Jo. We met at your office a while back."

"Hi, Jo," Brandon said. "Yes. I remember. Though, I have to admit I wouldn't have recognized you out of uniform. Welcome. Come on in." Brandon nodded at Sonny, and he smiled.

"Uh, mind if I take the night off again, Boss?"

"Of course not. You've been saving up vacation for what, like twenty-five, thirty years?"

They laughed, and Lucinda walked back into the kitchen.

"Hey, we were about to head off to grab some dinner," Brandon said. "You're welcome to join us."

Lucinda stuck her head back in the living room, looking at Brandon with a slanted eye.

"Oh, no thanks, Boss." Sonny smiled nervously. "That's okay. We've made plans already."

"Oh, of course."

Lucinda shook her head and disappeared back into the kitchen.

They chatted for several minutes before Sonny and Jo decided it was time to leave. "See ya, Lucy!" Sonny shouted.

She walked back into the living room. "Okay, Sonny. You guys have a good time."

"Be safe," Brandon said.

They walked out to Jo's car, and Brandon closed the door behind them and returned to his seat. Lucinda threw a towel and hit him in the head. It fell open and covered his face. "You're such a goober," she said.

"What?"

"He's clearly into her. You can't expect him to drag her along with us on a date." She smiled and shook her head. "Give me a minute to finish up in here, and I'll get ready."

Brandon went into the bedroom to start getting dressed. When he emerged in a suit and tie, Lucinda smiled and kissed him. "I didn't realize this was a *dinner* dinner."

"Only the best."

"Well, okay then." She went into the bedroom. When she returned, she was in her little black dress and made up to the nines.

"Wow!" Brandon said. Is that what you wore on our first date?"

"You remembered."

"How could I forget? Hey, I ordered up an Uber. Hope you don't mind."

"You know, I hadn't even thought about Sonny not being here to take us anywhere. Strange," Lucinda said.

"The guy needs a life."

"That, he does."

"The Uber is outside. Ready?" Brandon asked.

"Let's go!"

They loaded into the back seat of the car. Brandon had directed the driver to one of the finest restaurants in Sacramento. He drove away from the house. After they had gone several blocks, the driver stopped at a red light and was looking around at the traffic when his window shattered with a loud explosion. His body was thrown into the passenger's side, and blood splattered throughout the car's interior.

Lucinda screamed as Brandon grabbed her and threw her down into the floorboard, covering her with his body.

"Stay down! Stay down!"

Then they heard both front doors open, and Brandon looked up to see one masked man pull the driver's lifeless body out onto the street. Another masked man jumped into the driver's seat.

"Oh, my God!" Lucinda shouted. "What's going on?"

Brandon sat up and lunged forward to get the keys, but the man in the passenger seat swung his hand and hit Brandon on the side of his head with the butt of a handgun.

"Get back," the man shouted with a Latino accent.

"Who are you?" Brandon said, barely able to speak. "What do you want?"

The driver put the car in gear and sped off through the busy streets of Sacramento.

"Look, you guys. I don't have much money on me, but I'll give you what I have."

"Shut up," the driver said. He, too, had a Latino accent.

Lucinda was crying and had her head pressed against Brandon's shoulder. She had noticed the blood that sprayed on her face and arms and tried to rub it off. "Oh, God. Brandon."

He looked down at her and frantically started looking for wounds but found nothing. "Are you hit?"

"I don't think so."

"Here." He reached into his pocket.

"Whoa. Whoa. Whoa." The man quickly pointed his gun at Brandon. "Let me see your hands."

"I'm just getting a handkerchief for her."

"Move slowly."

Brandon eased the handkerchief from his jacket pocket, but when he had reached for it, his hand touched his cell phone, giving him an idea. He handed the handkerchief to Lucinda, and she started rubbing the blood from her arms and face.

"Come on. What do you want with us?" Brandon asked.

"Just sit back and enjoy the ride. You'll find out soon enough." He put the gun down to his side and turned to watch the road along with his partner.

Brandon looked down at Lucinda and squeezed her shoulder to get her attention. When she looked up at him, he looked down at his coat. She nodded and laid her head deep into his chest, acting like she was afraid. More afraid, that is, than she actually was. She slid her hand into Brandon's coat and pulled the cell phone up only enough to see the front, but it was still hidden from the two men in the front seat.

She slowly and quietly opened the messaging app and found Sonny's number.

The man with the gun turned to see why they were so quiet. Lucinda quickly closed her eyes and laid the phone against Brandon's chest. When she had opened her eyes enough to see that he had turned back around, she looked under Brandon's coat again and sent a text to Sonny.

911

CHAPTER 19

The car sped into an abandoned warehouse, and the dock door closed behind it. The men jumped out of the front seat, and there was shouting between them and others in the warehouse. Brandon recognized the Spanish language they were speaking but didn't understand enough to know what was going on.

The darkness blinded Brandon and Lucinda until their eyes adjusted. It was clear that they weren't supposed to get out of the car. "Did you send anything?" Brandon whispered, careful not to look down.

"I texted Sonny."

"Good."

Then both back doors flew open, and the two were forced from the car. The shouting continued, obviously orders, but they didn't understand. Brandon looked around but couldn't see the two men that brought them there.

Finally, someone shouted, "Get back!" He spoke English.

The crowd quieted and stepped away. "Did you check their pockets?" he asked. When nobody answered him, he screamed again. "Did you check their pockets?"

"No. We didn't have a chance." It was the man that Brandon saw in the car with the gun.

"You idiots," he said, grabbing Brandon's lapels and throwing open his jacket. He took the phone from the jacket pocket and threw it across the warehouse as hard as he could. He took Brandon's wallet from his other pocket and quickly looked through it before throwing it to the ground. When he reached for Lucinda's purse, Brandon shoved him, only to be met with a hard-right hook to the jaw. He dropped to his knees.

"Don't be a hero," the man shouted. He grabbed the purse from Lucinda's hand and rifled through it, then threw it to the ground. He took Brandon by the collar and jerked him back onto his feet and started patting his pants pockets and felt down the outside of his legs. He pushed Brandon toward another man and reached over to feel around Lucinda's waist.

Brandon jerked himself away and lunged for the man trying to frisk Lucinda before taking another punch to his ribs. He fell back to his knees. Blood ran from his mouth. The man turned back to Lucinda and felt around her waist and under her breasts, and then spun her around to see where she might be carrying something behind her. He reached under her dress and felt up onto her thighs. Lucinda cringed and looked at the ceiling.

"She has nothing," the man said. "Take them back into the office and tie them up."

Once they were seated and tied, Brandon and Lucinda were left alone in an abandoned office. It was dark, but they could see enough to recognize the file cabinets and papers tossed around in disarray.

"You okay, Honey?"

"Brandon, I'm scared."

"Yeah, me too. Try to stay calm. We'll think of something."

They waited for what seemed to be hours in the sweltering heat. Brandon's eyes had darkened bruises from the blows he took. Lucinda had fallen asleep with her hands tied behind the chair and her head hanging down with her chin nearly touching her chest. Then Brandon heard loud noises outside the door. It was several men, and he could tell they were getting closer. Lucinda awoke and raised her head when the door burst open, and three men walked in. The two surrounding a taller man in the middle were carrying guns.

"Get out. Leave me alone with them." The two gunmen left while the third man walked closer to them, coming into the light of a streetlamp leaking through a window covered in dirt. Brandon noticed that he was an older man with graying hair.

"Who are you, and what do you want with us?" Brandon asked.

"Shut up. I'll ask the questions."

"You know this isn't going to end well for you. Let us go."

"I said shut up. I know who you are, and I know why you are in California. The truth is, this isn't going to end well for you, my friend. You've made your last deal with your presidente. It is time for you to finally meet the fate of your predecessor."

Brandon looked at Lucinda with questioning eyes then back at the man. "What are you talking about? Who are you?"

"I am Fidel Escobar el Dios."

"Cártel del Mundo?"

"Ah, señor. You learn well. I am what you might call the drug lord. And now that you have seen me, you know you must die."

"Why didn't you just kill us?"

"Easy enough to do. But first, I wanted you to understand that now, you have come into my territory. Yes, California will split, but it will do so on my terms. You see, when your predecessor started working with your President Richland to eliminate my network in Washington, D.C., I had to put a stop to it. You understand, of course."

"Wait. You killed Bob McClellan?"

"Of course. Well, I didn't pull the trigger, but I ordered it, and I watched."

"My God. My wife. You killed Cassandra?"

"No. No. That was your agent, but he became a willing accomplice when we showed him what could happen to his family."

"And Jimmy? Director Cortez? Senator Sanders? All of that was you?"

"Well, the senator was probably more willing to work with us than you might imagine. Why do you think winning an election is like winning a lottery for your top-tier politicians? A lifetime of comfort and riches."

"You're an animal, you son of a bitch!" Lucinda shouted.

"Ah, and Miss Reagan. You show your feistiness once again. I bet you're happy that we got the girls' mother out of the way for you."

"You sick bastard!" she shouted.

"If you bring my girls into this, I swear to God, you're a dead man!" Brandon shouted.

"I don't think you're holding the cards here, Mr. McStocker. We're going to end this once and for all. California will be mine. What better way to let the country know who is in control here? I have thousands of employees working the streets of San Francisco, convincing the so-called activist puppets that they're doing the right thing. It's been working for years. Aren't you impressed with how we can even get laws changed here? No matter how bizarre, we get them passed."

"Why?" Brandon asked.

"Because there are people who need proof. Most of those people are now on my payroll. Those who aren't, are dead."

Brandon began to realize that with this killer spilling his guts like this, there was no way they were going to leave there alive. "Senator Wilhelm? You killed Senator Wilhelm?"

"Well, had him killed, would be more accurate. But again, I had to prove our reach to someone."

"My God. President Richland. You've been trying to play President Richland."

"We almost had him once, but you kept getting in our way. I wanted to take you out then, but you were too valuable for getting me California."

"So, you've been playing me, too?"

"Let's just say I've been watching you."

"Gentlemen!" Escobar shouted toward the door. "Come in here and make these two dead."

Lucinda lowered her head and started to cry.

"Again, Escobar. You aren't coming out of this alive either," Brandon said.

"Well, that remains to be seen, doesn't it, my friend?"

The two gunmen opened the door and entered the room entirely too eager to carry out the orders of their lord. One stood behind Lucinda, and the other stood behind Brandon.

"Goodbye, my friends. It will be my pleasure to finally get you out of the way."

"I love you, Brandon," Lucinda said through her tears.

"I love you too, Sweetheart. You've been my hero from the very beginning." He lowered his head, waiting for the end.

Both of their heads sprang up when they heard gunfire outside the door. Escobar ran for the door just as three more shots rang out from the small office window. Lucinda screamed. Escobar, along with the two gunmen, dropped to the floor simultaneously. Gunfire continued outside the door for almost a minute before everything fell silent.

Brandon and Lucinda were frozen for several seconds in shock and disbelief.

"Are you okay, Honey?" Brandon asked.

Lucinda looked around her body. "Uh, I think I'm fine. What the hell was that?"

The door burst open, and Sonny ran in holding his service pistol. Josh Bixby and Bruce Talbot followed closely behind him.

"Oh, thank God," Lucinda said. "Sonny, get me the hell up out of this chair." He quickly untied her, and she jumped to her feet and threw her arms around him. Then she ran to Brandon and wrapped her arms around his neck and began kissing his cheeks and lips.

"Okay. Okay," he laughed. "Untie me. I'd like to get up, too."

"Oh, sorry," she said as she struggled to get the ropes undone.

"Man, are we glad to see you guys. How did you know where we were? I saw my phone get busted to pieces."

"We didn't," Josh said. "Olivia did."

"What?"

"Brother, it worked," Josh said.

"What worked?" Brandon asked.

"That database she had her Smart Wad working on actually came through for us."

"Smart Wad?" Sonny chuckled and shook his head.

"Uh, I think you mean Genius Pod," Brandon laughed and cringed at the pain it caused to his beaten body.

"Whatever. They know where everybody is. The lords, the shooters, the dealers, everybody. All they had to do was watch the activity on the networked cameras, and they told us exactly where to come. Not only that, a dragnet is going out all over the state to pick up most of the others. It's going to be a busy day in the justice system."

"That's amazing. So, she did it," Brandon said.

"Hell yes, she did it," Josh repeated.

"She did it!" Lucinda shouted.

Brandon stood and turned to hug her. "She did it! Our girl did it!"

"Come on, let's get out of here," Sonny said. "We have a cleanup crew coming to process this scene. Let's get you guys back home."

"I need to let the governor know she did it," Brandon said. "He needs to know. This changes everything."

"Okay. Okay. But let's get you home. In fact, let's stop by the hospital first and get you checked out. It looks like you took quite a beating."

"He was trying to be my hero," Lucinda smiled.

"It's a wonder you aren't dead. You know who you were messing with, right?"

"Oh, I know. Well, I didn't at the time, but he finally came in and introduced himself." Brandon looked down at Escobar's lifeless body on the floor. "He tried to take out everybody that I loved. Why?"

Agent Bixby put his hand on Brandon's shoulder. "You had too much power, brother. Too damn much power."

"Well, they haven't seen anything yet." He took Lucinda's hand, and they walked out of the dark office, navigated their way through the bodies strewn around the warehouse, and made their way to where Jo was standing in the parking lot.

"Damn, you guys," Jo said. "I am so sorry you had to go through that. Now, I wish I hadn't taken Sonny from you. He should have been with you."

"Stop," Lucinda said as she hugged Jo. "Just stop. You've given Sonny a light that I haven't seen in him since I've known him. You keep that going. Keep it burning. We're fine."

Tears filled Jo's eyes as she squeezed Lucinda. The others followed behind them, got in their cars, and drove away. Brandon and Lucinda got in the back seat of Jo's car, and Sonny squeezed into the passenger seat.

"What about the Uber driver?" Brandon asked.

"Didn't stand a chance," Sonny said. "The local cops have located his next of kin and are taking care of it."

"God, that sucks," Lucinda said. "Have we awakened the proverbial sleeping giant?"

"Possibly," Sonny said. "But based on Liv's data, we've been able to mount a massive nationwide sweep. Josh and Bruce are headed to the CHP control center at the Capitol to oversee it."

"What do you mean?" Lucinda asked.

"Once the word is out that Escobar is down, the cartels are going to go nuts. We can't afford to let that happen. So, virtually every law enforcement officer and agent in the country is out of bed making busts. Even the National Guard is involved. Now that we know who and where the players are, we're about to incarcerate more prisoners than this country has ever seen. Unfortunately, many of the players are white-collar dealers. Far too many are well-known personalities."

"Where in the world are we going to put that many prisoners?" Brandon asked.

"Arizona has been setting up a makeshift colony in the desert west of Tucson. It'll be a temporary solution until Mexico can figure out what to do with them."

"Speaking of Mexico," Lucinda said. "Aren't we going to instigate a problem down there?"

"Oh, yeah. The president has committed troops to go down there and provide security in order for their president to get a foothold on some order. You know they're going to try to flex their muscles."

"Yep," Brandon said. "So, how has all this been going on without us knowing about it?"

"It's been in work for months," Sonny said. "We just wanted to give you plausible deniability. We didn't know we were going to have to pull the trigger quite so quickly. But we were ready enough with a ninety-percent solution. So, when I got that text from Lucy, my gut told me it was time to call Josh. He called Clyde, and we were off to the races."

"So, Richland knew what was going on?"

"Well, let's just say, he does now."

"Here we are," Jo said. "Let's get you in the emergency room."

"We're okay, really," Lucinda said.

"I know that's Brandon's blood all over him. I just want to make sure none of that blood all over you is yours," Sonny said.

"Okay. Okay. Fine." Lucinda opened her door and got out of the car.

Brandon got out and walked around to join her before walking into the ER together. Sonny followed close behind as Jo drove away to park the car.

As soon as they entered the large sliding doors into the emergency room, they heard a voice shouting across the receiving area. "Mrs. McStocker!"

Lucinda turned to see who it was.

"Mrs. McStocker!"

Lucinda smiled when she saw the nurse approaching her. "Willie!" It was the nurse that cared for Lucinda during her previous stay at the hospital.

"Mrs. McStocker. You're back so soon?"

"We just can't stay away. We had another incident, and this guy wants us to get checked out."

"Ah. Hey, Sonny."

"Hey, Willie."

"Hey, Mr. McStocker. You look like you took the brunt of the incident. Are you feeling okay?"

"Hey, Willie. For having just been beaten, I guess I feel okay."

"I have a room right up here. Follow me." The nurse looked over at the reception desk and shouted to the duty nurse. "I'll take these two. They're returning customers. He can check them in." She motioned to Sonny.

"On it," he said.

Once the nurse got Brandon and Lucinda settled into their room, she made eye contact with a doctor on duty and motioned for him to come in. He smiled and put the clipboard he was looking at down on a desk and went in to see them.

"Dr. Madison, this is Brandon and Lucinda McStocker," Willie said.

"Well," he said. "I can see you aren't in here for appendicitis."

"No. No, I'm not," Brandon chuckled with a grimace.

The doctor began asking questions as Willie took their vital signs and started a chart on the couple. After several minutes, Sonny spoke quietly through the curtain.

"Okay to enter?"

"Yes," Lucinda said. "Get in here."

He pushed his way through the curtain and saw the doctor looking over Brandon.

"Uh, I don't suppose you can take this call," Sonny said.

"Who is it?" Brandon asked.

"Well, you have a couple of daughters on the phone that are just a little bit anxious."

"It's fine," the doctor said. "You better take it."

Sonny handed Brandon the phone.

"Hey, girls."

"Daddy!" Olivia shouted. He pulled the phone away from his ear and smiled at Lucinda. "Are you okay?"

"Sweetheart, we're fine . . . thanks to you."

"Are you sure you're okay, Daddy?" Susan said. "You guys are scaring the crap out of me."

"Hey, Honey. We're fine, really. Liv, I don't know how you pulled it off, but these guys got to us just in time."

"Well, it was Trevor and his guys. The team put some pretty mind-blowing algorithms together in short order and were able to track a spike in activity out there. The system worked."

"Yes, it did. I think you all may have done some serious damage to the cartel today."

"Yes, you did," a voice said from just outside the curtain. "Can I come in?"

Sonny slid the curtain back. "Governor Truly?"

"Governor?" Brandon said. "Sir, what are you doing here?"

"The governor is there?" Olivia asked.

"Uh, yeah. Hang on, Honey. Governor?"

"Talbot told me what happened. I just wanted to get here to make sure you folks are okay."

"They're actually in pretty good shape, considering," Dr. Madison said.

"Thank you, Doctor. Can you two leave us alone for a few minutes?"

"Of course, sir." Dr. Madison and Nurse Willie left the treatment room and went about their business in the ER.

Governor Truly began speaking much more quietly. "Are you two sure you're okay?"

"We're fine, Governor," Lucinda said. "Obviously, Brandon took the brunt of it. It was damn scary." She began wiping the tears that streamed down her face. Sonny went to her and squeezed his arm around her shoulders. She turned, laid her face in his chest, and wept.

Brandon lowered his head. "I'm so sorry you had to go through that, Honey."

"It wasn't your fault," she whimpered through the tears. Sonny rubbed her back as he held her.

"Brandon," the governor said. "Is there anything my staff or I can do?"

He looked up at Sonny then back at the governor. "Well, sir. I could use a new cell phone."

The governor chuckled. "You got it."

"You've got that right!" Brandon heard Susan shout on the phone. It came across loud enough for Lucinda and Sonny to hear, and they all laughed.

"Honey, I'll let you know when I get it. Here, talk to Luce."

"Hey there," Lucinda said as she took the phone. She walked out into the receiving area to continue her conversation out of earshot of the others.

"Do you know if the president is up to speed on all this?" the governor asked.

Brandon shrugged his shoulders and looked at Sonny.

"I'm pretty sure he is by now, sir," Brandon said.

"I need to give him a call," the governor said. "I think this changes things."

CHAPTER 20

"Did you submit your application for candidacy?"

"I did, Mr. President. But only because Lucy wouldn't leave me alone about it, even after making fun of it. You can't seriously believe I would run, though."

"Why not, Brandon? This country loves you right now. I think you'd be a shoo-in. . . maybe even by a landslide. Something we haven't witnessed in a while."

President Richland looked at Olivia and Tim, sitting on the couch in the Oval Office. "Have you settled on any plans, now that you've finally tied the knot?"

"Well," Olivia said. "Somebody has to run the company."

Brandon sat up straight and looked at her. "What are you talking about? Don't assume I'm going to run, let alone win."

"You're going to win," Olivia chuckled.

"That's some pretty amazing work you've been doing, Liv," President Richland said. "I'm thoroughly impressed with what you've been able to do to track the cartel."

"It was the team, sir. Trevor Marshall headed all that up. He's an amazing guy. I just hope we can hold on to him."

"What do you mean?" Brandon asked.

"He and Darcy have been talking about going back to Kentucky to be closer to family."

"Really?"

"That's the talk."

Brandon smiled after a long pause. "Maybe I'll turn the company over to you, then retire and move to Kentucky with them." Lucinda looked at him and smiled, squeezing his hand.

"Oh, shut up," Olivia laughed.

"Mr. President," the press secretary said. "The networks will be ready for you in thirty minutes."

"Thanks, Margie," the president said into the intercom.

"Also, sir, Governor Truly just arrived."

"Oh, okay. Great. Send him in."

The president, along with Brandon, Lucinda, Tim, and Olivia all stood as the door to the Oval Office opened.

"Governor Truly," the president said. "Come on in. It's good to see you, sir. Or, should I call you President Truly?"

"Well, not just yet, sir."

"You ready for this address to the nation?"

"As ready as I'll ever be, Mr. President. It's been a long time coming."

"That, it has. And you were right. Bringing the cartel down changed everything."

"It did, indeed."

"Sir, the press secretary is here."

"Thanks, Marge. Well, everyone. Shall we make our way down to the studio?"

The door to the Oval Office opened, and the president's press secretary stuck his head in and nodded at the president. "Follow me, sir."

"Thank you for taking time out of your busy schedules to join us for this important announcement. As most of you know by now, for the past year, Congress has been working with my office and the State of California to try to resolve a decades-long problem. I wanted to come on to let you know the status of those talks.

"Since the CEO of one of our major contractors and his wife were kidnapped almost a year ago today, we have been able to significantly reduce the threat of drug cartels in California. We haven't eliminated the monster just yet, but we have cut off its head and rendered it useless. Thanks to the efforts of Brandon McStocker's daughter, Olivia O'Neil, and her team at McStocker and McStocker, we now know who these criminals are and where they hide.

"With that threat largely out of the way, we have been able to negotiate the withdrawal of California from the Union. Congress agrees that it will be in the best interest of the nation if we make this change a reality. The residents of the state let their voices be heard at the ballot box last November. While there is no precedent for this in the Constitution, Governor Truly knew that he had to lead his state out. But he also knew that it had to be done peacefully. I applaud the governor for avoiding the threat of a Civil War II—a fate that so many of us had feared.

"Without the cartels stirring the pot in San Francisco, the governor has been able to calm the anger and fear. But again, the independence that the state wants so desperately is now inevitable. So, as members of Congress, along with the governors of each state, work toward the best possible and legal solution, I anticipate having a bill to sign sometime over the next several months that will grant California their independence from the United States of America.

"But as you all know, we have to maintain a strong relationship with California, not unlike what we enjoy with our neighbor to the north, Canada. California will continue to provide food to the entire continent while the U.S. will continue to provide for their security.

"The governor and I also recognize that there are many in the state that do not want to transition to a sovereign nation. Their allegiance remains with the United States. So, I have asked Congress to include an annexation plan for the eastern parts of the state to be incorporated into Nevada and Arizona appropriately. The borders will have to be negotiated, and it will likely take years to become final, but it will not hold up the peaceful withdrawal from the Union.

"Governor Truly has also indicated to me that his state senate is working on a plan to have two states, possibly three, within the nation of California. NorCal and SoCal are the working names of these states as of today. But of course, the governor will oversee the evolution of that process.

"And, since we are undertaking such a massive policy change, I have also asked Congress to take up the issue of statehood for Puerto Rico."

Then the president finally broke into a smile. "If we bring Puerto Rico into the Union now, we can keep our flag unchanged."

Those sitting in the back of the room, behind the cameras, were shocked but smiled at the president.

"It is good that the residents of California can finally feel safe from the cartels. And the rest of the country's fear of the cartel taking over California has been put to rest. The system devised by the McStocker team is paying great dividends. I suspect that the topic of privacy will surround the conversation soon enough. But for now, Californians are elated to be safe again. But still, most of the population out there holds a very progressive world view not shared by the rest of the United States. I thank God for Governor Truly and his leadership.

"May God bless us all."

"Hey there," Brandon said as he walked past Mena's desk.

She jumped to her feet and walked around her desk to hug him. "We have certainly missed you around here."

"I've missed you all as well. Sorry I couldn't make it in yesterday when we got back into town. The Central House had us up to our ears in preparations."

"No doubt. It's been a crazy busy year."

"That, it has."

"How are the newlyweds?"

"They're great. Governor Truly offered them an all-expense-paid vacation anywhere in California for their honeymoon. So, they just headed home to pack up."

"Are you kidding? That's pretty ironic."

Brandon chuckled. "At least that."

"Trevor in?"

"Yep. He's in there working on something."

"Okay. I'll be in here catching my breath. Lucy will probably be along shortly."

"Yes, sir."

Brandon walked into his office and closed the door behind him. He threw his coat and briefcase on the conference table and sat at his desk. After spinning his chair around to look out over the city, he stood and walked to the window to get a more panoramic view. He scanned Lebanon, K.D. from left to right, then he smiled and shook his head. He took his cell phone from his coat pocket and sent a text.

Mr. President, K.D. will no longer be in the center. Please don't ask me to move it again.

He chuckled and threw the phone across his desk. He pressed the intercom.

"Hey, Trev?"

"Hey, Boss. You're back."

"I am. Got a minute?"

"Be right there."

Brandon sat at his desk and leaned back in the chair, locking his fingers together behind his head. He stared at all the pictures his daughters had hung since they moved into the building several years earlier. He smiled at the portrait of Bob and Anne McClellan.

Trevor tapped on the door and walked in. Brandon stood to greet him.

"Good to see you home," Trevor said as they shook hands.

"Great to be back. Have a seat."

"Sure. What's up?"

"I just wanted to tell you how impressed I am with how you handled that Genius Pod."

"Oh, that was all them, Boss."

"No. It was your leadership. Hell, you impressed the president and have gained the admiration of this whole country."

"Oh, stop."

"No, really. I want to thank you. You saved our lives."

Trevor dropped his head, and they sat quietly for a few minutes.

"So, what's this I hear about you two going back to Kentucky?"

Trevor's head shot up in surprise. "What do you mean?"

"Liv tells me you guys are talking about going back home."

"Uh . . . wow. Well, yes. We've sort of been talking about it. Darcy misses the granddaughters, you know. Of course, they're all grown up, but still, she misses everyone."

"I can certainly understand that."

"But there's been no decision yet. It's just been loose talk."

"Up for some pickin' Friday night?" Brandon asked.

"Can't wait. It's been too long."

"Indeed."

"Is that all? I'm kind of in the middle of something over there," Trevor said.

"Oh, yeah. Go. That's fine. I just wanted to check in."

"Thanks."

"We'll talk later," Brandon said.

"Of course."

Trevor returned to his office as Brandon picked his cell phone up from the edge of his desk and texted Susan.

Jam Friday night?
Of course! Yay!

Sonny drove the limo into the parking lot at Barney's with Brandon and Lucinda in the back seat. They noticed another limousine parked at the edge of the lot and the driver leaning against the fender.

"Who is that?" Lucinda asked.

Sonny opened the back door, and Brandon was the first out. "I don't know." He held Lucinda's hand as she got out, and they walked to the back, where Sonny had popped the trunk open. They got their instrument cases out and walked into the diner while Sonny took up his usual position at the fender of the car.

The bell over the door rang, and Susan looked up from behind the counter to see who it was. "Hey, you guys!" she shouted. "It's so good to see you." She walked out from behind the counter to get closer to Brandon and spoke quietly. "Hey, Daddy, the governor of California is here."

"Governor Truly?" He started looking around.

"I put him back at your table. Hope you don't mind."

"Not at all. Look, Luce. The governor's here."

"Let me take your cases," Susan said. I'll put them in the corner behind the circle."

Brandon and Lucinda handed Susan their instrument cases and walked to the corner table.

"Governor!" Brandon said. "I'm shocked to see you here. What a pleasant surprise."

Governor Truly stood and shook Brandon's hand. "I was in town, and I hear this is the place to be on Friday nights. I hope it isn't a problem."

"No problem at all, sir."

The governor took Lucinda's hand and guided her to the seat next to him and across from where Brandon sat.

"Why, thank you, Governor." She said. "So, when do we get to call you Mr. President of the nation of California?"

"Well, I think it's going to be pretty soon. It would seem that all the other states want us out as badly as my constituents want out, if not worse."

"Oh, I don't know about that, Governor," Brandon said. "You did an excellent job of leading the state through all that. But you said, 'worse than your constituents.'"

"Pardon?"

"You said the others want you out worse than your constituents. What about you?"

"What do you mean?"

"Are you looking forward to it, Governor?"

The diner got loud, and there was a ruckus at the front door. Everyone turned to see what was going on. Susan walked to the corner toward Brandon's table.

"What's going on, Suze?"

"Uh . . . well . . . Liv and Tim just showed up, and they're out in the parking lot talking to the president."

"What?"

"Yep. His whole entourage just showed up, and his agents are casing the place."

"What in the world is he doing here?"

The governor smiled. "As I said, it's the place to be on Friday night."

Everyone in the diner stood and applauded as Tim, Olivia, and President Richland walked in the front door with the first lady on his arm.

"Oh, my," he said. "Please. Please. Everyone sit." He laughed at the attention and followed Olivia to the table where her father sat. The diner eventually quieted, and everyone returned to their seats.

Governor Truly, Brandon, and Lucinda all remained standing.

"Mr. President," Brandon said. "This is a pleasant surprise. You and the governor both, right here in Barney's Diner at the same time. Who knew!"

Susan walked over and started moving chairs so she could slide two tables together. "Here you go, Mr. President. You guys have a seat."

"Glad you could make it, sir," Governor Truly said.

"Oh, so you two knew about this?" Brandon asked.

"We met earlier, yes," the president said. "When Sam said he was going to pay a visit while he was in town, I thought it would be fun to come listen to some good music."

"Well, we're glad you're here, sir," Lucinda said. "Hey, girl," she said to Olivia. "You're late."

"Yeah, I got tied up at the office."

"Everything okay?" Brandon asked.

"Oh, just some bad news. I guess I knew it was coming, but still. It's sad."

"Trevor?"

She looked over her shoulder toward the jam circle. "Yep, 'fraid so."

Brandon looked down into his coffee and shook his head.

"So, Brandon," the president said. "I saw you've thrown your hat into the race. You don't know how happy that makes me. But I haven't seen you out stumping. When are you going to get that campaign of yours off the ground?"

"Oh, jeez. I don't know, sir. It just isn't my thing. Besides, I don't even have a campaign manager."

"Yes, you do," Olivia said.

"I do?"

"Yes, you do."

"Who?"

"Me!"

"You're going to be my campaign manager?"

"Of course."

Everyone at the table laughed, and Brandon shrugged his shoulders, looking at the president.

"So, Sam. You ready to take the title of president out there?" President Richland asked.

"Oh, I don't know, Andy. I think the state is ready in all respects, but my wife and I have been thinking a lot about it."

Brandon looked at the governor and slanted his head. "You aren't staying out there, are you?"

"I've wanted to discuss it with you, Mr. President. We're considering a move back east to stay in the U.S."

Brandon slapped his hands on the table and leaned back in his chair. "I knew it!"

"Hey, Daddy!" Susan shouted. "They want you guys to come over there. Come on. Let's pick!"

Josh stood with his arm around Susan's waist.

"God, you don't know how happy it makes me to see you two together," Olivia said.

"A gorgeous couple indeed," Lucinda said. "It took you two long enough."

"Hey, that was her fault," Josh chuckled.

"Go ahead, Brandon." The president said. "You guys go have fun. We'll be back here rooting for you."

Brandon and Lucinda stood and made their way to the other side of the dining room, stopping along the way to greet their friends. Then they went to the corner, where Brandon took the guitar from his case and Lucinda took out her mandolin. They walked through the middle of the circle to the empty chairs next to Trevor and Darcy.

Brandon leaned against Trevor's shoulder. "So, you did it, huh?"

"Uh . . . Yeah. Sorry, Boss."

"Hey, don't apologize. You've done wonderful things at the firm, and nothing can take that away. I completely understand. Now, just enjoy the night. Let's pick!" he shouted.

Darcy started shuffle-bowing her fiddle and shouted, "Soldier's Joy."

Trevor joined in with a roll on his banjo while Brandon and Lucinda joined in. "Yeehaw!" Lucinda shouted.

After they had played for a few hours nonstop, Brandon finally took a break and placed his guitar behind him against the wall. "I'll be right back, Luce," he said, leaning down as the music continued. "I need to stretch a bit." She nodded and kept playing.

He smiled and made his way out of the circle and walked to the counter where he saw Pastor Emmet sitting and enjoying his root beer. "Hey, Preacher!"

"Hey there, Brandon. Sounding good over there."

"Thanks. Is this stool taken?"

"No. No. Have a seat. So, you're running for president, eh?"

"So they tell me." They chuckled.

"Doesn't sound like you're too attached to the idea."

"Not at all."

"Well, there's no doubt in my mind that you'll make a good one."

"Come on, Emmet. You of all people know what all I've been through. I'd be a mess."

"Yes. Yes. I know what you've been through, and I also know that you're a better man for it. You'll do just fine."

Susan caught her dad's attention from behind the counter. He shook his head, and she walked back into the kitchen.

"You know, Trevor and Darcy are moving back to Kentucky," Brandon said.

"Really? No, I didn't know. I'm going to hate to see them go."

"Yeah. Me too. I don't know what she's going to do with her music school, but they'll figure it out. We're sure going to miss him at Mac and Mac."

"No doubt," Emmet said.

"Well, I'll leave you alone to enjoy the music." Brandon stood and put his hand on Pastor Emmet's shoulder. "Thanks for the chat."

"Hey, Brandon."

"Yeah."

"Like you said, you've been through a lot. You've grown a lot. Follow your heart."

Brandon froze and slanted his head, still staring at the pastor.

He patted Brandon's chest. "Just follow your heart."

On inauguration day, President Richland sat watching while the president-elect stood to take the oath of office. The judge completed the oath and shook his hand. "President Truly. Congratulations, sir."

"Thank you, judge."

President Richland, his wife, Brandon, Lucinda, Tim, Olivia, Susan, and Josh all stood and applauded for the new President of the United States. President Truly walked over to greet Andy Richland and shook his hand.

"Sam, I can't think of anyone better to lead the transition of this new country of ours. You're a great leader, sir. I'm glad you decided to turn California over to Allen Pinkerton."

"Thank you, Mr. President. Allen will make a great president out there." President Truly stepped sideways in front of Brandon and Lucinda. "So, what's next for you two?"

"I'm retiring," Brandon said. "At least for now."

Lucinda grinned from ear to ear. "We're going to Kentucky!"

"Say what!?"

"This guy has turned the whole thing over to me," Olivia chuckled.

"And you, Susan? You've got a great little diner there."

"Thank you, Mr. President. You have an open invitation. Stop in anytime. On the house."

"I'm sure I will. Nothing new on the horizon for you?"

"Well, I have a wedding to plan."

"You do?"

The others looked at Susan with surprise. "What are you talking about, Sis?"

Susan smiled and winked at Olivia.

"Oh, my God. Sonny?"

"Yep. Sonny and Jo are getting married. Of course, he needs my help."

"That's great news," Brandon said. "Wonder why he didn't tell me about it."

"No doubt because of your bromance," Susan chuckled.

When the inauguration ceremony was over, Brandon and Lucinda joined Sonny at the limousine, where he was waiting with the back door open.

"I hear you have something to tell us," Brandon said.

"Your baby girl ratted me out, didn't she?"

"She did. So, it's true then?"

"It is. Be my best man?"

"You know I will." They got in the car, and Sonny drove toward the office.

"So, when are you all moving back east?"

"After the wedding."

He looked at Brandon and Lucinda in the mirror and smiled.

"I'll be in my office, Mena."

"Yes, sir."

Brandon closed the door behind him and walked straight over to the window. He stared at the panorama—the city he built. The city that Bob McClellan dreamt of. He was in a daze for several minutes before being jarred out of it by Mena's voice from the intercom.

"Sir, I have two young ladies out here who would like to see you."

He smiled. "Oh, send them in if you must."

Olivia and Susan were chuckling as they walked into the office and closed the door.

"Hey," Olivia said, walking over to join their dad. "You okay?"

"Oh, I'm fine. Just having a moment."

They each took an arm and joined him, enjoying the view.

"Sonny and Mena are going to stay with you," Brandon said.

"They are?" Olivia was surprised.

"Of course. They love you, Sweetheart. But they will both give you their resignations out of respect. So, the decision will be yours."

"Sonny doesn't want to go to Kentucky, eh?"

"Not even a little. He's a city boy."

"I wouldn't let him go anyway," Susan said.

"Have they set a date yet?" Brandon asked.

"Not yet."

Olivia's eyes filled with tears, and she began to sniffle.

"Oh, stop," Susan giggled as she too began to cry.

"It's okay," Brandon said. "I'm thinking of her too."

"I miss Mom so much."

"Me too, Liv," Susan said.

"I love your mom. You guys know that, right?"

They each leaned their heads on Brandon's shoulders.

"We know you do, Daddy," Olivia said.

Then Susan raised her head and looked at Olivia. Olivia raised her head to meet Susan's gaze.

"But Lucy is the bomb!" they shouted together.

They all laughed through their tears.

The End

**Thank you for joining Brandon and his team in Left Coast Left.
Did you enjoy the story? Here's what you can do next.**

If you enjoyed the book and have a moment to spare, I would really appreciate a short and honest Amazon review.
Your help in spreading the word is very important and greatly appreciated.
You can also sign up to be notified of my next book as well as prerelease specials and giveaways here:

www.TerryStafford.com/list

If you have fallen in love with Trevor and Darcy Marshall, read their Kentucky story in my award-winning novel, Strings of Faith. Available in paperback, hardcover, ebook, and audio formats.

Link directly to Strings of Faith on Amazon

And don't forget the first two books in the Brandon McStocker series, Kéntro and National Cross. If you haven't read the story from the beginning, you'll love reading about how the saga began. They are available in paperback, hard cover, and ebook.

Link directly to my Amazon Author Page

Who is Terry?

Award-winning author, Terry Stafford, came to writing in the second half of life. He uses his fiction to weave tales of music for readers who miss the good ol' days. Having a master's degree in management as well as a background in the U.S. Navy and later with NASA as a senior project manager, Terry saw how his experience could bring order out of creative chaos in his own writing life. He knows creatives often feel like scatter-brained writers and helps them become prolific storytellers. Terry lives in California's beautiful San Joaquin Valley with his wife, Gail. Both talented musicians, you can find them attending bluegrass music festivals or playing with the praise band every Friday night for the Celebrate Recovery ministry at their church.

Connect with Terry on his website at https://terrystafford.com and through one of these social media sites:

- *https://www.linkedin.com/in/terrystafford*
- *https://www.facebook.com/TerryStaffordAuthor/*
- *https://twitter.com/tlstafford*
- *https://www.instagram.com/tlstafford/*

Lightning Source UK Ltd.
Milton Keynes UK
UKHW012247250920
370542UK00001B/169